T2-CRY-240

BEFORE THE RUINS

BEFORE THE RUINS

A NOVEL

VICTORIA GOSLING

HENRY HOLT AND COMPANY
NEW YORK

Henry Holt and Company
Publishers since 1866
120 Broadway
New York, New York 10271
www.henryholt.com

Henry Holt® and 🅗® are registered trademarks of Macmillan Publishing Group, LLC.

Distributed in Canada by Raincoast Book Distribution Limited

Library of Congress Cataloging-in-Publication Data

Names: Gosling, Victoria, author.
Title: Before the ruins : a novel / Victoria Gosling.
Description: First U.S. edition. | New York : Henry Holt and Company, 2021.
Identifiers: LCCN 2020002138 (print) | LCCN 2020002139 (ebook) | ISBN 9781250759153 (hardcover) | ISBN 9781250759146 (ebook) | ISBN 9781250783516 (international)
Subjects: GSAFD: Suspense fiction.
Classification: LCC PR6107.O6774 B44 2020 (print) | LCC PR6107.O6774 (ebook) | DDC 823/.92—dc23
LC record available at https://lccn.loc.gov/2020002138
LC ebook record available at https://lccn.loc.gov/2020002139

Our books may be purchased in bulk for promotional, educational, or business use. Please contact your local bookseller or the Macmillan Corporate and Premium Sales Department at (800) 221-7945, extension 5442, or by e-mail at MacmillanSpecialMarkets@macmillan.com.

First Edition 2021

Designed by Meryl Sussman Levavi

Printed in the United States of America

10 9 8 7 6 5 4 3 2 1

To Joan

What, then, is the right way of living? Life must be lived as play, playing certain games, making sacrifices, singing and dancing, and then a man will be able to propitiate the gods and defend himself against his enemies, and win in the contest.

PLATO, *LAWS*

BEFORE

THE

RUINS

CHAPTER 1

GAME

THE YEAR PETER WENT MISSING WAS THE YEAR OF THE floods. I was on my way home from a meeting in Paris when the call came. It was a Wednesday, late April, and as the train hurtled toward London night was coming on. The heavy clouds were darkest blue and great pools of water lay in the fields like molten silver. I was on my laptop, reading about the latest in a series of leaked financial papers. When I glanced up, the last light slipped away, and my reflection coalesced upon the window as though the darkness was developing fluid.

My phone rang and I rooted violently for it in my handbag, alive with panic, as though I was secretly, desperately hoping for a momentous and life-changing call from someone who would ring only once and withhold their number. In my wildest dreams, I would not have guessed Peter's mother would be the caller.

"Andrea . . . are you there? It's Patricia, Mrs. White." When I didn't answer, she went on, "Is that you, Andy? Is it you?"

"Yes, it's me. How are you?" Had the vicar died? A quick, stabbing pain, deeper than I would have expected.

"We're both well, dear. You sound . . . a bit different." Thinking about it later, I would realize she meant posher. "Peter says you're doing very well."

Her voice was trembly. She had always been old, even when we were small. Her eyes were a pale china blue. When I used to knock at the vicarage door, her mouth would purse in disappointment as though she'd been expecting a boy, not a girl, but a nice boy called Rufus or Hugo from a nice home. But there I was with my crew cut and pink plastic earrings, smiling the gap-toothed smile of a master criminal and inviting Peter to throw sticks in the stream, by which I meant trapping a slowworm and posting it through Mrs. East's letterbox because I'd heard my mother call her a witch. We were always up to something or other. I had a weakness for games, a trait I shared with Peter.

"It's Peter, dear, I'm worried about him. We haven't heard from him. Not this past month. Have you spoken to him?"

"I'm afraid I haven't, Mrs. White." I imagined her standing in the vicarage front room, staring out toward the yew hedge, the vicar beside her with a crocheted blanket draped over his knees. It seemed wrong, talking to her on an iPhone. She came from a generation that knew rationing and hand-cranked their cars and had uncles who'd died in the trenches. A time of myth, it seemed now, like that of Arthur and his knights.

"It's been four Sundays now. He always calls us on Sundays after Evensong. I've tried calling him but I just get the recording."

I hesitated. My instinct was to cover for him, only I didn't know what I was covering for. It had been my birthday, my thirty-eighth, the previous week. Usually Peter remembered and sent a text, but not this time.

"I don't see Peter very often. We sort of move in different circles. And work is always so busy. I mean mine and Peter's. Have you tried calling him there? Or his other friends?"

"He told us he changed jobs. I thought I wrote the name of the company down but I can't find it. It was a foreign name, or names, a sort of string of foreign names. And he hasn't brought anyone home in . . . well, in quite a while."

No, it was unlikely that Peter would have brought anyone home.

"You were always such good friends. You and Peter. And Marcus and Emma, of course. But you and Peter were friends first. I know he always thought of you as his best friend, even after," she paused, "everything that happened."

Everything that happened. Peter had wanted to talk about it at the wedding, the wedding I invited him to and after which he'd disappeared, if only from Patricia.

"Have you tried googling him, I mean for his work number?"

"Googling . . . ? No, I was hoping . . . you will look into it for me, Andy? You'll find out what he's up to, won't you?"

After we hung up, I stared out the window. The train carriage was quiet. We raced past a string of streetlamps on an overpass, lights blurring so the night was stitched with golden thread. I wondered why I'd agreed. It might have been her calling me Andy. For well over a decade, Peter's mother was pretty much the only person to call me by my full name. But I have been Andrea, or frequently Ms. Carter, for many years now.

Then there was the fact that she had always loved Peter, fervently, protectively; when he was sixteen she was still cutting the crusts off his crab paste sandwiches, unaware that he'd been throwing them to the jackdaws in the graveyard since he was seven and buying chocolate bars for lunch with money he'd come by via the vicar's trouser pockets. Yes, Patricia loved Peter, and yet I don't know if she ever really knew him. She and the vicar had had some fairly clear ideas about who he should be, and in the end I think he consented to play pretend with them, to give them what they wanted, which meant, I suppose, that he loved them too.

At King's Cross I made my way underground. There, the walls were papered with moving, glowing dreams. Descending on the escalators to the Victoria Line, I found myself thinking that if ads were really dreams, the preoccupations of the unconscious, then all we wanted to be was sexy. Because they all said sexy—the women coy, or inviting, or half-naked, the men white of tooth and thick of mane—so that must be what we were buying. Not good, or kind, or honorable, the qualities the vicar had once struggled to impress on us, just sexy.

I forced myself to march the few streets home, wondering how quickly I could get into bed and fall asleep. I was always tired at that time. Doing my job, sleep came at a premium, but even when I did get a chance to catch up, it was a tiredness that sleep could not cure. If I had divided myself into parts—body, brain, heart, soul—I would have been unable to tell you which bit precisely was so exhausted.

Once home, I didn't immediately go to bed. Instead, I fussed about the flat, making tiny adjustments to things, passing a duster over the surfaces, even though the cleaner had been the day before. The fretfulness in Patricia's voice had got to me. I wondered what Peter was playing at, which made me think of the wedding, of the last time I had seen Peter. He had wanted to talk about the manor, but I had closed him down.

As I laid out my clothes for the next day, I had no inkling that, in light of Peter's disappearance, the manor and "everything that happened" there was a subject that was going to be thoroughly reopened. That in pursuit of Peter, I would see and speak to them all again except, of course, for the one who could no longer speak to anyone.

Slipping between the sheets, I checked my emails and scrolled through the news one last time, then turned out the light. In the darkness, I lay listening to the quiet street and distant sirens. In London, no matter where you live there are always sirens at night. I thought of the scenes the police were being called to, the people being raced to the hospital in the backs of ambulances. I thought of all the games no longer being played. Of all the games gone wrong.

All of which should have meant bad dreams, or at least unsettled ones, but in fact my dream was quite the opposite, although in a way that was worse, since waking from it was so painful. I don't remember all of it, of course, was left only with a few images and a feeling: my bare feet ankle-deep in the wet emerald lawn, the sun falling just so on the manor, and to the left the lake where the wind stirred the reeds and the little white temple cast its dark shadow on the ripples. The whole afternoon lay ahead, spectral in its perfection. The sky would stay its clear, glassy blue, the shadows would creep feline over the grass, and then as the sun sank, the stone of the place would begin to exhale the heat of the whole long day. And in my dream, I knew exactly which day it was. I knew that today was the day of the apocalypse, today was June 20, 1996, the day the four of us first went to the manor, the day we met David. Just before we found out about the diamonds.

CHAPTER 2

APOCALYPSE I

IT WAS MAY WHEN MY MOTHER CAME HOME AND, COLLAPSED upon the hall carpet, her face all concertinaed on one side, announced the coming of the apocalypse. It was coming, it was coming soon, and none of us would survive it.

"June twentieth," she said, "1996," and then she passed out. I rolled her onto her side and pulled down her wrinkled skirt, breathing in vodka fumes and the smell of her unwashed hair. She opened her eyes, blinking sleepily like a kitten, and lashed out, her fist connecting with my jaw. I swore and backed off to a safe distance. Then I went to the kitchen, put a bag of frozen peas on it, and waited for the murder to seep out of my heart. It'd been a while since she had caught me.

"It's coming! You're going to die too!"

I went over and slammed the kitchen door, sealing her off. I hadn't spoken to her properly in months. After a couple of minutes, I heard her shuffling into the living room where she slept these days, partly because she kept falling down the stairs, partly because it was as far away from me as she could get.

The door clicked shut. The radio came on. I swapped the peas for a bag of fish sticks, reaching deep into the frost-encrusted maw of the freezer compartment and hauling them out in a shower of ice.

Ultimately, she was right though. Not about Armageddon, but about a coming end.

* * *

It became a thing, the apocalypse. Like lines from films we watched together, the in-jokes we curated, and the impressions we all did, even Peter, of Peter's father.

"So Mum says the world is ending on June twentieth." Nothing my mother said or did surprised them, and the hash we smoked, sat in the back of Marcus's uncle's van parked up at the castle or in a quiet spot in one of the lanes, meant our reactions were often muted and slow to load—although at the time the comparison would have conjured Atari computer games, rather than YouTube videos or Facebook Live. Porn was still a dirty magazine passed around class. We saved up for CDs and taped songs off the radio. I didn't have a TV because my mother wouldn't pay the license fee, so news came from skimming week-old copies of *The Sun* or *The Evening Adver* in Darren's office.

Outside the van, the hedgerows were clouded with cow parsley and hogweed. Peter, Em, and I were eighteen. Marcus, my boyfriend, was nineteen. I was sitting wedged under Marcus's arm with a toolbox sticking into my back. His other hand held the ashtray, an empty paper coffee cup, and rested lightly on my thigh. Sometimes I wished we could stay in the van forever. I couldn't remember meeting any of them. We had gone to the same schools, right from when we were five, all the way through. We had a common language and a shared reference library of teachers, landmarks, and local legends. It was as if they had always been on the edges of my vision: Peter in a stripy scarf, aged six, hopping across the playground; Em arriving at junior school each day with a red teapot slung over her shoulder on a string; Marcus, a good-looking boy in the year above, endlessly chasing a football across a field. While we had always known him—because everyone knew everyone, because of who his uncle was—Marcus had been the last to join our tight-knit group. He had left school at sixteen but come back in to retake his English GCSE on his Uncle

Darren's orders. There had been an empty chair next to Peter and Marcus took it, and at lunchtime trailed after him, looking awkward and asking questions about King Lear, and then about what we might all be doing later on or at the weekend, and scowling at anyone else who came near us. I was tempted to tell him to get lost, but Em said, "He's all right, Andy. I mean, he's not doing any harm." Until suddenly we were four. And four was enough for me. Four was plenty.

"So no exam results then?" Em was sitting beside Peter on a rolled-up bit of carpet; Em kneeling, her fringe over her eyes, Peter—all ankle, knee, and elbow—with his long skinny legs drawn up under his chin.

"No Oxford?"

"No, Peter," I said. "After the apocalypse there will be no Oxford. No more school of any kind."

"And Reading?" Marcus had his eye on a ticket to the festival.

"Canceled due to the sun turning black and the heavens being rolled back like a scroll."

Peter reached in and plucked the joint from my fingertips. "The Lord giveth, and the Lord taketh away," he intoned. Sometimes it was almost like having the vicar in the van with us.

"But if the apocalypse is coming," I went on, "we can do exactly what we want, and only what we want. Until June twentieth, that is."

People had been talking to us about the future ever since we could remember, particularly in Peter's case, of whom great things were expected. The idea of deleting it, and ending its hold over us, was worth exploring. In the van, wreathed in smoke, nostrils filled with the smell of grease and oil and the tang of hash, we talked about what we'd do. Who would die painfully. What we'd steal. The things we'd try, mostly things we'd seen people do on TV that were supposed to be fun. There was an edge of hysteria to our laughter. Em had to scramble out, bent over at ninety degrees, and pee behind one of the back wheels, getting thistled in the arse in the process.

They would have let it drop, however, had it not been for me. The apocalypse called out to something lodged under my skin, the longing for destruction perhaps, for erasure—of everything, of everyone, especially myself.

* * *

We dropped off Peter at the vicarage and Em at her family's cottage on the Hungerford road, and then Marcus and I drove into the Savernake Forest, ancient woodland where Henry VIII had once hunted, home to deer, walkers, and courting couples, site of murders, and rumored wandering place of a headless horsewoman. We parked the van and walked out to the Big Bellied Oak, climbing up till we reached a seat among its thousand-year-old branches. A little starlight crept through the new leaves. I thought of dead stars, dead events, all their rage consumed millions of years ago, just a memory of fire reaching out across the universe, and for the first time since the punch I felt better, more normal, and not like my hands were twitching to strangle someone.

"You all right?"

I nodded. Marcus had a chivalrous streak. He was protective. Only a month ago, he'd sent Greg Martin sprawling for trying to put his arm around me. But my mum was a woman, and by Marcus's code you never hit women, never lifted a finger against them. His uncle said men who did that were no better than dogs. Still, better not to say anything.

"Just stoned," I said.

"Me too." With one arm gripping a branch, Marcus leaned in to kiss me. His mouth was warm and tasted, not unpleasantly, of cigarettes.

We'd been going out a year, since I'd heard rumors of a girl out at Bishopstone who liked him. It wasn't just the prospect of losing the lifts, or my Saturday job at his uncle's office, or the fact that with

Marcus around no one dared give Peter any trouble, not in the roughest of pubs. I liked Marcus, although it was sometimes hard, with all the other stuff in the balance, to know how much.

He drew back and let out a quick breath. "If I close my eyes, I feel like I'm falling." He wrapped both arms around the branch and glanced downward. "Oh, that's weird."

"You've got the fear."

"A bit. It'll pass. Hey, what are you doing?"

What I was doing was unbuttoning his Levi's. One of his legs began to tremble slightly, dancing in the air. I wondered what it would take for Marcus not to respond to my hands—more than the prospect of a thirty-foot drop, it seemed.

Something was rustling about in the undergrowth over to the left. The moon was peeping. I liked having him where I wanted him. I liked the fact that like this, he could not touch me back, so I did it slow. Before he came, he said my name, quickly, with a furrowed brow, like I troubled him, like I pained him. I wiped my hand off on my jeans.

"I think you hit the headless horsewoman." But part of my brain was thinking, *Well, that's that done for a while.*

Later, in bed, floating on a little hash cloud, I thought of the world after the apocalypse. I saw Marlborough empty of people, its supermarkets abandoned, its shops looted. I imagined packs of dogs marauding up the high street, and the great stone fountains of its famous college dry and full of leaves. At our own school, Saint John's, our work peeled from its sugar-paper mounting on the display boards, and in the canteen, the linoleum shrank and cracked, and the enormous saucepans rusted where they hung on the kitchen walls.

It made me feel something, something shimmery, like the times in the church, years before, when I would hang over one of the creaking pews till my hair touched the flagstones and Peter would ring one of the hand bells right next to my ear. Even after the sound had faded and my ears had stopped ringing, something in my brain would go on resounding, as though deep inside me a tiny cliff was shearing off into the sea, a tower block collapsing soundlessly.

So I kept bringing us back to it, asking Marcus and Peter and Em again and again what they would want to do if they had one more day, just one more day.

* * *

On June 20, dawn broke the color of Mrs. East's roses. After much consideration, I'd decided not to kill my mother. Instead, I made myself pancakes for breakfast. I put all the golden syrup I wanted on them, which turned out to be all the golden syrup there was. Then I licked the plate.

The lane into town was narrow and windy. When cars came along, I waited on the verge and then wandered out again to the middle of the road where it was sunny. The woods exhaled cool air. At some point I started jogging, and then the jog became a sprint, just for the hell of it, in and out of the sunlight and the dappled shadows on the road, until I was winded, and slowed, panting, to a lope.

A tractor was haymaking in a field. I passed the rugby club, and then the corner of the common where the circus tents of the Mop would set up every autumn, and where certain girls would sit near on the grass banks in summer, waiting for cars to pull up and take them out to some quiet spot in the Savernake and—almost always—bring them back.

When I got to Marlborough I went to the bank, and since it was the last day on earth, I took out every penny I had, which added up to nineteen pounds and seventy-eight pence.

* * *

The manor lay empty, with a chain and padlock on the gate and signs that said the property was patrolled by guard dogs. It wasn't. Men working for Marcus's uncle Darren had put the signs up a few years back, when the family who owned it got into trouble with inheritance taxes and had put it on the market. It had sold, a year or so ago, but there was still no sign of the new owners. A couple of times squatters had gotten in, but Marcus's uncle had ways of dealing with unwanted visitors, involving his Alsatians, Arnie and Sly; balaclavas; and a couple of his bricklayer friends. Last time, he let them leave with what they could carry, burnt the rest of their stuff, and gave Marcus the thumb-sized piece of hash he'd taken from them.

As we came down the hill along the A436, from the van's passenger seat I could see the manor's shingle roof and then, for a split second, I was allowed a glimpse of its lovely face before it was swallowed by the line of firs that stood along the front boundary, shielding it from the road. On the double-decker to Swindon, from the top deck, you could keep it in view for a few more seconds, and on school trips, or the annual Christmas excursion to see a show at the theater, I had always looked out for it, greeted it as a secret friend, like the mysterious, bowing blue-robed figure in the east window of the church.

Marcus parked the van in front of the gate and we climbed over quickly and moved up the driveway, out of sight of the road. There were weeds growing up through the gravel and the lawn was knee-high in wild barley and thistles. As we drew nearer and the sound of the cars—already muted by the firs—diminished, I became aware of the murmur of bees in the grass. I suppose there were crickets and hornets and wasps as well, but what I remember was that heavy, satisfied sound that bees make. The brick had weathered to a darkish pink, and each one was surrounded by a rime of white mortar. With the morning sun upon it, it made my heart quicken.

We stopped a few feet away from the front door and dropped our bags on the stone steps. Peter peered in the windows and as I bent over to untie my laces, I heard him bang the knocker against the door, and the sound echoed through the empty building. Marcus was standing with his hands in his pockets, gazing upward.

The manor was three stories high. On either side, set back a little, and a story shorter, were wings. The roof was shingle, the facade brick, and around the mullioned windows, the builders had incorporated seams of local flint. Further on, if you followed the drive round, were stables and a clutch of outbuildings.

"Are you going to take that side?"

With his chin, Marcus indicated left. That way, the climb was fairly easy owing to a chimneypiece edged in sticking-out brickwork, and nearer the top, a string course, a line of bricks that stuck out edge-ward from the wall.

No other route was immediately obvious, but I knew that Marcus had found one, and that it was hard, which was why he was nudging me toward the easier climb. Every way I looked, the eaves were the problem. Then I caught Marcus cast a quick look right and, following his gaze, I saw in the shaded corner where the wing met the main house, there was a tree. Tiny green-and-brown dappled pears hung from its branches and, while it barely reached to the first-floor windows, coming halfway down the wall was a piece of drainpipe, and above that a series of jutting cornerstones.

I went to stand beneath it with Marcus at my heels.

"I'll take the tree and the pipe. You take the chimney," I said.

"You sure?"

"The world ends today."

"Right." I wasn't going to be told what I could and could not climb and Marcus was smart enough to know it. Besides, it was one of the things he liked about me. His mum, Darren's sister, was a bag of nerves, forever calling up Marcus or Darren and asking them to drop whatever they were doing because she thought she smelled gas or the fridge was making a funny noise.

"I'll watch you."

"Peter can do it. I'll meet you at the top."

He looked at the route up and poked the toe of his trainers into the ground. The lawn at the base of the tree was soft and springy, but even so.

"You fall, Andy, you're fucked."

"Think so?" Our smiles met. Peter, hearing his name, ambled over, a finger thrust between the pages of a book to guard his place.

"There's a piano inside."

Em was sitting on the lawn and had taken out her sketchbook. She lifted her skirt so the sun could get to her legs, her gaze settled upon the fountain and its stone cherubs, and she sighed contentedly.

I stepped into Marcus's cupped hands, swung up into the pear tree, and a couple of birds shot skyward. Following the trunk, I hauled myself up and then, as I got higher, shifted my weight so that the tree bent over toward the wall of the house. As it did so, I pushed off with my feet and caught hold of the drainpipe. It was easy and within a few seconds, I had shinnied up and got my hands around the first of the cornerstones. There was a breeze higher up. A little winged creature, a beetle with petrol-blue iridescent wings, landed on my forearm. I got my feet right up under me and grasped for the next cornerstone and then the next, feeling the oil from my palms seeping into the stone.

The guttering was choked with rotting leaves and bright green moss. I reached up and put my hands on the roof. The shingles seemed firm, but they were old and I wondered when was the last time a human hand had touched them. It seemed likely that they would take my weight, but I wouldn't know until it was too late. There were no handholds on the tiles, so the thing was just to get the feet up and run, keeping low and hunched forward. I got the first chimneystack in my sights, drove up with my legs, and went for it.

By the time I got my hands to the stack, I was panting. The chimney pots were covered in bird shit and I held on tight to them, managing a single whoop as I caught my breath. Marcus was coming up over the other side. From the other chimney he walked the length of the roof to me as though along a tightrope, his arms held out for balance. I swiveled round to get my first look over the back of the manor.

I would get to know it all well: the courtyard with the remains of a once-fine rose garden; the walled kitchen garden where a few fig trees, spliced against the crumbling walls, dropped their fruit onto stone pathways where it split and rotted; the derelict greenhouses full of empty snail shells, spiders, and broken glass. My gaze passed over the tangled orchard of apple trees and the remains of a rotting summerhouse. Further away, bordering the property at the back, was a copse and then the pale yellow of barley fields which rose to the horizon. Then I glimpsed the glint of sun on water and saw, to the left, at the bottom of the sloping lawn, a small lake, half choked with reeds, and there on its far side, a folly, a little white-pillared replica of a Greek temple.

Marcus kissed me, a quick, juddery kiss as we held on to the chimneys. Down below, a wood pigeon flew to a perch atop the pear tree and when I looked up toward the sun, the sky was clear as glass, and specked with tiny flying insects. The shingles were like scales under my feet, like the scales of a great dragon. The shimmery feeling was back, and I did not think I could contain it. It tempted me to flinch, as though the joy of it would break my heart. For a second I thought Marcus was going to say something and I turned to look at him, at his gleaming face, wet with sweat from the climb, and ever so briefly he appeared to me like a stranger. But before he spoke, if he even intended to, I saw the white flash of Peter's waving hand and looked down to see, standing next to Peter, a real stranger looking up at us, face shadowed by the hand that was shielding his eyes from the sun.

CHAPTER 3

WEDDING

JUST BEFORE HE DISAPPEARED, I INVITED PETER TO A WEDDING. He came, but arrived so late I'd given up on him coming at all. Dinner lay in ruins, the father of the bride was inching toward the summit of his speech, when suddenly I caught sight of him, slipping around the edge of the room toward me. The wedding was at the Savoy, in the Lancaster Ballroom, and the room was a sea of pink roses, of gleaming points of light flickering from candle to crystal to chandelier. Waiting staff dipped among the tables, and the mirrored walls made it seem like there were more of them than there were, more of everything. For a moment I lost sight of Peter, then he was there, right beside me, the same dark hair and widow's peak, the aquiline nose and bone-white skin.

He gave me a quick squeeze of the shoulder by way of apology, and then gestured to a waiter to fill his glass. The others at the table, strangers all, appraised him: so tall and slender, so well dressed, the keen and handsome face, and then . . . Ah! They'd seen it, what people have always been able to see in Peter, even children who don't know the name for it yet, even when we were tiny, long before Peter himself knew what it was.

"Three?"

"Oh, four at least." But before we could agree on how many

hundreds of thousands of pounds the wedding had cost, it was time to raise our glasses to the bride and groom. I felt Peter take in my dress and then glance at my face, so that I tipped my head forward into the light to give him a better look. His fingers quickly reached out and touched the back of my hand, and then just as quickly retreated. He smiled at me. I smiled back.

"How long has it been this time?"

"About six months," I said.

The last time I saw Peter, I'd gone to meet him and some friends of his—or at least people he knew—in a bar on my way from somewhere else. Peter had bought round after round of drinks and had his arm slung around the shoulders of a young Norwegian who looked at him with hopeful bright blue eyes.

Later that night, toasts finally over, I asked him about Anders as we strolled through the Embankment Gardens.

"Torn apart by wolves in Regent's Park. A very sad business."

"And the one before, wasn't he . . . ?"

"Made into black pudding by a German cannibal? Yes. I had to testify at the trial. Shocking." I suspected he left them, most of the time. Or perhaps they tired of being kept at arm's length. "Nothing to report on that front, I'm afraid. Are you seeing anyone?"

I shook my head. The Thames was a sheet of rippling darkness. By the wall, Peter turned to me.

"Whoever are these people?"

"I only know the groom, Oliver. He's my boss. You know the type, but we get on. I think her dad owns British Airways. Or Bahrain Airways. Something like that. It's his second go. Her first." I paused. "I wasn't going to come, but then I thought it might be fun. If you came too. Isn't this where they arrested Oscar?"

Wilde, patron saint of queer and clever boys, was once Peter's darling. I remember notes passed in the classroom: *Oscar said this, Oscar said that,* as though Wilde was climbing up the ivy and in through the vicarage back bedroom window each evening. We would have been about twelve. Em was already our friend by then, Marcus still a few years off.

Peter did not reply. I was struggling to judge his mood. The air was cold, and I gripped his arm. Even in heels I barely reached his chin.

"Silly shoes." I pointed at my toes.

"Pretty."

"Christian."

"You naughty thing." But he didn't want my hag routine. Instead he ran a hand through his hair and sighed and I was possessed by a memory of Peter turning to me at our infant school thirty years earlier and whispering, "Your Ws are like wobbly bottoms, Andy. Like bums. Fat wobbly bums. Mine are much better. See."

I scavenged a cigarette from a young man with glistening eyes standing among a group of smokers by the River Doors. A pale bridesmaid in light blue chiffon hung from his arm as he cupped his hands to offer me a light. I walked back to offer it to Peter.

"Shares?"

"Of course."

We took another turn of the gardens. The young man was watching us. I handed Peter the fag. He inhaled and then made a face. "I think we should get very drunk together."

"Really, Peter?"

"Oh absolutely. Don't you think so?" There was a note in his voice. If I hadn't known better, I would have said it was need. And I suppose I heard in it another kind of offer, one I wanted to grab with both hands: *Get wasted with me, get happy with me, like old times . . .* So I replied quickly that of course I thought we should. Even though I'd already had more than enough, even though there are compelling reasons why I shouldn't drink at all.

* * *

When he was a child, Peter's parents told him there was an angel writing down everything he did in a book. There were two columns, one for the good things and one for the bad things. When I first knew him, when I was the rough kid with a kitchen-scissors haircut, hunched over my free school dinner, knife and fork clutched in my fists, there was a sort of physical stutter to Peter, like he couldn't ever trust an instinct, not even to get out of the way of a ball hurled at his face, without checking in first with his angel. I don't know if that was what marked him out. I would have been the more obvious target—no dad, jumble-sale clothes, mum off her hinges—but then my teeth and claws were sharper.

Back inside we fetched drinks and went to stand in a corner with a good view of the crowd. I watched Peter as his eyes moved over the guests and wondered if the angel was still there, invisibly keeping track of accounts. I showed Peter the keycard to my room.

"Why not a taxi?"

"Treating myself." I had also thought that if the evening went well, Peter might stay too. I had imagined us lying on the bed in hotel robes watching clips from YouTube on the flat screen. On the website it said that a chef was available around the clock and that special requests were catered for, and I'd coveted the idea of us lying there giggling and ordering up strange creations from room service.

"Work must be going well."

I shrugged. "Yours?"

Peter nodded and then looked away. I was not quite sure what Peter did. His degree had been in law. Now, his job was something to do with navigating the intricacies of international tax legalities for a series of companies I'd never heard of. It involved a lot of travel, and he was paid a lot of money, that was all I knew. My own job, compliance officer for an investment fund, drew similar reactions. People asked. I told them. After a few seconds their eyes glazed over, and the next time we met, they would ask again. Of course, after he went missing, I regretted not pressing him, accepting the averted gaze as a sign of boredom rather than evasion.

Peter fetched more drinks.

"Shots, Peter?"

"Shots *and* champagne."

"Well that's all right then." I thought again of the room upstairs, the gorgeous, very expensive room only a few doors down from where Wilde and Bosie had enjoyed their trysts. My nightie was laid out on top of the covers. Next to the bed, there was a glass of water. In the bathroom, I had lined up the comb, toothbrush, toothpaste, makeup remover, eye makeup remover, cleanser, toner, moisturizer, eye cream, and hand cream. Small tasks performed for the benefit of my future self. It was a law I had come to live by: *Thou Shalt Not Lay Mines for Thy Future Self! Thou Shalt Not Create Great Piles of Shit for Her to Shovel!* But then sometimes it left me feeling like a butler to a cold and demanding stranger: the pension contributions, the long hours at work, the time put in at the gym, the eternal vigilance. Because what about me? What about the me now?

"You'll make sure everything ends well?"

"Didn't I always look after you?" Peter said.

I wanted to answer that it had been the other way around. Instead I said cheers because I couldn't think of a better toast—absent friends was out of the question—and Peter said cheers too, and we drank the shots, and then the champagne, and then we drank lots more.

* * *

But I do remember. Most of it. We circulated and looked at all the money. Was that so-and-so? Hadn't that old lady once dated Mick Jagger? In the Manhattan Room we discovered that it didn't matter how much money was spent on a wedding, the music could still be wrong. After a couple more drinks, we danced anyway and I thought how the dress I was wearing had been worth all the money and the swimming disgust paying for it had made me feel.

In the atrium, we watched a wicked-looking old gent try his luck with a pair of fifty-somethings. They were far enough away that we couldn't hear them, so I voiced the old chap and Peter the ladies.

"You're both as lithe as eels."

"Octavia and I have very strict rules when it comes to three-ways."

I remember needing to pee but not wanting to go because Peter's eyes were suddenly gentle and unguarded, and then really having to pee, dashing to the ladies', whacking on some lipstick, and then quick to get more drinks, because I didn't want to lose it, that lovely cloak of gaiety and wildness and freedom, with its concealed lining of panic.

The young smoker was waiting at the bar. He looked like an advert for a very expensive, morally dubious product.

"How old are you?" The words slipped out of my mouth. He leaned in to whisper an answer. "As old as all that?"

When his bridesmaid showed up, I slid off the stool and laughed at how regretful he looked.

We kept circulating, Peter and I, drinks in hand, floating down green marbled corridors, descending carpeted stairways where there were giant vases and tiny couches for passersby to swoon upon, overcome by the weight of their vast fortunes. So I swooned, falling like a leaf and landing to show the maximum of chest and leg.

"Fucking socialist death duties, Darling! I'm going to have to sell Granny's island."

"But Kirrin's been in the family since William the Conqueror, Bunty!"

I laughed harder than the joke deserved and glanced in the mirror, at my stockinged legs and lipsticked smile, at Peter's tie undone just so. The self-assured handsome man, the black-haired laughing lady reclining in her midnight blue silk dress. Look how well we were doing in our adult disguises! The children we had been—a boyish girl, a girlish boy—no more than tiny points of light under the skin.

* * *

Oliver, patrician as ever, came over to say hello. His bride was waving to him from the other side of the ballroom, and Oliver waved back, beaming, as though he hadn't seen her in years. I complimented him on his speech. It had been rather good. He'd started off by saying something provocative, about getting married in an age when two-thirds of marriages ended in divorce. Then it had been witty. He'd got some laughs talking about how sweet Aria was, how trusting and kind and determined to see the best in people, which meant that if they ever divorced, he could take her to the cleaners. Finally, he'd arrived at sincerity: He couldn't imagine not being with her, but if anyone was going to break his heart and ruin him and leave him a shell of a human being, he wanted it to be Aria, because she was worth it. His voice got a little thick toward the end and my eyes had pricked with tears, and I found myself thinking that Oliver would be all right now, that Oliver would be safe, as though marriage was, despite all evidence to the contrary, a sheltered harbor, an Ithaca beyond war and monsters and the wrecking storms.

"You know, I thought you might be Andrea's mystery man," Oliver was saying to Peter. "We all think she's got one, you know." Then he asked what I had been like when I was younger.

"Oh Hobbesian. Absolutely Hobbesian." Oliver didn't get it, so Peter explained. "Nasty, brutish, and short. From Hobbes's definition of the life of mankind." Oliver had looked away. Peter swallowed and just for an instant a crack opened up and I glimpsed another Peter. The Peter who was always quick and clever, but not quite clever enough to hide it, so people were unkind to him, how unkindness seemed to follow him wherever he went, till he took on a hunted, slinking quality, which was when it really got bad.

My eyes fell on the smoker. There was something about him. He threw me a wink and then mimed smoking a cigarette from where he sat at a table of friends. When I turned back, I thought I heard Peter say, "She was our queen."

"I'll be right back."

I made my way to the River Doors. It was raining and everyone had gone inside. I counted to three and turned and there was the smoker, and didn't he look happy. A couple of cigarettes, my drink, a slug from his hip flask, and the evening began to tear like tissue paper. It was like ripping the wrapping off a gift. Inside was a box of glittering fragments and darkness.

We wandered a few steps into the gardens until we were under a tree. I felt the old, careless joy. *Oh Andy? She'll do anything, she will.* The cold rain fell on my bare arms and it fell on London, filling the gutters and flowing into the storm drains. Elsewhere, it fell on woods and fields, on the Savernake Forest and the old earth fort at Barbury, on the manor and whoever lived there now, and—a little further still—on the gravestone at Saint Helen's, where I still thought nothing on earth would ever bring me.

"You should have a coat on," he said. I put my hands inside his suit jacket. The heat was radiating through his shirt. He put his hands on either side of my waist. Even in the heels, I had to get on tiptoe. White shirt, white teeth, dark blond hair. His name is one of the things I lost. I kissed him. Or he kissed me. And it was like finding a door to a warm room unlocked on a cold night and slipping inside. Lovely, until the bridesmaid showed up.

* * *

When I finally found Peter, he was sitting alone in the American Bar. I thought he'd gone, that I had, not for the first time, ruined everything. I called a waiter and ordered us two glasses of champagne, feeling the panic draining away. The smile Peter gave me was thin.

"Some things don't change."

"You were four hours late."

Peter looked at his hands. His voice was tight. "It has, of late, been hard to get away."

But I didn't ask. Once again, I missed the chance.

"Did you have fun?" When I didn't reply, Peter said, "He looks like David. That young man. When you think about it." It was a little bit like having a bomb thrown at you from a very great height, watching it turn as it fell toward you through the air.

"Do you think so?" I took my drink in a gulp.

"Is it because of David that you're not with anyone?"

I signaled the waiter for another. "Do you remember when everyone used to say they didn't mind gays as long as they didn't ram it down their throats? But it's heterosexuality that's rammed at people, Peter." I started laughing. "Like a shopping cart, right in the back of the knees." I got up and mimed it for him, earning a worried look from one of the barmen. "Seeing someone nice?" Ram. "I know a lovely chap, just your sort." Ram. "What about kids?"

Next, I remember standing at the sink in the marble bathroom. In the mirror, the bridesmaid's hot, hurt eyes were boring into mine. Beside her, I looked like the wicked queen: black hair, now turning to frizz, gray eyes, mouth red, like someone'd slapped it.

"Sometimes I look so much like my mother," I told her.

Two whiskies, and the night was black streamers. I had Peter's hand in mine, and we were dashing up the Strand and then along the Mall. Saint James's Park was a pool of darkness and as we slipped in among the pathways, I asked Peter if he'd ever gone cruising there.

"Not even a little? Not a Coldstream Guard or a member of the Household Cavalry? No, not even a little member?"

He shook his head. The water gleamed. There was no one there, not a dog, not a jogger.

"I'm thinking of inventing an app," Peter was saying, "and when you open it, it will give you a history of all the crimes that have ever taken place in the surrounding area. All the murders and robberies and incidences of gross indecency and . . . slight indecency? Minor indecency? Going back to when records began."

"Here Bishop Barnaby famously burned on a pyre his loyal servant Robert for serving his tea tepid."

"Exactly."

The cold was getting to my head. I crouched down and put a hand on the grass to steady myself. The earth was folded in on itself. Bleeding cold. I felt it reaching up my arm.

"'And no birds sing.'"

"What?" Peter said.

"Where's that from? 'And no birds sing'?"

"Keats. 'La Belle Dame sans Merci.'"

"Ah, the one about the fairy who enchants the knight." I owed my reading to Peter. He was my friend, my special friend, my very best. I demanded a haircut like his, shoes like his. I tried complaining that I couldn't see the board in a ploy to get glasses so I could be like Peter. No one expected anything of me, but if Peter was on the clever table, then so was I, even if it meant murder. I wasn't going to let him escape me through the pages of a book.

My fingers sank through the grass into the dirt. To lie down, to get inside it, to be covered over. Just for a bit. Drinking thoughts. Peter pulled me up and led me over to a bench.

"Do we have anything to drink?"

"Nope."

I opened my handbag and inside there was someone else's pack of cigarettes, and a clutch of bar miniatures.

"Looky, looky."

"That's the girl I remember." Out in the darkness, I heard the water part and glimpsed a serpentine neck dipping beneath the surface. He fell silent for a moment. "I saw David, Andy."

I'd always thought it was Peter who was keeper of the great silence. Had it been me? And if so, for how long? I opened another little whiskey, a fairy-sized bottle of oblivion.

"And?" I felt a little rocket of rage going up. At an airport baggage carousel, wife and child in tow? On YouTube or giving a Ted Talk? Crouched on a pavement, begging for spare change?

"Does it matter?"

"How did he look?"

But Peter didn't answer. Instead he asked me if I was happy.

"Delirious, Peter. Absolutely delirious."

"Why can't you just be fucking happy, Andy?" He rubbed at his eyes. "Just be fucking happy." And for a horrible second, I thought Peter was going to cry.

"Look, I am happy. We've gone to the ball. We're having a nice time, aren't we?"

"We've never really spoken about what happened at the manor. Not just . . . I mean all of it."

"Accidents happened at the manor. Just accidents. It wasn't anyone's fault."

"There's something, something I should tell you—"

"I grew up," I said. I don't know why I thought that was the correct response. Everything was getting away from me. "I grew up!"

"Is it because of Joe?"

The reflex, never buried that deep, surfaced in one white-hot second: I curled my fingers round the little bottle and lashed out with my fist, catching Peter on the brow.

Horrible. Horrible. I took off along one of the paths. I could hear him calling for me. Saying he was sorry. My breath was all wrong, sawing in and out, and I heard myself crying, distantly crying, the sound of a woman in distress. *Someone should help that woman,* I thought.

Emerging from the park, I found myself stumbling under the faded neon of the streetlamps in front of Buckingham Palace. Further on, there were guards up by the gates. The palace looked like an enormous wedding cake, white and clean and gleaming; a wedding cake or a doll's house, a doll's house built for a nation. I wondered which room the Queen was sleeping in? Or was she awake, peeping out from behind a curtain at the nocturnal subjects of her realm? I wondered if we ever kept her up nights with the worry of us.

There were steps up on the left. I sat down on them, or sprawled. The *Mail* was missing a tremendous opportunity for an upskirt pic.

Joe had been my mother's last boyfriend. He'd made my life hell from the age of thirteen to fourteen, before going out one night in his car and never coming back. Joe was the reason I couldn't stand Midlands accents and disliked beards and never took unlicensed cabs, in case one day I got in and Joe's eyes met mine in the rearview mirror. Joe was why I would never have a dog, because you owned a dog and put it on a lead, you told it what to do, and made it love and fear you, and that sort of thing was up Joe's street, not mine.

When Peter arrived, I was gazing up at the palace facade, working out if it was possible.

"Easy."

"What?" He sat down beside me and gently put my bag in my lap.

"To climb."

"Think you could still do it?"

"Maybe not in these shoes."

Peter gave me a smile that was just a twist of the mouth. I took his chin in one hand and touched his brow lightly with the fingers of the other. Peter winced.

"Sorry," I said.

"Me too. For all of it."

I could have said *all of what?* But I didn't, because I was afraid there were things we might say to one another that would mean the end of everything. And I couldn't afford to lose Peter. That's what it came down to.

After that, I got what I'd wanted, because we went back to the beautiful and very expensive room, and we lay upon the bed in the dark and I think I remember Peter taking my hand. But the sadness had arrived. It was always sad to see Peter, really. That was why we saw each other so rarely.

He was gone when I woke, along with a few chunks from my own personal wedding video. I didn't call him. I remembered enough. I didn't want filling in. I thought that by not calling him, that night could become just one more thing we didn't talk about. Instead, I collected my things and took the tube home, public transport as a form of penance. On the way from the station to my flat, I stopped and bought twenty quid's worth of low-end, highly processed sugars and fats, because I was already convinced that at home an episode would be waiting for me there. And it was.

But what was waiting for Peter? That was the question. What was waiting for Peter that caused him to break the habit of twenty years, the habit he had kept religiously, of calling his mother every Sunday after Evensong?

CHAPTER 4

APOCALYPSE II

WE TOOK MARCUS'S WAY DOWN FROM THE ROOF. AS I DROPPED into the long, wet grass, I felt a snail shell shatter under my heel, then something small and slimy squish against the ground. After wiping my foot on the grass, I went over to where I'd left my shoes and sat down to put them on. Peter left the stranger talking to Emma and shot over.

"He's a friend of the family who own it." Marcus had gone over to investigate. I saw him shrug. "He's at school with their son. His name's David." Peter stopped. A bubble of enthusiasm had been rising in his voice. When he spoke again, he had assumed his lazy, lecturing tone. "The parents are in America. They're British but his father's got business there. They're coming back in the autumn."

David was about our age. His hair was on the blond side; he had nice jeans on and a faded T-shirt in forest green. I could feel the day threatening to turn. He had more right to be there than we did, but he was uninvited. He came and the day I had planned so carefully was turning. Some people spoiled things. I cast another look at him, only to find him watching. He was humming as he came over and it took me a couple of seconds to pick up the melody.

"But if you're the queen of the castle," he said, "does that make us the dirty rascals?"

I had begun building a spliff. Now I let the lighter go out and blew out the tiny ember from what was a fast-diminishing eighth. The hash gave out a little plume of smoke. A few paces away, Em had her arm through Peter's, as though holding him back.

"You tell me," I said.

He sat down on the step, but not too close, and leaned back on his elbows, the toes of his shoes burrowing among the gravel. He was humming again and looking out over the lawns. Together, we followed the path of a white butterfly as it danced toward a sunken little pond, its surface covered in lily pads.

"These parents of your friend not about then?"

"In Boston for the summer," he said. His voice was neutral, not posh, but not local either.

"And you're what? Keeping an eye on it for them?"

I handed him the joint and his eyes met mine for a second before I could look away.

"Something like that," he said.

* * *

We ate the picnic I'd brought under the pear tree. There were mini pork pies and Scotch eggs, pasties, a Walkers multipack of crisps, and everyone's favorite chocolate bar: a Crunchie for Em, a Boost for Marcus, Peter's Wispa, and a Mars for me. Em snapped a bit of her Crunchie off and gave it to David and then we all followed suit, so that there were four little pieces of chocolate lined up before him on the blanket like offerings.

"What should I have brought you?" I asked. We waited expectantly while he thought about it. Would it be something posh? Cadbury's Bourneville, or—worse—a red Bounty? Perhaps he only ate Ferrero Rocher. In town, the nice cars had a tendency to slow down to let the kids in Marlborough College uniform cross the road while ignoring the rest of us. Then there were the plummy, carrying voices in Waitrose, the shops that sold evening wear, skiing and sailing kit, or displayed magnums of champagne in the window with strawberries around Wimbledon.

"Imagine it's the last day on earth, just before the apocalypse. It's the last chocolate bar you're ever going to eat," Peter said. I flashed him a look.

"The apocalypse?" David said. "Well, in that case, I think it would have to be a Curly Wurly."

"But a Curly Wurly is all holes!" Em's voice was hot with outrage.

David lay back on the grass. He was lean and a little shorter than both Peter and Marcus. Whereas Peter burned, Em freckled, and Marcus and I tanned, the sun turned his skin a tawny color. His hair was a dirty blond, the kind that would lighten in streaks. He made me think of summer, not June, but of the shorter days of July, the heavier quality of the air.

"It's the holes I want it for. They have a very special flavor," David said.

After a bit, I offered him the hash and he took a turn skinning up. He did it neatly with deft fingers. David had nice hands. It was the first time I remember noticing whether someone's hands were nice or not. The joint went round. There was a little rabbit-shaped cloud up above all on its own. At some point, Peter started up. When I tuned in, he was talking about Oxford.

". . . an offer from Balliol. Of course I have to get the results. Law's very competitive." He was starting to speed up. "Do you know today's the apocalypse? Andy's . . . well, someone said it was going to be today, so we decided to pretend that it was, which is why we came here. Andy's idea. She has a bit of a thing about this place. What would you do if it were the last day on earth? It's funny, because I'd still want to know what happened at the end of my book. So I'd probably end up reading right through it." On and on it went, without a pause for breath, Peter, like a trackside bookie, giving David the inside information on all of us. ". . . and Marcus's uncle keeps an eye on it for your friend's family, and Marcus is learning the business," and "Em's an artist, very talented. She's really into Blake," and finally, "Andy just wants to climb, she wants to be the English Catherine Destivelle."

I preoccupied myself with looking at my hands and willing him to stop. It would have been bad anyway, but being stoned made an agony of it. It was the braying edge his voice took on, his tone both superior and queasily desperate. It was almost as if he was trying to make you hate him, when of course, his intention was the exact opposite.

When he did suddenly stop, I glanced up to see David had laid a hand on Peter's forearm. The touch can't have lasted a moment. I wasn't sure if anyone else had even seen it. In the silence that followed, someone suggested leaving.

* * *

David walked us to the van where Marcus rummaged until he found a pen so we could write down our numbers. When it was my turn, I hesitated.

"You can try this if you can't get anyone else."

"It's for the box. Andy doesn't have a phone. You have to call the phone box at the end of her road and sometimes she answers and sometimes no one answers, and sometimes you get a passerby," Em said.

David folded the note and put it in his pocket. "Although if this is the last day ever, I guess there isn't much time for me to use it." While he was not looking at me in particular, in fact was turning from me to pat Peter on the shoulder and tell him that he must come back and try out the piano, I thought I felt the slightest stillness among his words, like the spot in a stream where the blank surface hides unexpected depths. And then, as we piled into the van, he glanced my way, as though to see if I had noticed it.

On the way back, we were quiet. I turned round in the passenger seat. Em was flicking through her sketchbook, but Peter's eyes were closed, his arms wrapped around his knees. I figured that he was hating himself for his performance back at the manor. I had a way of bringing him out of it when he got like that; the trick was to make him focus his disgust on something outside himself. Shit music. Shit telly. Shittest album, actor, newsreader, DJ, politician. Biggest prick at school among the sixth form, biggest prick among the staff. Get the venom going, get the fangs bared and pointing outward.

But this time, I turned back to look at the road and left him to stew in it. It was not just that Peter was leaving, it was that he was so desperate to be gone; to embark on a new life at Oxford among his future friends, a cast he'd assembled from the pages of books by Evelyn Waugh, and men he referred to initially by surname—Wilde, Huxley, Auden—and then, as though they had, over crumpets and tea in their rooms, moved on to first-name terms, as Oscar, Aldous, and Wystan.

"You'll come back to see us, won't you?" I'd asked.

"I expect we'll motor back for the odd weekend."

Because that is what Oxford promised, weekends of motoring in the countryside, picnics under trees with companions who would, after the wine had gone to their head, rest their cheek upon his arm, sigh and close their lovely eyes. It was his grail and I had no role to play in it.

When I was fourteen, after Joe had gone, after I dared believe it was for good, I had stopped going to school for a while. I found other companions, other ways to have fun. When I came back, I'd expected the crevasse between me and Peter to disappear, but it didn't. Half the time it was like he wasn't even there, like he was off somewhere in his own head, and he never wanted it to be just us, just me and him. If I suggested we go off on our own, he made excuses. At first, I'd thought he was punishing me for disappearing, but it wasn't that. It was like I wasn't safe anymore. That was how he'd treated me, and even now the unfairness of it made my eyes sting so I had to stare hard out the van window at the blurring hedgerows.

On the high street, Marcus pulled up and Em and Peter got out. Em had choir and despite my threats of rivers of lava and Death on a white horse, she'd pledged to go out with a handful of old ladies singing Queen medleys. We were the same height, but that's where the similarity ended. She was a fawn, Em. Not a pick over seven stone, and all fringe, eyelash, and skinny leg to my tits, arse, and lip. The same guys who at school shouted at me to get my tits out got tongue-tied around her, but I could never push her around.

"Em?"

"Not possible." It was what she always said when she didn't want to do something. A sad shake of the head, a sigh. "Not possible."

"Pete, we pick you up at eight?"

"I'm going to stay home and revise. I've got that last exam, remember."

"Pete, please!" It was Peter I wanted really. It always was. Games weren't the same without him. "It's the end of the world." But he shook his head. He wasn't playing anymore.

We went for a drive, stopping for a pint in the beer garden of the Red Lion at Avebury where we could look out at the stone circle. Marcus had a shandy because he was driving.

"You could get drunk if you wanted to. Won't matter if there's no tomorrow."

"If I got caught driving Darren's van pissed, I'd be praying for the apocalypse." He looked away. I had the sense he was tired of it, that he wanted me to let it drop. But that wasn't quite it.

"Andy—" Marcus looked about the garden, as if for help. Two women, a decade older, were sitting at a picnic table a way over with crisps and Cokes. One of them caught Marcus's eye and I saw her whisper something to her friend and they both laughed quietly. On Friday afternoons and Saturday mornings, I worked in Darren's office, sorting out the timesheets and helping with payroll. There was a new computer program that would, once it was set up, calculate everything automatically, and I was learning it since the two women who worked there refused to go anywhere near it. Most weeks Marcus picked me up after football, often still dressed in his kit, and Jules and Karen were the same as these two, purring and cooing over him, asking if he'd scored any goals, telling him he was the spitting image of Michael Owen, and offering him Jaffa cakes.

"What is it?" My voice came out less friendly than I intended.

"Uncle Darren phoned this morning."

"Yeah?"

"And he needs me this evening. He says it's important. Some travelers have got into one of the sites. They've got a sound system. If we don't get them out now, it'll be rave central. Then there'll be no getting rid of them. You and me can do something tomorrow."

"There is no tomorrow."

"Come on, Andy. Don't be—" He looked at me helplessly. He had brown eyes. They weren't like Peter's, which in some lights appeared almost orange. Marcus's eyes were depthless, a hardwood brown. I never wondered what he was thinking. But he was quick to put his hand in his pocket, and didn't count what I owed him, and he drove us about, and other girls wanted him although he acted like he didn't know it. "We can stay here for a bit. Get some chips in town."

I told him not to bother, and on the way back I gave one-word answers to his attempts at conversation, relenting only when we pulled up a hundred meters before the house, at the spot where he always dropped me off. I gave him a quick kiss, since it didn't do to push Marcus too far, got out, and watched him execute a three-point turn in the lane and drive off.

Our house was on the end of a row of farmworkers' cottages. They were tiny, with thick walls and small windows. The council owned them. In the seventies, indoor bathrooms had been added on the back, but ineptly, with minimal insulation, so that in winter it was like trying to wash in the middle of a freezing field.

Mrs. East was standing by her garden gate. A pack of B&H king size sat atop the low brick wall and as I came nearer she picked it up and shook it at me. I took one and she lit it with the lighter made out of a bullet casing that her husband had brought back from Germany after the war.

"How's you then?"

I shrugged. Mrs. East's hair hadn't gone white or even gray. Peter once suggested she blacked it with shoe polish. After we'd put the slowworm through her letterbox, terrified that we'd killed her, we'd plucked and left a rose on her doorstep each day for a week. From her own front garden. While we intoned the Lord's Prayer. We only stopped when we heard her cackling through the door.

"Have you seen her?"

"Not today. You had your tea? There'll be cauliflower cheese in a little while. *Countdown*'s on in ten minutes."

"Richard Whiteley's a tool."

Mrs. East let out a plume of smoke and cocked an eyebrow. It was not how I had envisioned the day panning out, but it was better than going home, and in the event, I wouldn't have changed things, since not only did I beat Mrs. East for the first time ever, but the word I got, ABALONE, was a seven, a personal best.

Mrs. East saw me out. At the gate, she stopped a few feet ahead of me and pointed skyward. A hawk was hovering over the field opposite the cottages. The sun was setting, and in its rays Mrs. East's ears were translucent, pink as seashells and tracked through by tiny veins. I looked up. The sky was whitening, the bird barely moving. For the briefest of moments, I felt myself disappear, had the disconcerting sensation that I was both the hawk and whatever creeping thing it was tracking, and then the feeling was gone and what remained was a sickening jolt of déjà vu and in the red phone box, the telephone started ringing as I had somehow known it would.

CHAPTER 5

TOWER

TWO DAYS AFTER PATRICIA'S PHONE CALL, I ARRIVED AT work to find, on my desk, a copy of a best-selling book. It was a memoir of a middle-class white woman who finds happiness by going on a long holiday, dabbling in soft-core spirituality, and getting a man. Oliver. Six months back I'd made the mistake of getting drunk with Oliver. I'd only meant to have one or two, but the brakes had utterly failed, and at some point into the third bottle of wine I had said something to him about wanting to change.

"Change what?"

"My life."

Now every once in a while Oliver would reference the moment. He had sent me a link to a video of an old Tampax ad in which a woman roller-skated joyously on a beach. Another time, he'd signed me up to a sponsored parachute jump. A letter had arrived at my flat thanking me for my interest in building schools in Africa. I dropped the book in the trash and opened my email.

There'd been no answer to the thirty or so calls I'd made to Peter's phone. Nor was there a reply to the string of emails I had sent. Now I typed another: *Patricia is worried. It's time for a turn.* And then, as an afterthought, *I am worried too.* A turn. That was what we called it when it was time for Peter, Em, or Marcus to return home and reassure various parties that they were still alive. *A quick turn, I'll be back after dinner!*

Even after I sent the email, I struggled to focus. The office was open plan and from my desk I had a view over the atrium and the desk-bound gatekeepers nineteen floors below. It was a tower, a tower whose music was air filter and fan, rap of heel on polished floor, tap of fingers on keys. There was not a blade of grass or a breeze, not a creature, only a tinny fountain in the marble foyer and a few captive plants, and yet how the shoulders around me hunched over the screens, how the eyes were fixed. We worked long days. Much of the year, we hurried home in the dark and hurried back before it got light, only to find the work was no closer to completion, as though our dreaming selves had unpicked it overnight. It had no magic, but it was not unenchanted. I had come to London when I was twenty-one. Seventeen years it'd been my home. Of those, seven I'd spent here.

Before me, a cursor flickered against a bright white page, empty save for the title *Compliance Initiatives in Response to New Regulatory Safeguards*. It was my job to write such reports, and shout at traders, and sign off on deals, enforcing the rules of the game that accounted for 11 percent of the UK's economy. But I did nothing, because I was harried by visions of Peter, not latter-day Peter but original Peter, ur-Peter, on the stone bench in the playground alone, jiggling a foot. Hunted down the corridors by bigger boys for wearing a homemade cape to school. I told myself that Peter was a big boy, able to look after himself, but all I saw was Peter as a small boy, Peter and I chasing raindrops down windowpanes with our fingers on wet days at school, our breath clouding the glass. On very rainy days, they sometimes gave us hot squash. We liked hot squash.

On a piece of paper I scribbled down the options. What I was left with was 1. Peter was not answering his phone or emails because he didn't want to. 2. Peter was not answering his phone or emails because he couldn't. This second possibility led to further options:

a. Peter was dead. b. Peter was sick or injured. c. Peter was being prevented from answering his phone or emails by person or persons unknown.

I found myself wanting to tell someone. Oliver? He would be dismissive. I thought of other colleagues I was on friendly terms with, with whom I occasionally lunched or grabbed a quick drink at the end of a particularly long day. Over the years I'd been confided in. Steph's messy divorce, James's stint in rehab, Petra—her face entirely expressionless—telling me that she wished she'd never had children. But none of them would do. Suddenly I knew who I wanted to talk to.

Not possible. Not possible.

Midmorning I called around the hospitals to ask about unidentified admissions. They told me to contact Missing Persons, but that would be a job for Patricia if it came to it. Instead, I searched the Internet for Peter. I sought him here. I sought him there. But he eluded me. There were so many Peter Whites, enough to fill a football stadium, and although I peered among their ranks, I could not find the distinguishing mark that would identify my own. Nor was I surprised. Peter had given me his views on social media, on "maintaining an online presence" during a stroll by the river a few years before.

"You've heard of Bentham?"

"'Fraid not, Peter."

"He was one of those eighteenth-century types. Did a bit of everything, philosophy, law, social reform. When he died, they stuffed him and put him on display at UCL."

"Seems a bit harsh."

"Oh, it was what he wanted."

The Thames hurried past like a man on urgent business. The rain and wind were coming every whichaway and had deterred most other strollers. I had come out without an umbrella, so Peter was trying to shield both of us with his.

"I think you're digressing. Tell me how Bentham has prevented you from posting updates about your cats on Facebook," I said. "Mittens seems a bit sad today. Or, Mittens stole my sandwich."

"Jeremy had a dream. It was for a prison. But being a progressive, kindhearted man, Bentham shied away from the kind of dungeon intended to either kill you or terrify you into behaving yourself for the rest of your life. He envisioned a Panopticon Penitentiary, a prison built in such a way that the inmates would all be visible from a central watch post, but would be unable to tell if they were being watched. They might be being watched all the time; they might not be watched at all. He believed that even the possibility of being observed would change the behavior of even the most hardened of sinners. He said it was a new mode of obtaining power over people in a quantity 'hitherto without example.' But even his ambitions pale into insignificance now."

"Not even LinkedIn, Peter? It's for business." He shuddered visibly. We were both wet. There were tiny droplets on his glasses, and his face was gleaming not only from the rain but with the come-to-life quality he took on when speaking about something he was interested in. I didn't quite believe him, was sure there was a Romeo or Grindr account somewhere with his profile picture on it, if not his name. But perhaps not. For some reason, I found myself thinking of Peter's angel.

By lunchtime, my insides hurt, as though something within me was rupturing, perhaps the place in which I kept the past safely lidded. I gave up on getting anything done. Instead, I googled Jeremy Bentham and read that along with his other achievements, he had coined the term "deep play," which he defined as a game with stakes so high that no rational person would engage in it. There was a portrait of him, a fleshy man, with shoulder-length white hair and a bald pate. His face wore the expression of someone eminently capable of filling heavy books of tissue-thin paper with minuscule print, the kind that with a pistol pressed against your head and forced to choose, you'd rather eat than read.

The news websites were full of atrocities and celebrities. There was more about the endless rain, and on a couple of sites these stories ran side by side with updates on the latest leaks, as though there was a connection between them, the falling rain, and the drip of confidential information about offshore bank accounts and secret payments and highly prominent world figures. It was all there, from tax avoidance by famous actors known for their public moralizing, to billion-dollar money laundering schemes run on behalf of criminal empires. And the corruption and embezzlement and outright theft were on such dizzying scales that the celebrity articles were a relief, a mildly poisonous anesthesia with which I tried to obliterate the feeling of helplessness.

I sought to lose myself in clicking, like a child following bread crumbs in the forest, not even looking for Peter anymore, but still possessed by the sense that I was somehow following a trail, a trail with an end to it. And I thought that perhaps that was what everything in my life had in common: work, and buying things, and going to the gym, and eating meals, and looking at things on the Internet, that they felt like necessary work, resulting in progress toward an unspecified goal.

I bought a coat, some cosmetics, a pair of flip-flops, a bottle of high-end vitamins, spending £400 before I knew what I was doing. I accidentally saw a photo of a man moments before his beheading, eyes wide, head pulled back. And so the day passed.

Everyone else started to go home. Nothing had been achieved. I had a trapped and hopeless feeling. The last thing I watched, before finally leaving around seven, were a few unboxing videos. I had stumbled on this particular series a while ago. They were oddly calming. In each one, a pair of smooth white hands, employing a small pair of scissors and occasionally a craft knife, opened a package containing a desirable consumer item, usually something electronic. The unboxing was always done against the background of a blue cloth and the maker of the video had added an unobtrusive soundtrack, over which the occasional small sigh could be heard when the pair of hands encountered an obstacle—a particularly resistant flap or bit of tape. The process was neither rushed nor unduly lingered over. In each video, the sequence happened in the same order: First the exterior packaging was opened and discarded, then any accompanying information, instructions, and so forth were extracted and held up to the camera, then came the turn of the accessories—chargers, batteries, and so forth—if they existed. Finally, the interior packaging was inspected and the product itself withdrawn, cleared of any protective sleeves and displayed by the hands from each angle. And every time, when the moment finally came, I wondered if the hundreds of thousands of other people who watched these videos felt the same as I did, the same anticipation, the same surprise, and ultimately the same disappointment—that what was inside the box was just a thing.

CHAPTER 6

APOCALYPSE III

I COULD SAY IT GAVE ME A MOMENT'S PAUSE, GOING BACK out to the manor on my own to meet David, but that would be a lie. I was sour at the others for leaving me to spend the apocalypse with my mother, as though they had conspired to make my worst nightmare come true—me and my mother, the last people on earth, locked in battle.

She called out my name a couple of times. Her voice was plaintive. I was in the bathroom, door bolted, and didn't answer. Soon she went away. I didn't want to fight with her, but I just couldn't find it inside myself, a kind word, a peace offering of any sort, even as I forced myself to think that it was the last chance I would ever have. Later, when I found out she'd eaten all the bread from the bread bin, a whole loaf that I had bought and paid for because she spent most of her giro on cans, I would be glad.

I ran a bath and slipped into the water. It was lukewarm and three inches deep. I got a washcloth and ran it over myself, climbed out and fought my hair back into a plait while looking in the bit of mirror we kept propped against the window, and in which I saw only pieces of myself, rubber lips, small chin, round grayish eyes. In the pane I could see a second reflection, whole, colorless, a mere outline superimposed over the field. In the twilight the barley was fawn and swaying where the breeze touched it. I waited there, watching, and it seemed that they were playing, the barley bowing to the breeze, the breeze gusting then abating. When it was gone, the barley seemed to wait, to tremble for it. It was like watching lovers.

* * *

When I left, the TV was off, but she had the radio on. Nights, if she was home, she liked to listen to the local show where people called up to talk about what was on their minds, in the middle of the night phoning in to get things off their chests about crop circles and ley lines, car clamping and the Criminal Justice Bill. My mother listened from the sofa, or paced the room. I sometimes imagined she was waiting to hear someone in particular, or for one of the speakers to say something, magic words perhaps, that would release her from her spell. Now I wonder if it wasn't simply that she had gone beyond music, that listening to it confused and disquieted her, like someone hearing a language they had once understood well, but which was now lost to them.

I took the Ridgeway back to the manor, jogged the three miles there swinging my arms. The track led across the Downs, a pale chalk road. I heard rabbits bolting in the darkness, pebbles skittering under my feet. I put home out of my mind and it was easy, like switching off a light. Midway, the track went through a copse where it was lightless, where the night was thicker, and my body shied like a blinkered horse as though sensing something my eyes couldn't see.

At the manor, I found David in a room on the first floor. I called for him and he answered, so I followed his voice through the dark rooms and up the creaking stairs and then down a black corridor toward a little flickering light. He was at the window, lighting a cigarette from a candle.

"Every time you do that, a sailor dies. But I suppose it doesn't matter now." David turned to me. "Will it be very violent, the end of the world? The dead bursting out of their graves and so on."

"Possibly," I said.

"Then I am glad you're here." The room was blue and the candle burned with an almost white flame. It did not seem end-of-the-worldish, but there was something old about it, as though the moment was not as freshly minted as others I had known. "Do we know when it is going to end exactly?"

"No."

"So it could be any moment?"

"Yes."

"Well then," he said.

"Well then what?"

"Well then, I should probably tell you something."

* * *

David was a liar, a thief, and in considerable trouble. It made me like him, when before I had not been sure. I liked stealing too. I liked things that were stolen. That morning, the last of my money had got me a half bottle of rum and two liters of supermarket brand Coke. I also had a crumb of hash, which we smoked out in the rose garden sitting on the stone bench where Mortimer had died, not that we knew it at the time. The beds were a tangle of weeds and thorns, but peeping out from among them were roses, still unfurling from their buds. While we talked, I tore off their heads and shredded the petals between my fingers.

There had been some kind of school trip to Italy. He had borrowed a coat and gone out and met some people and decided not to go back. Or not decided, one thing just leading to another. Only the coat had had credit cards and quite a large amount of money in it. And he had spent the money, and used the card a couple of times, three times at most, while thinking about what to do. Then, when he had decided he ought to go back, say sorry, and promise to pay back the money, etc., it was too late and the police were looking for him.

"Whose was the coat?"

"A teacher's."

It wasn't the whole of it, but I didn't press. I wasn't seeking a hold over him, at least not then.

We took the rum and Coke and went down to the lake, following the path round to the temple, where we inspected the plinth, which bore a stone head of Athena. Then, sitting cross-legged on the leaf-littered floor, we watched the moon slipping down into the water like a bather.

"Isn't it supposed to become as blood?"

David told me that in Rome, site of his recent troubles, there were great oil paintings of the apocalypse, and catacombs under the city, and that aboveground the city was full of statues of great men whose faces had been destroyed, the noses chiseled off by waves of invaders, and that right in the center were the ruins of the giant Colosseum, where you could sit on stone seats, look down, and see the underground passageways where the animals were led or kept chained before being released to gobble up Christians.

"They used to damn people to beasts." His voice was dreamy. "I had a dream once they set a fanged giraffe onto me. If you killed a parent, they put you in a leather bag full of vipers and then drowned you all together in a bucket."

He told me he'd been at the manor four days, that he'd walked a mile to the nearest pub to call me, and was about to give up when I answered.

Something slapped upon the surface of the water and the bathing moon broke into ripples.

"It's the kraken," he said. "It wakes up at the end of the world, says so in Revelation."

"Peter's father is a vicar," I said. "But he never reads from the good bits. I think he's embarrassed by them. It's all love and peace and Christian fellowship with him."

"Clever Peter," he said, "who's missing the end of the world in the service of algebra."

He touched my arm. The skin of his palm was dry. I followed

him back down the path to a spot on the lawn by the water's edge where we pondered the reeds in silence. I was waiting for him to try something. After all, he'd called me, not one of the others. I'd come because I wanted to know what I'd do. If I would turn my back on him, or laugh, let him kiss me, or say something mean. But David didn't do anything, even though I was standing a small step closer than was necessary, even though afterward he could say he was drunk, even though it was the end of the world.

Instead, he stood there, eyes to the sky, waiting. The moon was her fat self, pouring out a cold, pale light that put the stars to shame. I stole a couple of quick glances at his face and then back to the night. We waited and I could tell David was listening, so I listened too. The road had fallen silent, and in the quiet it was possible to feel, if not to hear, the music of the place, the manor itself, and of the great chalk ridges of the Downs, and the moon's chilling melody.

And David standing there, tensed, as though the heavens were just about to be rent asunder. For a funny moment, the game became real. That's the only way I can describe it. A shudder passed through me and then, as though it had leapt from my body to his, David shuddered too. It went on a little longer, the moment, until its edges trembled and it collapsed inward, and in the aftermath, as though from very far away, I heard the laughter spilling from us both, spilling like water.

* * *

We stayed up the whole night, waiting for it to happen, but it still didn't come. The sky was reddening in the east, as though a great fire were burning, but soon it faded and the light was pale and colorless.

We lay on the bed, on a sagging mattress. Heads in opposite corners, feet in the middle, not touching. We were weeks away from touching, and even then David would never touch me first. He brought you close with talk but did nothing. It made a space. With Marcus, he was always there before me. He wanted me and was prepared to stay close, to queue patiently for whatever I would dish out, till I felt like a hair-netted, apron-wearing server in a canteen. But with David there was space, and in it I would learn what it was to burn for someone. Only a forewarning, then, on the musty sheet, a far-off siren, no cause yet for alarm.

Below a wood pigeon, breast thrust out like Napoleon, strode across the lawn. I thought of the day to come, of all the days to come, of my mother in her room at home; once she had had fresh starts, heralding spring cleans, swearings off, jacket potatoes and tuna, but there were no fresh starts now; the days were a pack of cards wiped clean of their faces. A pack of days to come, and among them the possibility of a black jack. The sound of the old Merc's engine behind me in the lane. Joe at the wheel. Peter always said he was gone forever, but what did Peter know?

David went with me as far as the gate. On either side of the drive, the grass was sopping with dew. At the bend near the front of the house, there were bicycle tire tracks in it, just for a couple of meters, as though the rider had wobbled off course.

"Did you call anyone else? Before me, I mean."

"No. Just you."

"If I hadn't answered, who would you have called next?"

"I don't know. Will you come back?"

"So you're staying?"

"I need to think what to do. And I like it here. Don't you, Andy? There's something about it." David smiled. The top incisor on the left next to his canine was chipped sharp. In combination with the smile, it made him look a bit fox-like.

"I suppose." As though I could have stopped myself coming back, even if I tried. There had been that moment, you see, that moment with David at the lakeside when I had felt something, something rare. As a child I would have called it magic. As an adult, you weren't supposed to believe in magic, even if you needed it, even if you needed it desperately.

* * *

Mrs. East's front door cracked open and she beckoned me over.

"Saw you coming back down the lane. I'd give anything to sleep like I did when I was your age, and there's you wasting it. Tea?"

Inside, her house was the same as ours, save it looked like the person who lived there liked it. There were family pictures on the walls. A grainy black-and-white of her parents. Her son, Ian, a boy in a donkey jacket with a puppy, a man with a bow tie and a lost expression. My favorite was the one of her husband in uniform during the war. He was wearing an army cap and smiling. It was a picture taken to give to a woman. The eyes were promising.

Mrs. East told me once that while he'd been away fighting the Germans, she used to go dancing with airmen from the RAF camp. She told me she couldn't sit at home for five years and that there had been an American who told her he painted her name on the side of the big bombs before they flew them over Germany. "He told me I set Hamburg alight," she said and I knew he was her lover, the American, and I wondered if her husband had known it too.

After Mrs. East had poured the tea, she got the frying pan out and put four rashers in it. When it started to sizzle, she went and stood over it, giving the bacon the odd idle push with an egg slice. Only after I started talking, telling her about David and the manor, did she take a couple of the rashers out of the pan, sandwich them between two slices of bread, and hand me a plate along with the sauce bottle.

As I ate, she came over and I felt her pick up the end of my plait and hold it between her fingers for a second. "Don't get old, Andy."

"I'll try not to."

"This lad, blond haired or dark?"

"Blondish."

"Blond men go bald early. Such a shame." Her smile was quick and wicked. "What's he like then?"

What was David like? I furrowed my brow.

"Oh dear, oh dear!" Mrs. East let out a dry laugh that turned into a coughing fit. Finally, between wheezes she got out, "You'll have to dance with him. We always said you could tell what a man was like by dancing with him."

"I'll bear it in mind."

Mrs. East slid the pack of cards out of the drawer. Usually, we played chase the ace, trumps, or gin rummy. Mrs. East liked to win too. "Before the war the manor took a lot of staff from Marlborough and villages, maids, gardeners, all that."

I dabbed the last crust in the puddle of bacon grease while she shuffled, the cards making ripping noises between her hands, which were all knuckle and vein and gleaming ring. I slid a B&H from the pack, lit it, and passed it to her, and then lit one for myself.

"Poacher."

I had a look at my hand. It was not bad, not bad at all. Mrs. East ran her tongue over her teeth and exhaled smoke out of her nose in two plumes, like a dragon. She fanned the cards and studied her hand, looked up.

"Maybe you'll find the diamonds, Andy."

CHAPTER 7

TELEPHONE BOX

PETER WAS FINE, PETER WAS ALMOST DEFINITELY FINE. I swept my trolley down the frozen aisle under the neon strip lights. Peter was having a small existential collapse, an episode, hopefully somewhere warm where it wasn't pissing down.

After work I had gone home, and then, unable to settle, I had come here. The supermarket was open till midnight. I liked it best near closing time. Without the hordes, it was a soothing place to wander, a hypnotic dreamscape, a place I felt myself largely absent, as though crowded out by the spirits of my ancestors, the thousands of generations who had starved in winter and tottered about in rags and watched their children die of scurvy, who knew that the moment I was living was an anomaly—a brief comfort-saturated flaring in which the human race burnt through everything it had, like a wild sailor on shore leave—and who wanted to enjoy the moment, to roam the aisles of the supermarket and choose between thirty-three types of bread.

The past, what I had escaped, what I had lost, were not what I wanted to think about. Peter could have any number of reasons for going AWOL. Instead, I lingered over toiletries and cleaning products and condiments, hand hovering as I selected and rejected. Teams of people had spent many hours ensuring each item was as convincing as possible. I let the waterfall of words—jalapeño, Californian, corn-fed—wash over me, maneuvering my little trolley, comforted by the anonymous presence of others. Was I close to running out of Worcestershire sauce? How were stocks of dried goods? These were questions I could answer.

I chose the last remaining cashier over the self-service checkout. She smiled at me and I smiled quickly back. The total came to £19.02 and I gave her a £20 note and the extra two pennies and I got another smile as she handed me the shopping bag with my items and the receipt in it; between us, we managed the whole thing so deftly and humanly, I felt quite reassured. Just before the automatic doors, for a split second I was tempted to go back and ask the cashier if, broadly speaking, she thought everything was going to be okay.

The rain danced on the road and the cars swished past, their lights shimmering in yellow and red on the wet tarmac. I hung the carrier bag from my wrist, put my umbrella up in one smooth movement, and stepped out resolutely onto the pavement. Cold droplets bounced upward, beading my tights. I hurried on. Up ahead, something fell down in front of one of the streetlamps, a fairly large item and heavy, since it fell so fast. I heard a man cry out, a rough shout of fear, and then I saw another person run across the road in front of a car.

I could not tell what had happened, but my instinct, honed by years of living in London, was to turn on my heel and find an alternative route home. *Man run amok at Waterloo? Then I'll take the Northern Line via Bank.* As I hesitated, a small crowd drew up around something. All of a sudden, the situation, like one of those pictures of a platter of fruit and vegetables that turns out to be a man's face, resolved itself. Someone, or something, had fallen from the roof. If it was a something, it had hit a someone. Someone was on the ground.

I cried out, "Peter!" I think I cried it out more than once. A charge volted through me from the roots of my hair to my fingernails. Peter was lost. Peter might be hurt. Where was Peter? I wanted Peter.

I barged my way forward and knelt. It was a man, a man in a

beautiful navy-blue cashmere coat. There was quite a big pool of blood. The rain was falling upon it. I reached out a hand and touched the man's hair. It was dark, but it was not Peter's hair.

"Don't touch him," someone said. "You're not supposed to—"

"He's dead," I said.

"But you have to wait. You can't move them. An ambulance is coming."

"Do you know him then?" A woman this time.

"No." I stood up.

One of the men was looking upward. "He came off the top," he said. "And he came all the way down." He was a big, bald man. He spoke almost with reverence. There was the approaching throb of a siren.

As children, Peter and I had dreamed of coming across a great mystery, a puzzle that only we could solve by means of deciphering various clues. What was in it for us? What reward had we expected?

More recent arrivals pressed forward. There was the urge to see. The man was hidden again from sight by the crowd. The ambulance—or was it the police?—drew nearer. Either way, soon the real detectives would arrive. They would get their tape out and seal off the area. Out would come the notebooks, the pencils to take down the answers to their questions. I had seen it all before.

* * *

The phone at the Whites rang and rang. I hung on grimly, estimating the time it would take for either the vicar or Patricia to lay aside their book, put on their slippers, and descend the long and winding vicarage stairs. Eventually, Patricia picked up.

"Peter?" Her voice was flustered, hopeful. I imagined her hurrying down in her flannelette, gripping the bannister, thinking I was her son. I felt bad for not waiting till the morning.

"No, it's me. It's . . . Andy."

"Oh."

"I'm sorry it's so late."

"Is there news, dear?"

"No, not yet. Listen, are you sure you can't remember who Peter was working for?"

"No, I told you. I thought I had it written down, but I've been through everything, everything in the bureau, and all of Richard's papers in case I'd . . . It was . . . it was two names and one of them was a foreign—" She was as close to tears as I had ever heard her.

"But you do have Peter's address? Thing is, I thought I'd pop round. I mean, it's late but he's likely to be home now. If he's not gone away, that is."

I waited while she fetched her address book and made her repeat it to me until I had it by memory. Birthday cards, Christmas cards, thank-you cards—to Patricia, they were what separated us from the beasts. I didn't doubt she still sent cards to people she hadn't seen in fifty years.

"He might be cross. Do you think he'll be cross, Andy? When he was still at home, he'd have the most frightful rages if I went near his room. His bed would be full of toast crumbs and there wouldn't be a teacup left anywhere else in the house . . ." She trailed off. "You'll let us know, won't you?"

I said that I would. As I waited for the taxi to arrive, I tried to remember Peter's "frightful rages" but couldn't really. What temper Peter had, he kept in check around me. When I looked back it was always me throwing my weight around, losing my rag. But Peter? Peter had gone underground. He had been evading me for so long, it was hard to say exactly when it'd started.

The cab pulled up and I got in. As soon we pulled away, I realized I had neither my umbrella nor my shopping, but I didn't think for a moment of turning back. I felt it, bone deep, the sudden conviction that Peter was not dead, that Peter was hiding, and I was going to find him, really find him, as I always had in our games of hide-and-seek—crouched behind the holly bush, or lurking in one of the

Hacketts' calf pens. I heard it faintly, a far-off cry echoing down the years, *Coming Peter, ready or not!*

* * *

His flat was in Vauxhall, not far from the station. The building was twenty stories high, new, its surface sheer and glassy. Most of the apartments were owned by foreign investors and left empty, nest eggs, to minimize tax liabilities and be turned into cash when the need arose. A few apartments were illuminated, but the majority were dark.

I presented myself to the doorman as Peter's cousin, Peter's worried, trembly voiced cousin, sweet and uncertain. The doorman buzzed Peter's flat.

"Mr. White is not answering." He was reading *The Abuja Inquirer* online and, as I leaned in over the desk, I saw he had his shoes off. A half-eaten ham roll was sitting in an open drawer. He looked at it guiltily and slowly rolled the drawer shut.

"Do you know if he is there? Have you seen him today? Recently then?"

A shake of the head. "But I do nights. Eleven till six. I haven't seen your cousin in some time, but that doesn't mean he's not here."

"His mother asked me to come. She doesn't want to call the police yet, but we're all so worried. He might be in there. He might be sick." My voice suggested the edge of tears, it suggested that upstairs my cousin was dying, his phone just out of reach. The doorman's name tag said Adewale. I could see the word "mother" affected him. I tried it again. "You have to let me in so I can see if he's all right . . . for his mother."

From my handbag, the statement handbag that I had placed on the desk with the globally recognizable logo pointing right at him, I took out my phone. "You know what my cousin looks like, you've seen Peter?" I showed him the selfie I had taken of us at the wedding. "Me and Peter." He looked down at the picture as though an answer would be found there. "Come up with me. If he isn't there, no one will know you ever let me in. If he is, then he's in trouble and you'll have done the right thing."

I waited while he put his shoes back on. He looked frightened. It was the fear of getting things wrong, of getting in trouble. I pressed on before he could think of someone he should call. I had the sense he was a newcomer, to the job or the city. I knew how that was, the shallowness of the hand- and footholds. Only I had been able to assimilate, to make myself indistinguishable from those who ran things.

"You have keys, don't you? Keys to the apartments?" He fetched a bunch from the drawer.

"I can't be gone for long."

"We'll be quick."

The lift rose up into the night sky. I could see the doorman's face reflected in the glass. A struggle was going on inside him, and without saying or doing anything, I focused on exerting my will over him.

The lift opened onto a corridor, pale and empty.

"It's so quiet. Does anyone live here?"

He nodded. At one of the apartments, he took out the key and slipped it into the door. Then he stopped, wide-eyed. "Maybe he isn't alone." He paused. "Your cousin has visitors sometimes. Visitors at night."

So we knocked and called his name through the door. Then, "I am opening the door, Sir. Your cousin and I are coming in." But the doorman, Adewale, lingered on the threshold. We had seen too many films, the both of us. We knew how it went, the corpse like an unwrapped gift, the blood spray up the wall. Gay men, like women, were most likely to be killed by the people they had sex with. Perhaps that was why we bonded so well over cosmos.

I tottered inside, calling Peter's name. The room was vast, white walled, except for the expanse of glass that faced out over the river. On a sunny day it might have been lovely, but now the darkness pressed against the pane, as though it was peering in. There was a tang in the air I couldn't place, that was neither cleaning product nor food. Three rooms led off the main room: a bathroom, a bedroom, and a study or second bedroom that was totally empty. Peter was not there, nor were there many signs that Peter had ever been there. Where were the books? Where were the records? Peter had liked to express himself through content, back when we didn't call it content: well-thumbed copies of yellowing paperbacks, videos of foreign films taped off Channel 4 after midnight, vinyl when everyone else was showing off their CDs. All hoarded up in the hope that someone, the right someone, would see them and know him for who he really was. I was the one looking, the one paying attention, but I was never the right person for Peter.

In the wardrobe, there were expensive shirts still in their wrappings. In the bathroom cabinet, a half-empty box of antidepressants. In the shower, hotel soap and shampoo. In the fridge, a flat bottle of tonic and an array of condiments.

Peter slept on a mattress thrown in the middle of the floor, a few short steps from the gleaming black kitchen. The bed was unmade, the sheets in need of a wash. Among the pillows, I spotted a bag of mint imperials and a smile came unbidden: a geography teacher, Mrs. Haines, catching him at it, week after week. Her back to the class as she wrote notes on the board:

"Mr. White, I hope you've got enough of those for everyone."

Until the week he replied that he supposed he did, actually, and she had him get up and divvy them out, only hardly anyone ate them, because they were Peter's.

The dishwasher had a hint of foulness. I stared into its mouth, and into the pristine oven and the empty bin, and I ran my fingers over the cutlery in the drawer and banged it shut, so that Adewale looked at me in alarm.

An armchair was placed by the window. Was this where Peter had his cornflakes in the morning? Or where he sat in the evenings, at night even, before or after his visitors had come and gone? Upon the glass, an oblong smear. I sat down in the chair and leaned forward to rest my forehead against the window. Below me, the glutinous river snaked toward the sea. When I drew back, some inches below the first smear was now another. And I thought, *Oh Peter, this is not what we planned. This is not what we planned at all.*

Which was when, looking down, I saw it, at the foot of the chair, as incongruous as a dream image: a red telephone box, six inches high and made of molded plastic, the kind sold in the tourist traps around Piccadilly alongside models of busby-hatted soldiers and teapots in the shape of Big Ben.

This one had been customized. I picked it up and held it in the palm of my hand. The windows of the telephone box were blackened and in places the plastic had melted and twisted. As I turned it this way and that, a sooty, oily residue came off on my fingers. It smelled poisonous, like the bonfires Mr. Hackett used to have at the back of the cowsheds, old tires and baler twine smoldering away in a metal drum.

To almost anyone else it would have meant nothing. But I knew it. I knew what it meant. It spoke volumes to me, and I waited there, holding it in my hands as the minutes stretched out.

Later I would wonder why I was so convinced, how I had taken off so keenly down the wrong path on the basis of such a small thing. Perhaps because it chimed with certain thoughts I'd had over the years, certain suspicions. That melody on the piano, Peter's face when I came in the morning we found the body. The possibility that in the book written by Peter's angel was an entry I'd do anything not to read.

Or perhaps it was because—unable to imagine a future, little better than asleep in the present—there was something I had lost among the ruins of the past, something of myself that I had to retrieve. That, in the end, the clue said nothing about Peter and everything about me.

CHAPTER 8

DIAMONDS

LIKE ALL CHILDREN, I KEPT A LIST OF THE THINGS MY mother didn't give me. Mine was more substantial than most: a father, siblings, family in fact of any kind, answers to the most basic of questions. What I had was Peter, and to some extent the Whites—usually good for a roast dinner after church, despite Patricia's mixed feelings about me—and I had Mrs. East. Mrs. East, who made me cups of tea, and doled out fags and sponge cake, and told me things. Like, when I was a babe in arms, my mother had turned up with me one day in a taxi. Colin, Mrs. East's husband, had come out to see if he could help with the bags and she'd told him to piss off.

And she told me that during the hours of wakefulness, in the night, in the gray dawn, she would time travel, reenter the past in reverie, that there was a trick to it, like threading a needle with your eyes closed. Done right, she could live it again, certain moments, certain days, not as herself, but as a witness, a will-o'-the-wisp, shadowing younger Mrs. Easts, reliving days fifty, sixty years old:

"I was out at the castle. I used to go there to watch them come home, the bombers, to count them in like hens into the coop. Listening out for their engines. Scanning the skies. I used to think if I could be there to count, I could keep them safe, stop the fox from getting them. I was wearing the lilac cardigan and my brown shoes. The bomber made a funny noise as it came in, the engine stuttering.

On the airfield, the men came running. Tiny, they were. The noise stopped, the engine noise, and they were coming down. I felt my heart stop. It stopped in my chest. All the birds lifted from the fields below. They came up and the plane came down over my head, so close I could see the bullet holes."

We were standing at her back window, watching the day leaving. Late September sunset: a rollout of radiant pink, the sun offering a rose-gold wreath to the earth; the light touched the mist rising from the harvested fields, and the vapor became corporeal, the body of a god as a shower of golden light. Her head lay on my shoulder. She made a gesture with her hand, the one that would have also belonged to one of her parents and charmed those who loved her, a sort of circling indication meant to firm up meaning, to locate it in the ether, when she felt her words were not enough.

"Andy, I think sometimes of all the jobs people don't have anymore: cartwright, and plowman and lamplighter, coalman, quarryman. It's like even the words are becoming ghosts, are vanishing into the mist. It's like souls dying."

The last times I saw her, in the hospital in Oxford—my third year in London, fourth?—she took my hand and told me that she was sorry she hadn't done more. "I should have stuck a carving knife in him, Andy my love. That Joe. It's the only thing I regret."

"You still haven't got a nine at *Countdown*, Mrs. East."

"I did so."

"'Seraphims' isn't a word, my darling." And I kissed her bony hands, and the creases on her cheeks, and when I fell asleep in the chair I thought I heard her say something, one last thing, but my eyelids were too heavy and I missed it, I missed the last thing Mrs. East ever told me.

But on the subject of the diamonds, Mrs. East should have kept her mouth shut.

* * *

From Mrs. East, the bones—a famous theft, a prominent local family, an unsolved mystery. Mrs. East remembering the newspaper reports from the year she was twelve, the gossip raging for months in town, the sightseers who came down from London to stand at the manor's gates and gawp, before heading to The Polly Tearooms for scones. The flesh we added from books Peter found or ordered from the library, a guide to local history, a compendium of unsolved crimes, a biography of Lady Mary Ashton, the owner of the diamonds. The case we assembled went like this:

In 1936, a diamond necklace is stolen at the manor. The manor, then as now, is three stories high, built of redbrick and sandstone. A small portion belongs to the sixteenth century, most to the seventeenth, and of course there are the later additions: the outbuildings and stables, the Georgian folly of a Greek temple in Portland stone down by the lake. There are sixteen bedrooms on the two upper floors, not including those in the servants' quarters. On the ground floor, there is a library and a drawing room, a dining hall and a room for billiards. There is a boot room and a run of sculleries and pantries.

The road that passes in front of the house is at the time little more than a cart's width wide. Even in 1936, it's a rare day that sees more than a handful of motorcars, which is to say cars are noticed.

The manor's heyday is long gone. It is the same all over the country. The estate is being sold parcel by parcel to pay taxes and death duties, to make up for investments gone south with the Wall Street crash. The family cannot get the staff. There are factories in Swindon and Oxford where the wages are higher, where the young people don't have to bow and bob, where there are bosses, not betters. Still, the staff—all old hands (too old it is lamented), all trusted faithfuls, no newcomers, no one who can't be vouched for—do a fine job, the all-important appearances are maintained.

The manor has been in the family since Queen Anne. They won't sell it until they have to. In 1936, having to is twelve years off, when the Denfords' boy is dead and Lord Denford, shunned from 1940 onward for his vocal support of Hitler in the years before the war, for having stood up in the House of Lords and sung "Land of Dope and Jewry" to the tune of "Land of Hope and Glory," finally accepts that the writing is on the wall.

Back to the manor: Beyond the grounds, there is a small wood that rises to the horizon; the surrounding farmland is made up of rolling fields which grow wheat and barley. There are racing stables and gallops and, on the higher ground where the Downs are steep, flocks of sheep. Just to the south, there is a hamlet that bears the same name as the manor. It has an inn and a small church with a graveyard where those who have lived in the house are usually buried, those who did not die in foreign wars or marry into families who claimed them for their own.

We are close to the Ridgeway here and not far from the White Horses, the stone circle at Avebury, various long barrows and Iron Age earth fortifications. Marlborough is three miles as the crow flies; the nearest train station is in Kendon, two miles to the north.

On the night the diamonds go missing, all is swathed in snow. Overnight a thick layer has fallen to blanket the house, the fields, the lichen-speckled graves. All is white, save the shadows, which are blue, and the lake, which is black in parts and gray where the ice is spreading, growing over the surface like a cataract forming over an eye.

It is the dead of winter, and the dead of night, and there are tracks, human footprints, in the snow, beginning in the courtyard, at the door to the library. At first, they follow the path toward the outbuildings and then past the stables, moving in the direction of the road, but at the foot of the drive they falter and then halt, perhaps contemplating the drifts of snow ahead, the likelihood of any vehicle at all being able to reach the manor, no matter what plans have been made, no matter how vital the mission.

After that, the footsteps double back, briefly disappear into the tack room adjoining the stables, and then reemerge, this time leading down through the drifts to circle the lake, tracking across the film of snow that has blown over the floor of the little temple, until at its center they turn and, very distinctly, the toes point out over the lake, as though their maker paused here to contemplate the frozen reeds and thickening film of ice.

When they leave the temple, something new starts to happen. The drifts on the lawn are, in places, knee deep and as the tracks return in the direction of the house, they begin to wander. Here and there, the snow is greatly disturbed and, once back within the walls of the kitchen garden, the tracks become smears. Finally, by the stone bench in the rose garden, they stop.

The scene is one I have visited in my dreams, both sleeping and waking.

A man, a Mr. James Mortimer, is slumped on the bench, his panting exhalations creating small puffs of smoke in the freezing air. He is dying, and James Mortimer is not his real name. It is the name he assumed when he befriended Lord Denford's son at the races, when he offered him good tips that led to fair-to-middling wins, when he coaxed and flattered and listened his way into Clive Denford's trust. It is a name that leads nowhere.

In his lap lies a small tin, its two halves prized apart. Later they will test the tin for poison but find instead gelignite. Mortimer took it for his heart. He is looking down sadly into the empty case, panting as he dies.

"It would have been all right, I suppose, if it wasn't for the snow."

Mortimer doesn't look up. You would think that it would be better to die looking up at the sky than down at your knees.

"There was an accomplice, wasn't there? They were supposed to come and spirit you away. Except it started snowing and it didn't stop."

A bubble forms on his lips and bursts. Behind us the house is quiet. There are seventeen souls inside: the four family members, six servants (the four who sleep in and two who have accompanied their employers), and the seven weekend guests, the men there to shoot, the women to gossip and play cards. There are four more hours until the stable boy and scullery maids get up, seven more till Sir Thomas Denford and his weekend guests have their tea taken up, and Lady Mary Ashton realizes her diamond necklace, her famous diamond necklace, is missing, its velvet-lined case empty and the door to her room—which she swears she locked from the inside—open, the key missing.

"Where's the necklace?" I ask. "Where did you put it? We looked everywhere. Em always said it was in the lake."

I sit down and reach over to tilt Mortimer's chin up so that he gets a view of the night sky. There's no moon, but the night is aflame in blue and white.

He's not going to speak to me. He never speaks to me, not even to tell me his real name.

Mortimer has stopped panting now. He seems to have given up exhaling. Instead he takes a series of tiny in-breaths while his eyes scan the heavens left to right as though reading a book. I try one last time:

"Where is it, James? Where's the necklace?"

But it's useless. He's leaving, taking his secrets with him.

What we know about him—the racing tips, the paternal interest he showed in a somewhat lost young man, the promise of a lucrative business proposition—is all we'll ever know. Eight years later, Clive drowned in the shallows of a Normandy beach during the D-Day landings. Four years after that, his father, Lord Denford, sold up and moved to a house in the village of Ramsbury. When he died, a former domestic told the papers he kept a picture of Hitler and a revolver in the top drawer of his bedside table.

James Mortimer expires, becomes extinct. The papers have a field day. Half a million replicas in glass are made and sold in Woolworth's. When the police fail to find the diamonds, Mary Ashton's family hires a private detective. The search goes on for months. For years the theories multiply—an insurance swindle, an inside job. People claim to know who Mortimer was, or that they've seen the diamonds in Rio de Janeiro, or Sydney, around the neck of a gangster's moll in Chicago. None of it comes to anything. The story fades, is revived first on the occasion of Mary Ashton's scandalous divorce and then upon her death. It lingers in the minds of locals like Mrs. East, enters the annals of local history, becomes an anecdote here, a footnote there.

It was enough for us. More than enough. We spent the summer playing a game in which we searched for the diamonds. The game was a ritual, the ritual a spell. As though from above, with an all-seeing eye, I see the five of us, each of us a finger of a single hand, probing the manor's nooks and crannies.

I used to try to hear the diamonds. When we played the game, I used to listen for them, very hard, making myself quiet, as though they would speak to me and tell me where they were.

Perhaps a month before the end? An August rain falls from a cloudless sky and dries instantly. I am barefoot by the stables. I have been balancing on a rotting rain barrel searching the guttering. My hands are green with slime. David is walking toward me. He has been wading in the fountain. Wet footprints trail behind him. His T-shirt and shorts are soaked through. He is wearing an expression of mild surprise. It is an emptying thing to play the game. The hours slip by. The past and future retreat to dark corners far away. Something inside, in the heart, is being worked upon. There is an unlocking feeling, an unlocking feeling in the chest.

So David wears a surprised smile, a dazed look. His expression is reflected on my face. Our smiles touch first. I turn and go back toward the stables, toward the open door to the room full of birds' nests, spiderwebs, and old bits of tack. David follows me. His footprints shrink and disappear.

In the stables it's cooler. I have pretended for a long time that I am not frightened of anything, that there is nothing left that can frighten me. I have removed myself to a safe place, so it is so. My self comes back to my body, unsteady, circling. David shivers and I shiver.

I put out my hand and put it over his heart. After a moment, he does the same. The pads of his fingers pressing gently against my chest through the cotton of my shirt.

This is the other game, and I do not know how to separate them.

CHAPTER 9

ENCHANTED PALACE I

FRIDAYS AND SATURDAYS, I WORKED FOR DARREN IN THE office, matching purchase orders with invoices and delivery notes, then stapling them together. I slid the drawers out of the big metal filing cabinets and rifled through pink carbon copies for serial numbers matching the ones on a list Jules had given me. When that was done, I fired up the computer and played about with the payroll program with the manual open on my lap until Marcus came to pick me up.

Em finished at the tearooms at three. She came out in her black and whites with the little cap still on and got changed in the back of the van as we took the road out to the manor.

"Tips any good?"

"Busload of Americans!" She was unpinning her cap, her hair—mouse brown and poker straight—falling over her face.

"Did you get us anything?"

"Might have a few scones about my person, my love." She smoothed down her hair and began unbuttoning the white frilly blouse they made her wear. Marcus kept his eyes glued to the road. In stillness, she could sometimes take on the look of a lady from an old painting, keen-eyed and white-throated, with a smile that guarded secrets. But Em was not often still, and when she spoke it was broad Wiltshire. The tights and skirt came off. The maid disappeared. She had on a cream satin padded bra we'd nicked from Dorothy Perkins and a pair of yellow Snoopy underpants, then a T-shirt and shorts.

"Where's Peter?"

"At a wedding I'm guessing." Peter picked up tidy sums playing the "Wedding March" and "Jerusalem" for couples getting hitched. "Least no one was answering when I called."

But I was wrong, because when we got to the manor, Peter was already there, quite at home, sitting on a blanket I recognized from the vicarage conservatory, David beside him in the sunshine.

* * *

He told the others what he had told me. The school trip to Italy at Easter, the theft of the coat and cards. Same details, same confidential tone. I tried to look like it was news.

"How did you get back into England?" Em asked. "Didn't they have your name on a list at the airports?"

"I hitched lifts with lorry drivers. I came across on a ferry from Calais to Dover with Bob from Barnes and a load of Parma ham. At customs, they barely even looked at my passport."

"This teacher, what's he like?" Peter was scratching his shin where an ant had bitten him. My eyes wandered to his bike. It was on the grass, back wheel spinning slowly in the breeze.

"Badger? All right, I suppose." David swallowed. "A bit funny maybe, even for a teacher, but easy enough if you stayed on his good side." David had been at boarding school on a scholarship, but because of the business in Italy, he'd missed his exams.

"You could get a caution," Marcus said. Sentencing was a matter of interest among his friends. What you got for doing what.

"Don't know if they have cautions in Italy."

"Or maybe you can get the charges dropped, get him to say he'd given you the card, or it was all a mistake."

David looked a bit queasy at that.

"Not impossible," he said. "But I think everyone should cool off a bit first. Then I was thinking I might write him a letter." He was still looking for the right move, or perhaps for the problem to just go away. David didn't believe rules applied to him. "Maybe," he said, glancing at Peter, "you can help."

"Won't your parents be going mad with worry?" Em asked.

"I sent them a postcard." Later, he would describe them as "Nice people, you know. Nice, very law-abiding." He gave a suffocated laugh. "Dad's desperate for me to get an apprenticeship. Mum writes down everything she spends and eats in a little book. On Sunday mornings they test the smoke alarm."

David got up and we followed him into the house. The kitchen was cold enough to bring out goose bumps. There was a table, chairs, and a deep enamel trough. He'd found the mains and turned the water back on.

While the tap ran, we got some cups together. David handed me water in a tea-stained mug and our fingers touched.

We went out again, this time into the courtyard, and from there into the rose garden. David's head was inclined attentively to Peter who was talking about a book he was going to lend him. Marcus slipped his arm around my shoulders. Em skipped ahead. We had come to stand in front of the stone bench where, all those years ago, mysterious Mr. Mortimer had been found dead. I cleared my throat.

"So, Mrs. East says . . ."

* * *

In the beginning, it gave us a reason to look around as much as we liked. We talked about hiding places, the places where, had we been Mortimer, we would have chosen to secrete the necklace. We had to remember it was freezing, and the middle of the night, and that we had a heart condition, that we were panicking!

The diamonds were not under the old terra-cotta flowerpots.

Nor did we find them in the shallows of the lake, the wet mud squidging between our toes.

Not among the spiders in the cellar or with their cousins in the attics.

Or among the rotting tack in the stables.

Or in the greenhouses, as we tiptoed among the broken glass and the empty snail shells that littered the floor like spent bullet casings.

Still, I felt a singing feeling in my blood, as though Mary Ashton's discovery of her loss, the following uproar in the manor, the arrival of the police, were not events long past, but just about to happen.

"Diamonds," Em sang. "Oh diamonds, where are you!"

And David smiled at everyone with his eyes, and it was like a lamp shining. It made you want to get closer, because David thought he was special, and within the ring of light he cast, you were special too.

Still, I kept a careful distance. For Peter's sake, for Marcus's.

Later, parked up in the lanes, Marcus leaned forward to tune the van's radio.

"It's nice for Peter, you know, to have someone, a friend, isn't it? Peter's important to you, kind of like a brother." His eyes flicked from the dial to my face, looking for confirmation of something. Later, when I kissed him, I tried to give him the answer he was looking for.

* * *

Peter photocopied pages from the books in the library. A photograph of Mary Ashton as a debutante, flanked by a Mitford and an Astor, the diamonds slung around her neck, remarkable only from the other baubles on view by the single teardrop diamond, glistening like a fat tear in the suprasternal notch. There were a few black and whites of Lord Denford himself, and one of young Denford in uniform—his pose heroic but his eyes terrified as though he was facing down, not the lens of the camera but the barrel of a gun. Perhaps most exciting of all, was the picture of James Mortimer, an artist's sketch of the dead man's face printed in newspapers across the country in the hope that someone would come forward to identify him.

I kept a folded copy of it in the back pocket of my jeans. Over time, the image became less and less like something human, and more and more like a fortress, a silent fortress, built to guard a secret. I liked to take it out and look at it when no one was watching, the face of the dead man, a blind seer, a map to nowhere on earth. Some things touch something inside you, and you don't know why. Then you get a feeling, not a usual feeling, but something special, like there were two of you, the everyday one and another. The other was often absent, not there, or asleep, a Merlin buried deep under his mound, and the special feeling was an awakening, an eye inside sliding open.

I've read about people feeling such things when they are in love, an awakening, a coming alive, but I was not in love, not yet anyway.

* * *

In the rose garden, David emptying cans of beans into a saucepan. The sun was already gone, but in the west the clouds were raging crimson and pink and orange. Swallows dropped from the manor's eaves, to bob over the lawns.

A fortnight in and we had the place kitted out: a camping stove, a set of pans, torches, blankets and sleeping bags, cans of food, cereal, coffee, long-life milk. The camping gear was ancient, had belonged to Peter's parents.

"Have you mentioned us being here to Uncle Darren?"

Marcus shook his head.

"He wouldn't mind though, would he? It being us?" I had my head on his knee. I looked up, as sweet-faced as I could manage. In the corner of my eye I checked to see if David was watching. I avoided looking at him directly, but Peter made up for it. Marcus looked at me, and Peter looked at David, and David and I did not look at one another, and Em looked at all of us, pencil in hand, sketchbook on her lap.

"Wouldn't have thought so. But he'd want to be asked."

"But then he might say no. I don't think you should say anything, Marc."

I think we all shared Peter's alarm. Darren saying no. Or perhaps even worse, him saying yes, and it not being secret anymore. I liked Darren. In the pub, he drank pints of orange juice and lemonade, never a sip of beer, but he had a drinker's complexion. Even his hands were red, as though he had more blood than the rest of us. There were rumors of him putting a Paddy in the hospital for smashing up one of his diggers.

When Marcus was tiny, his dad had run off to Spain and not come back. There was a black mark next to his name that was never quite explained. It had been Darren trying to squash himself onto one of the school's plastic chairs come nativity. Darren standing at the side of the pitch cheering encouragement and shouting at the ref. And when we were twelve and they'd started a trampolining club, Darren drove the minibus, turning out every week for a term to give a handful of us a lift there and back, playing what he called proper music and asking about school. Darren had left at fourteen, kicked out for punching out a teacher who'd tried to cane him. How we'd loved to hear that one! When I got something right in the office, he'd say, "Good girl," and I'd feel a sort of doggy joy.

Still, I don't think any of us fancied the idea of Darren dropping in to enlighten us about the Yardbirds or the Moody Blues in the rose garden, to tell us at length about the problems involved with modernizing old plumbing.

So we left it at that. I laid my cheek back on Marcus's thigh. He held the end of my plait between his fingers. Once, before we were going out, I'd had him brush my hair. His mum was out and we were up in his bedroom. The curl made it knotty. I'd shown him how you had to start at the bottom. He went so slowly, like I was made of something much more fragile than I was. By the time he finished his breath was all funny.

Em took up a spoon and began stirring the beans. For a second,

I thought I saw a flicker of irritation cross her face, but then she said, "Happy memories," in a passable imitation of the vicar. "Did I ever tell you about our honeymoon, Patricia's and mine, hunting for fossils on the west coast of Wales?"

* * *

The game was Em's idea too. She found the diamonds in a charity shop. When the old died, their families emptied their wardrobes and dressing tables and took the contents to Sue Ryder or Prospect. In and among the usual rubbish, there were musty morning suits, monogrammed golf clubs, cashmere twin sets, satin purses embroidered with seed pearls, clip-on earrings like great dazzling barnacles in trays of costume jewelry.

In the manor kitchen, Em took the necklace out of her bag. We were in the big room, where it was always cool and dim. There were giant flagstones on the floor. We made tea there on the camping stove, and in its deeper recesses, the milk would last for days.

The diamonds were dull until she took them to one of the low, long windows and held them up to the light.

"They've got the right shape, with the big tear drop. Same as in the picture. There were loads of them." She coiled them up and then rubbed them on her shirt. "Mum says I should put them in bicarb."

Peter stretched out his hand for them. "They're heavy."

We passed them round. By the time it reached me, the necklace was warm. It did have weight to it. The stones were square cut, apart from the teardrop, which had come from India, a gift to a Colonel Ashton from a maharaja for saving him from a tiger. Had this been real, how many carats would it have been? The settings and the clasp were tarnished, it was impossible to see the color of the original metal, but it was probably nickel, at most silver-plated.

"How do we know these aren't the real ones?"

"Because they cost three quid?"

But if you'd laid the real necklace, also dirty, also tarnished, next to this one, I doubted I could tell them apart, the real from the fake. When David was gone, I'd trust myself even less.

Em had found them, so the first time Em hid them. We waited in the kitchen, listening to her footsteps disappear, trying to hear the creak of the stairs, of the opening of a door; and when she returned searching her face for clues, for traces of the hiding place. She did a good inscrutable. She was a good keeper of secrets.

If you found them, you hid them next time. We played it for weeks, never tiring of it, which isn't so odd when I think about it. There are other games, far more boring games, I've played, games that have gone on for years on end, games played routinely, with no hope of reward.

* * *

In the beginning, when we were small, I gave Em a hard time. Some days I would speak to her, some days I wouldn't, acting like she'd done something wrong. I told her the teapot was stupid till she stopped wearing it. I stole her lunch a week running. When we were taken for swimming lessons, I lingered in the changing rooms and put her knickers in the bin. On her pencil tin, she had Tipp-Exed the initials MF and a heart, so I told Martin Frost and he punched her on the arm.

It was malice I was after. I was waiting for the smug look on her face when she told on me. Or weakness, sobbing, *Please don't be horrid to me, Andy!* I mined for them with a passion, but came up empty-handed. In the end, I gave up.

When we were thirteen, she reminded me. I was sitting on a chair in her bedroom with a towel round my neck. Em was tickling at my face with her mum's makeup brushes, her breath warm on my skin.

"Remember when you used to bully me?" Her smile was impish.

I squirmed in my seat. She was doing my lips so I couldn't answer back. I had to suffer in silence while she went through it all, till her mum shouted up that dinner was ready.

When we came down the stairs, she said, "Don't you both look glam! You deserve to be on *Top of the Pops*." Em had turned veggie, so it was Linda McCartney sausages and mash. June let us take it back up on trays. But I couldn't eat. There was a pain in my stomach. I wasn't a very nice person. I'd always known it, but a lot of the time I managed to keep it buried away, out of sight.

"It's all right, Andy," Em said. But I couldn't look up.

"This tastes like shit. I don't want it. I want to go home."

Tears sprung in Em's eyes. I sometimes wished I could cry, but the feeling got stoppered in my throat.

"Really, really, really, Andy. I wasn't getting at you. I always knew we'd be friends." She put her plate down and seized my hand. Em was quick to accept fault in a way I never could.

I stayed over, chrysalissed in a sleeping bag on a foam mattress dragged out of the wardrobe. In the dark, we whispered. The cottage walls were six feet thick so there was no need for it, but it was thrilling to whisper, to share things you wouldn't tell anyone in daylight when they could see your face.

"So what's this new bloke of your mum's like then?"

"Joe?" I said. "He's all right."

And it wasn't a lie because in the beginning he was.

* * *

Em was waiting for me at the telephone box. Monday to Friday Marcus worked for Darren, although to be fair plenty of times he got off early or went in to be told he wasn't needed. When he couldn't give us a lift, we took the Ridgeway path together, trotting the three miles as the haze lifted from the horizon and the wheat goldened and the air began to tremble slightly in the heat. Then we went down, cutting across the fields to the stile and then traversing the nettle patch and briars to the old gate that took us onto the manor grounds.

"Keen as a fox, you."

"Today's the day, isn't it?"

"And if you find them, Andy, the real ones, what'll you do then?"

"The real ones?" I hadn't thought that much about it. It was the hunt I liked above all.

"Peter kissed him," Em said. I stopped and turned to face her. "Last time, when we were leaving, I went back for my sketchbook and I saw Peter kiss David."

"What kind of kiss?"

"Not the kind he gives his mum."

"And what did David do?"

"Nothing. I mean, Peter kissed him, and then after a moment or two, it ended and David sort of patted him on the shoulder, and then he said goodbye."

"Patted him? Like a dog?"

We came out a couple of hundred meters from the manor among a small group of apple trees. Their branches bent to meet the long grass. They'd had it really, but they still fruited, round hard little apples that as summer went on glowed red like lanterns.

"He shouldn't lead him on." The words felt funny on my lips. It was what some boys said if you were friendly to them or looked too good.

"Maybe he's not," Em said.

From the manor, I caught the sound of the piano. So Peter was already there.

They could not have numbered that many, but in memory it feels like there were a thousand of them, those beautiful mornings, the manor waiting. Peter playing a melody, something of his own devising he was working on. David lying out on the lawn, or frying eggs on the camping stove. As often as not, as we approached, he wouldn't even say hello, just lift his eyes and smile, as though among such good friends welcomes were unnecessary.

* * *

The swifts were crying, the evening light creeping away like it couldn't bear to leave. Marcus had built a hearth out of loose bricks and was trying to cook sausages over a bit of wire mesh. A little smoke snaked away across the grass. Em poured vodka into plastic cups. They were both happy, I think, and Peter was happier than I had ever seen him.

He and David were walking toward us over the lawn. Peter was not bad looking, I realized. At school, he'd been called all the ugly names there were, daily, for years. A tide of hostility toward him, because he was awkward, because of the way he spoke, because he was clever. Sometimes it ebbed, sometimes it flowed. It'd come to feel real. I thought of the last couple of years, how there'd been something hunched about Peter, something drawn, almost—now that I thought about it—like he was cradling a wound, only apparent now that it was gone.

David was laughing at something Peter had said. Peter's lips were curved in a smile. His hair was a bit longer than I'd seen it. In the light there was a reddish hint to it. He was filling out, growing into his height. On the grass their long shadows overlapped.

Great things were expected of Peter, and I had the sudden appreciation that he would get them. Prizes. Glitter. Entrance to new worlds. A sudden and horrid vision—us bumping into one another in a supermarket many years in the future. Peter, all expensive, braying, "Well if it isn't dear old Andy," while lifting an enormous bottle of champagne into his trolley, and me in tracky bottoms and rags clutching a pack of value fish sticks. Or two liters of cider. Or the sticky paws of snotty triplets. The pain in my guts was so visceral that I had to turn away.

I didn't mean to hurt him though.

* * *

Em found the diamonds around the neck of one of the stone cherubs that adorned the fountain, Peter among the weeds of a flower bed, Marcus inside the back of the old piano, David in an empty bird's nest in the stables. Em found them most often, I think. They were always the ones we had hidden, always Em's charity shop diamonds, never Mary Ashton's.

The white burning sun was just above the treetops, the wood beneath was blue. July days. August around the corner. When I closed my eyes, I could still see the sun, burning dimly behind curtains of orange, a red mark.

Victory for Andy! The diamonds were sitting in the fork of the pear tree. I put them on, fastening the clasp around my neck, and then I took off my shoes and climbed up. Through the first-floor window, I could see Em and Marcus. They were on their hands and knees peering under dust-sheeted furniture.

"Oi!"

When they turned, I indicated my neck with a finger and watched their faces sink. Then I went on up, taking the drainpipe again. Only when I got to the roof, I couldn't get up. I just couldn't make my legs do it. Strange. I gave the order again, but my body said no.

I went back down. David was waiting at the foot of the tree.

"Lost your bottle?"

I sailed past him. What did it mean, the nerve being gone? In stories, there were magic mirrors that showed what was inside people. In reality, you couldn't see. It was dark in there and you were left to guess.

I took him by surprise, putting a foot behind his and pushing. He went down into the grass easily. I knelt over him.

"No."

"I see."

I watched his chest rise and fall. His lips were coral pink. His eyes shifted color depending where he was. Now they were blue-green, like spring grass.

David put a finger up to touch the necklace. "They suit you."

* * *

The keeper booted the ball long and it came down over the halfway line. Marcus got a toe to it, but one of the Pewsey players barged him and sent it back up the pitch.

Em and I were sitting with Darren on a wooden bench they'd brought out of the club hut. Every time something exciting happened, Darren stood up and the bench heaved like a seesaw. It was Saturday afternoon, a grudge match, and we were two-nil down near the end of the first half.

Darren rubbed his face with his hands. "That ref got dropped as a baby."

The whistle blew and someone's gran brought out the orange slices and squash. I wondered what Peter and David were up to. What I saw in my mind's eye made my cheeks burn.

An ice-cream van pulled up and Darren dug out a tenner. "I'll have a Mr. Whippy."

"With a Flake?"

"Don't be daft. Of course, with a Flake."

I got three. On the way back, one of the Pewsey players jogged past. "I'll give you something to lick if you want."

Marcus came over. "What did he say to you?"

"Forget it, Marc." But he made me tell him and when he went back on the pitch, he was a bottle of rage.

"Shouldn't let hisself be wound up like that. He'll get sent off." Darren ate the last of his cone with a crunch. Em screeched in my ear as Marcus took a shot at the goal, but he was miles off target. Then he got a yellow card for elbowing. "Wait for it," Darren said.

But Marcus was carried off, not sent off. An opponent went in with a two-footed tackle. "Foul," Em howled, "that's a fucking foul! Sorry, Uncle Darren."

It was his ankle. He lay there clutching it and writhing. Darren was all over the ref. By the time they brought him into the clubhouse, the joint was swollen up like a grapefruit. Marcus held a bag of ice to it, jaw set.

"I can't play with you here."

Darren whipped round, voice molten: "Don't you blame her because you can't control yourself!"

We went back in Darren's car. Em in the front, me with Marcus's head in my lap in the back. The house Marcus shared with his mum was a new build, one of Darren's, with thick carpets, a fancy kitchen, and dimmers on the lights. The double glazing was so thick, you couldn't hear anything from outside.

Marcus's mum was home. She always seemed to be home. All those white goods to look after. I think I made her nervous, but then what didn't?

Em had a shift at The Polly at four. I was relieved when Darren put his head round the living room door and said he'd drop us both back in town.

"Come see us yeah? Tomorrow?"

I dropped a kiss on Marcus's forehead. "Course."

Traffic was heavy. Darren pulled into the market square and Em hopped out. They docked her pay if she was late.

"How's Peter? What's he up to today?" Darren was always asking about Peter. Back when he took us trampolining, he used to call him the Professor.

"He's all right."

"Reading a book somewhere I 'spect. And you, Andy? Things all right with you?" As I got out, he beckoned me back. He wasn't smiling now. "You ever need anything, you come to me."

* * *

Two days of getting the bus out to see Marcus was enough. His mum didn't want us up in his room, so we sat on the cream sofa, Marcus with his leg up on a pouf. His ankle was all the colors. There was nothing on telly. We couldn't even talk about the manor because his mum was always in and out, giving a little cough in the doorway in case she was interrupting anything.

We ate lunch at the table. "Markie likes his yolks runny. What about you, Andy?"

There were photos everywhere, mostly of Marcus, a couple with Darren and some old people. My eyes lingered on a picture of his mum in her wedding dress on her dad's arm. It was up on a top shelf and turned a bit to the left, like whoever put it there wasn't sure they wanted it to be seen. I moved closer.

"Andy! Put it back." In the photo, she looked about twelve with long, straight seventies hair. Her smile went from ear to ear. Marcus was struggling to his feet.

"All right, all right." I set it down and came and sat down next to him. "You never hear from your dad?"

Marcus shook his head. "Don't want a bar of him. She says the only good thing came out of it was me." He took my hand. "When you marry someone, you look after them. Treat them right. And you should wait, shouldn't get married young. You should be at least twenty-one."

The bus didn't come for another hour.

I chose a seat on the top deck on the way back, feeling the breeze pour over me, listening to the twigs scratching on the roof. There weren't many people on. Two ravers a few rows back were talking about e; Double Doves and Mitsubishis; how you wanted a line of whizz on the way up and a bong for the way down; Lakota vs. the Brunel vs. Gold Diggers; the trippy carpet at Membury Services.

"You want to listen, you come sit with us."

So I did, sliding across the seat as the bus shook round the corners, and listening to Scuttler and Lee—both on the simian side, both wearing clothes sizes too big—tell me about their weekend adventures like soldiers recounting legendary battles. They worked at B&Q in Swindon and spent most of the time smoking weed in the stores, or sleeping off their comedowns in the cardboard recycling container.

"It's quite comfy in there," Scuttler said.

There were summer jobs going if I was interested.

By the time I got off in Marlborough, I was twenty quid lighter and with three pills, brown-speckled like hen's eggs, in my back pocket.

* * *

"Best not tell Marcus, because of Uncle Darren." Darren didn't hold with chemicals. A bit of hash was okay, but that was it.

Peter surprised me because he said, "Fuck Darren." He'd not been keen to try e before, but now he was. Em had a shift at The Polly, so it was just me, Peter, and David. We dropped a half each in the manor's kitchen.

Butterflies gave way to tingles, to an urge to move. I raced them round the lake, but stopped halfway overcome by a drenched, sicky feeling.

I bent double, panting. Peter put his hand on my shoulder softly. "You want us to hold back your hair, Andy?"

"I'm all right. I'm all right." Better than all right, floating. Then suddenly, good so good, and David and Peter feeling it too.

"Let's go up the castle," I said.

"But it's miles."

"Not cross-country it isn't."

The path went up through a sea of emerald nettles, dusty and going to seed. Just past Ogbourne, a track led up to Smeathe's Ridge. On either side of us, the land fell away. Further on, there was an ordinance survey marker that showed north and south, east and west. To the north, far away, there was the motorway, the M4. Cars were flowing in either direction, a steady flow for as far as I could see, and it conjured the image of a ribbon drawn in either direction, a ribbon being tied around the earth. A breeze was blowing. It plucked at our T-shirts and blew my hair about my face.

"I don't want it to end," Peter said. But it seemed like it was already seeping away, so we took the other halves, only to find ten minutes later we were peaking again. When the second halves kicked in, Peter dropped to his knees in the grass.

David turned to me, pale, his pupils black and dilated. He looked like a rare and exotic flower, impossibly beautiful.

Dry mouth. Thudding heart. Skin burning. I sat down and closed my eyes, lost in it. When I opened them again, both Peter and David were lying on their backs staring at the sky.

"I'm going to go. I want to see my mum. I want to talk to her."

Peter raised himself up on one elbow.

"Bad idea. Bad idea. Stay with us."

But I shook my head.

"Really, Andy? You're going to go?" David said. "Can't you talk to her later? You were going to show me this castle."

"Come on. Listen, let's have a cigarette. Let's go threes." Peter started fumbling in his pocket. "There's something I want to tell you, Andy. It's bad but it's good. It's really bad, but it's also good. Stay. Don't go."

But I did, leaving the pair of them sprawled on the hillside.

By the time I got to the lanes, I was seeing fractals in the clouds, trails when I moved my hands. I got within a couple of hundred yards of the house, and then I climbed over the gate and lay down in the grass at the edge, hidden from the road by the hedgerow.

All the things I wanted to say to my mum were gone. Instead, I watched the barley rippling—the many thousand, thousand assembled ranks of stalks, the lifted ears—and I felt such tenderness for them. The clouds passed. At dusk, a field mouse crept between the rows, such a tiny thing, so busy, seemingly about such important work. I stayed there till it got dark and the ground grew cold.

* * *

Marcus was pissed off I hadn't spent more time aahing over his ankle and listening to his mum chat on about three-piece suites. He was driving again, but at the manor he wouldn't play the game, said he had to rest his ankle. I'd hidden the necklace, so I waited with him on the blanket while the others looked.

"What's up with those two?"

David and Peter were coming round the side of the house, Peter almost on David's heels, David with his eyes fixed on the ground. Something had happened after I'd left them on Smeathe's Ridge. Whatever it was, it hadn't done Peter's cause any good.

"Dunno."

"Lovers' tiff?" There was an edge to Marcus's voice. I could have placated him by saying something mean in agreement, or putting my hands on him, but I didn't feel like it. It was a relief when he went back to work.

* * *

We only went out together once, to celebrate our exam results. Mine were solid. Em got an A in art, which was all she cared about. Peter's were outstanding. Balliol would take him to read law starting October. I'd known it was coming but still had to swallow back the bitterness that flooded my mouth.

"A night on the tiles then?" Em's mum stuck her head round the bedroom door. She was carrying a plate of cheese on toast, the bread cut into little squares. "To line your stomachs."

When we were a bit younger, I'd made Em go nicking with me. Never in Marlborough, in Swindon where the shops were bigger. She was surprisingly good at it. Afterward we'd come home and divide the spoils. But we hadn't been in ages, and I didn't have anything nice. Em wanted us to wear dresses.

"I haven't shaved my legs."

"You can use my dad's electric razor. I'll tell him it was Faye." Faye was her little sister. I tried on all of Em's dresses, then we hit her mum's wardrobe. June had been a teenager in the sixties and had the miniskirts to prove it. Em was swishing this way and that in a long paisley number as her mum came up the stairs.

"You put everything back afterward." She stopped and leaned against the doorframe. "God, I used to be thin. Looks good on you, Em. Very romantic, very Joan Baez. You found anything, Andy?"

I shook my head and she went over and rifled through the rails.

"How about this?" It was violet, very short with a little collar and buttons down the front. "Go on. Try it on. It'll go perfect with your coloring."

It wasn't like anything I usually wore. When I came out the bathroom, a bittersweet look passed over her face.

"I'll tell you what. The pair of you can borrow them, but only if you let Faye join in for an hour. Slap some makeup on her. Let her show you her dances."

Before we left, she made us stand together for a photograph. I don't think I ever saw it. "Such young ladies," she said and pressed the button.

Lady. Girl. Female. Woman. Each of the words made you feel a bit different, act a bit different even, when it was applied to you. They weren't the only words for us, of course, only at Em's house it was possible to forget the other words existed.

* * *

The club played guitar bands, the crowd a mix of grungers, indie kids, Britpoppers, plus a few lost-looking goths and metalers, the remnants of dying species that had failed to evolve.

David wasn't sure about going.

"I don't think there will be any wanted posters up," Em said.

When he was out of earshot Marcus said, "He's going to have to face the music at some point."

Later, I wondered whether there hadn't been someone in the crowd who recognized him. Later, sitting out on the step, waiting for the phone in the telephone box to ring, I would wonder about all kinds of things.

But it was a good night. We did shots. When songs I liked came on, I danced with Em. She was all lit up with booze and mischief. Elbowing our way through the crowd to the toilets, I asked her if she fancied anyone.

"Maybe the one with the Bob Dylan hair."

So when we went back, I made sure we danced right up by him till he got the message and led her off upstairs to the balcony, but she came back after twenty minutes shaking her head. With boys, it was like she was always comparing them to someone in her head who was better.

When we left, the night was cool after the hot club. We had to wait ages for a minivan taxi. The driver wanted to know why we were getting out in the middle of nowhere.

"My uncle's got a caravan in the next field."

After he sped off muttering about pikeys, we waited till the road was empty and climbed over the gate. It was like the first day at the manor, only now it was night, and there were five of us, not four.

In the rose garden, the air was heavy with scent. Em had made colored-paper lanterns and put tea lights inside. She borrowed Marcus's lighter and managed to set fire to two before he took it from her and did the job himself.

"Why don't boys dance?" When she was drunk, Em sort of looked out of one eye at you.

"There were plenty dancing."

"But not you three. Sitting in a corner drinking like old men." She had the radio in her lap and was sliding the tuner between the stations, slipping between voices and static and crackling music, and I was struck by the otherworldliness of it, as though the stations were not channels but glimpses of other times and places. Suddenly a big band, loud and clear, the kind Mrs. East listened to.

"Andy and Peter can dance," Em said. "Mrs. East taught them. Show them. Show them how you do it." And she wouldn't give up till we did, demonstrating the few steps we knew, gliding up and down the worn stones.

Peter's touch was light. I fought the urge to hold him, to dig my fingers in. I had that last feeling—last orders, last dance, last summer, last goodbye. The song ended and he let me go like it was the easiest thing in the world.

Em wanted a turn with Peter. Marcus wouldn't dance with me, wouldn't let me pull him to his feet, so I asked David. Mrs. East said you could tell what a man was like by dancing with him. David was careful, attuned to everything, pleasant, a quick learner. I saw him cast a glance at Marcus.

"Sure you don't want to take over?"

So I learned nothing new from dancing with him, unless it was that he didn't want to be known.

But then, when the music came to an end and we stepped apart, David gave a little exhale when he let go of me. It was the kind you might make after crossing a fast-flowing river via a slippery log. The kind made when you thought at last you were safe.

I heard it and looked up, and saw David realize he'd been found out. But he didn't look away, and there passed between us something I can only call complicity.

And that was it, I think, the real beginning. That quick out-breath.

CHAPTER 10

SWIPE LEFT

THE BUS RATTLED OVER VAUXHALL BRIDGE, AND THE Thames—black and gleaming—ran beneath us. So much water, as though somewhere a dam had broken. On my lap I held the telephone box from Peter's flat in a carrier bag Adewale had given me.

"It's mine," I told him.

"Of course," he said carefully, and then, "Please will you go now?"

I rather wanted to stay. I had a friend once, an Irishman, Danny, who let me keep him company during his night shifts. He worked security at a shopping center in Stratford, ignoring the flickering feed of empty aisle and car park in favor of books he bought at a market by the river, rubbing his grizzled chin as he tried to teach me chess in the small hours. On Sundays, we walked the city.

"This is where Shakespeare washed his socks." Or, "Here's where Jonson killed his man, Andy."

Danny promising to show me Galway, never showing a sign of wanting to lay a hand on me. There had always been people I wanted to talk to, and people I wanted to touch. On the whole, they had been distinct groups.

On my fingers, I counted the years since I'd been with someone, since I'd properly made an effort to get to know someone. To let someone know me.

At the lights, as though following my thoughts, the bus gave a mortal, shuddering sigh. A taxi would have been quicker, but the bus had been approaching and going in the right direction. Perhaps I'd wanted the company.

All around, heads were bent over phones. At each stop, the eyes flickered up. Danny had been proof that kindness was unavoidable, even if you weren't looking for it. Still, who knew when one of us would start knifing another or kicking someone down the stairs. A group of beery lads got on and the beauty in the row in front turned toward the window and brought her arm up to shield her face, like a rich man concealing his Rolex within his sleeve.

The cafes were closed now, and the restaurants. A take-away glimmered here and there like hope eternal. In Chelsea, the hospital rooms were darkened, the corridors emitting a weak fluorescent glow. At Sloane Square, a man swung into the seat beside me and opened Tinder, swiping left at each woman's picture like a person with a nervous tic. *What's wrong with that one, or that one?* I wanted to say. *You'll run out if you go on like that.* Only he wouldn't, of course.

I snuck a glance at his face, youngish, not un-handsome, but his brow was furrowed, his cuticles gnawed raw, as though rather than looking for a potential date, he was grimly searching for the perpetrator of a crime that had been committed against him. The thought made me smile, and I turned to the window before he could notice.

I imagined turning back to him and saying, *My name's Andrea! I like working and have no hobbies whatsoever. Bet you can't guess what's in the carrier bag.* And him drawing down his finger across my face. Left or right?

But after he got off, and for the last leg of the journey home, I took my phone out and quickly found myself doing exactly the same. Looking at the potentials in their sports kit and on beaches, holding puppies, or leaping out of planes. Swipe left. Swipe left. Swipe left.

Because there were so many faces, but none of them—it appeared—ever the face I was looking for.

CHAPTER II

ENCHANTED PALACE II

WE PLAYED ON THROUGH AUGUST. THE ANIMATING SPIRIT that kept the game alive, kept us circling the manor's grounds, kept up its whisper. Under my feet grass, stone, wood. The birds at dusk. The air so thin, so endless. The light draining, the dew falling. The moon hung over the cornfields and the clouds ran in herds over her face.

David standing beside me on the steps, the shadow of the house cutting across them like a saw blade. Summer was teetering at its height, poised to fall.

Come September I'd work for Darren full-time, do bookkeeping and computer classes in the evenings. Marcus would be Darren's right hand. Em would do her art foundation. In October, Peter would go to Oxford. David would write the letter, get off the hook. I asked him what he'd do then.

"Why don't you look at me when you're talking to me, Andy?"

I repeated the question. "Re-takes then Uni? Travel? A job? Must have lots of chances. Dads of kids you went to posh school with."

"And you? Going to stay here and become a child bride? Look at me."

I looked at him. Tiny flecks of amber ringed his pupils. In the right light, scowling, Marcus looked like a Levi's model, but David, his bones were just right. I liked his skull, and teeth, and hair. His skin. He moved just so. I begrudged him all of it.

"Peter talks a lot of shit sometimes, doesn't he?" David looked uncertain. He was being serious. "I mean, a pinch of salt. After we took the pills, after you'd gone, he was coming out with all kinds of stuff."

"What's he been saying?"

David was good with words, but he didn't have the right ones now.

The shadow was moving. I could feel it passing over my skin till I was in the plain sun. Even then, a terrible cold wave swept over me, because I suddenly knew what David was getting at. Peter had been talking about me, about my mum, and how awful it had been for me, growing up like that. I could hear it, in my head, all the details, everything that David would be allergic to. He'd probably told him about Joe as well, creating intrigue, his voice full of drama, stringing it out for attention.

Joe could still come back. The feeling, when you opened the front door, when Joe was inside.

"Sent your mum to the shops. Now what you've been up to?" Joe was quick on his feet, the chair skidding across the kitchen, blocking the door before you could get back out.

I heard Peter leaning in to whisper the things he thought he knew. A sold-out, hollowed-out feeling.

"Pete wants to suck your cock. He'd tell you black was white if you let him. Are you going to let him?" I smiled, showing my teeth.

"Jealous?"

"Don't flatter yourself."

"I wasn't talking about me. You know, they all do what you want all the time, because if they don't, you're a royal pain in the arse. Tiptoeing round you the whole time."

"And you make people like you so they give you stuff. Or just to win them." Saying it, I realized it was true. It was why Peter had no power over him, because he'd been so easily won.

David licked his lips, took a quick step forward, and then stopped. From a distance, a shout of triumph. Em's voice.

"She's found them again," I said.

"Fuck."

"But not the real ones. Not Mortimer's ones."

"No. Because I'm going to find those." David said it lightly, but he meant it. It was what made the game real, what kept it going. David's belief the diamonds were there and he would find them.

"Not if I do first," I said.

* * *

In one of the tiny servant bedrooms, I found David peering out a dusty window. I stood in the doorway waiting for him to turn. But he didn't, even though he must have heard me coming. I didn't go in. I knew if I went in, something would happen.

I began to know where he was. I was listening for the diamonds, but it was David I heard. During the game, while we played, roaming the house and grounds, it came to be that I could feel where he was.

Even with my eyes closed, my awareness followed him—as he bowled tennis balls at Marcus who sent them flying with an ancient cricket bat, ricocheting off the walls or further smashing what was left of the glass hanging from the frames of the greenhouses. Or as he lay sprawled out at the top of the lawn, his toes pointing down toward the lake, talking to Peter about something or other, his hands occasionally lifting into the air to describe a shape or emphasize a point.

There was a gossamer thread stretching between us. And, as time went on, I began to feel it even when I wasn't at the manor. At night, for example, lying in my bed, I felt it still, fine as silk.

I'd known something like it once before, but that had been about fear, about knowing where Joe was so I could be as far away as possible.

I tuned in to it, the feeling between me and David. I blocked everything else out. At night, my mother had taken to shouting. Short bursts. Rarely intelligible. Sometimes I woke, sometimes the shouting entered my dreams. Waking, I would not know if it had been real. Neither awake nor asleep did I reply. I thought it could last forever like that. That I could punish her forever.

* * *

From out of a clear sky the drops came fat and far apart, then faster. Like a silvery applause, then drumming. I was caught out on the path by the lake, the rain cold, roiling the surface. I took off for the house yelling. A deluge. Above the sound of the rain, voices calling from one of the upper windows. Coming up toward the back of the manor, I slowed. What was the point; there was no getting wetter. The water in my shoes, in my ears, blurring vision.

Instinct? Premonition? I ducked left toward the greenhouses. David was sheltering under the bit of glass roof that was still intact.

"Nice and dry, are we?" But he couldn't hear me over the rain. He said something I couldn't hear either. The manor was only a looming shape. Water ran in sheets from the glass ceiling, a waterfall around us.

David was still talking, his eyes full of mischief. What was he saying? I took a step closer, and another. I brought my ear to his mouth, but he was only mouthing the words.

His body was warm and dry. I wrapped my chilly arms round him, my wet skin, my soaked T-shirt. I made him shiver. David's dry cheek pressed against mine. I held David in my arms and he held me back. Wanting meeting wanting. The feeling of touching him this huge relief, like I'd been holding my breath for it.

If there are moments that do great harm—the cruel word said, the fist swung, the bomb detonating in the packed marketplace—could the reverse be true? Not the long slow knitting of bones, or the wound puckering, turning to scab, then scar, but a magic reversal?

They were calling our names from the manor. As I let him go and stepped back, I saw something moving outside, a shape going back around the corner and out of sight.

I put my head out. The rain was falling more softly. When I turned back, David had knelt and was lifting a large piece of slate.

"What are you doing?"

"Looking." Under the slate were earwigs, a long pale worm, white roots. "I think we're going to find them soon. Don't you think so?"

* * *

Night was falling but Marcus wanted to drive, just the two of us, after we'd dropped Em home. We passed the standing stones at Avebury and I waved at the Devil's Chair. At the bend in the road, Silbury Hill looked like a giant sandcastle, an upturned teacup of soil upon which the grass had inched over the ages.

Marcus seemed to be struggling with something, but I wasn't going to help him.

On the lane toward home, a leveret leapt out in front of the van and bounded ahead of us in the yellow light of the headlights, till we'd clocked it breaking the thirty-mile-an-hour speed limit before it leapt into a gateway.

In the lay-by, Marcus killed the engine and in the sudden darkness leaned in to kiss me. After a few moments he drew back. He let out the slightest of sighs, the smallest of reproaches. I let go of the door handle and put my hand on his thigh. I kissed him again, this time properly, feeling his breath quicken and his body respond. It was mean of me, but it made me think of one of the Hacketts' old Labradors, how you only had to drop a hand to it and it'd be felled, on its back, imploring for a belly stroke with dying eyes. Marcus kissed my neck, one hand on my back, the other slipping between us. I could tell he felt he was owed it.

"We could go out Friday. Into town. Up to Bristol if you wanted, see a band. Just us two."

"What band?" I cracked the door.

"I don't know. Could see if there's something on at the Thekla."

"If there's anyone good, it'll be sold out."

"Don't you ever get bored of hanging round with him?"

"What are you getting at?"

"I know you and Peter have always been mates—"

"Yes," I said. "Yes we have." And I got out and slammed the door.

A light was glowing in Mrs. East's kitchen. I heard the van swing round and drive off. She came out onto the step and beckoned me over.

"Saw your mum take a fall today." She indicated a spot a bit further up the road. "I offered to call a doctor but—" And she shrugged.

"Was she pissed?"

"She was in a bit of a state. A bit . . . confused. Have the empties been stacking up?"

I tried to think. "They could be in her room. Or out the back."

"Might want to check on her, Andy."

"I'll look in."

But I didn't. I looked for cans or bottles, but there weren't any. I stood outside her door awhile, a long while, staring at the doorknob. She was breathing at least. Part of me wanted to go in, but it was small and weak, and a much larger part of me wanted to be elsewhere, and before very long that was the part that won.

* * *

David was sleeping, lying on his back with the sleeping bag drawn down about his waist. The moon was waxing again. On the side was a pack of cigarettes. I guessed Peter had bought them for him. I slid one out and sparked it at the window. I fancied I could feel him wake, that there was the slightest perceptible change. He didn't ask me what was up or why I was there.

Eventually, I said, "He hid them at night. We haven't played at night yet."

"Just us?"

"Yeah." I heard him get out of the bag and slip on his jeans.

"Do you have them? Am I hiding them?"

"I want us to look for the real ones, for Mortimer's ones."

We went down the stairs in the darkness and then out into the courtyard.

The diamonds were there, I knew it. The lake shimmered and the wind swayed the trees. We looked together for an hour, maybe two. No luck. No luck anywhere. I sat down on the stone bench where Mortimer died and the tears rolled down my cheeks.

"What's all this?" he said.

When I reached out for him, it was like grabbing a handhold because if you didn't you were going to fall.

Did I cry because I wanted him to touch me? Possible. But I couldn't have stopped it. Once we started touching, I couldn't stop that either.

* * *

"Did you turn him down?" We were in the little room at the top of the house, pink sunrise flooding in so it was like being inside a jewel. I had my hand on the small hollow that lay in the center of David's chest, a few inches down from his heart. Outside, under the eaves, the wood pigeons cooed. They were so fat now they could barely get off the ground, wobbling and bobbling their way across the lawn, fanning their tails at one another, courting.

"Not in so many words, but yes, I suppose I did."

"You didn't get off with him?"

"Would it make a difference?"

"I'd feel worse."

"This makes you feel bad?" David turned on his side and laid the fingers of one hand on my stomach. The thing was, it should have, but it didn't.

* * *

Three weeks? Less than a month certainly. Going back nights, waiting until Peter would have departed to meet his curfew. Then threading my way across the Downs, the rabbits bolting, the stretch through the copse, Crow Wood, lightless, where the night was thicker, heart picking up—the feeling of a presence there, nothing human, nothing in time—then down over the field, over the gate. The lawn wet. Looking for a light in the window.

I wouldn't have given the journey up. Going through the dark alone to find another person, even if they were crooked and not offering anything.

"Here, I'm over here."

My body drenched, the fear melting when he kissed me. It was like my heart was in a lift, and the lift would suddenly just fall, and then judder to a stop, and then fall some more. On the bed, in the darkness, I pressed down on David's hands, my hair falling to cover his face, and I didn't recognize my own voice.

* * *

One morning, slipping back in at five, I found my mother sitting at the kitchen table. My lips were tender, my whole skin felt raw. She looked up slowly, her face blank. Nothing dawned in her eyes. It was like she didn't know me from Adam.

Maybe I didn't know me either.

Who else knew? Em with her keen eyes? I watched Marcus go for a guy who squeezed up against me in a pub and thought *maybe*. Peter? A cold stream flowing between us, a bewildered, hurt look that made me wince. Not enough to stop.

* * *

"There's jobs on the Greek islands. Bar jobs. Not now, but in summer. You can make good money." I was testing the waters, not sure I could leave, even if David agreed to it. What would become of my mother without me?

"How much?"

"A few grand at least."

David grimaced. He got up swiftly from the bed and went over to the window. I knew what he was thinking. David had spent a lot of time around rich people, at the fancy houses and holiday homes of school friends. It was where he felt he belonged. It wasn't the money, he said, it was what it bought you, which was freedom. The freedom not to worry all the time, to not test the smoke alarm on Sunday mornings or write down everything you eat and spend in a book.

"How much would the diamonds be worth, do you think, Andy?"

But he came back. Lying down beside me, our fingers lacing. His lips on my collarbone.

When I awoke, David was gently shaking my shoulder.

"Is it time to go?"

"No."

"What then?"

"You cry in your sleep."

"I was crying?"

"You've done it before."

I brought my hand to my face and it came away wet. Was there the slightest tinge of accusation to his voice?

"Peter said—"

"What?"

But he didn't go on. Yet that final week, every time he looked at me it was like he had something he wanted to say, but then drew back from saying.

* * *

Mrs. White pointed me in the direction of the church. As I walked down the familiar stone path, the bells were silent in the tower. One was cracked. It always rang flat, a weird dissonant BOOOONG, clearly audible among the peals.

Peter was sitting at the organ and as I entered the nave and walked toward him down the aisle, he toyed with a number of chords, first this one and then another. The pipes breathed out and the air within the church hummed.

"What's that you're playing?"

"I'm just fiddling really." I went to stand at his side, the place I took when I turned the pages for him. His long white fingers moved over the keys as though he was searching for something. "I suppose I was thinking people are like chords. I mean they can be. Listen." His left hand roamed toward me. He played something that sounded like a wet fart and raised an eyebrow. "Doesn't it make you think of Mrs. Duncan?"

Mrs. Duncan had been a dinner lady at our infant school, a gigantic, myopic Scot forever bursting into tears.

"I see what you mean. And what chord am I?"

Peter shrugged. His fingers picked out again the notes he had been playing with when I came in. His brow furrowed. Who was he thinking of? Then I knew who he was thinking of.

"Peter? What have you been saying about me to David?"

"Nothing."

"Because if I want to tell people about myself, I will. Just like I let you tell people about yourself."

"Not everything is about you."

"He said after the pills, you said stuff. You don't get to talk about me. You don't get to tell people things you think you know, when you don't know anything. I never told you anything. When Joe was around you hid in your bedroom with your head in a book while downstairs your mum cooked your tea. Then after, you treated me like I had a disease. Telling me he wouldn't come back, because it was what you wanted to believe, like life's fucking wish fulfillment—"

"Joe's not coming back." Peter pushed the stool back and got up.

He looked sick, the color draining from his face. I followed him back down the aisle. "Just leave me alone, Andy, for fuck's sake."

Suddenly, he was on the verge of tears and my own eyes prickled in response. He had his back to me, taking long strides I couldn't match. He couldn't wait to get away.

* * *

On the last morning, I stayed till it was light. David walked me part of the way back. I had to go to the office to do the wages. I kissed him at the stile. When we drew apart, the wind dried the kiss on my lips.

When we touched each other, it was like we were drawing a map, a map of a place that we never spoke about. I wasn't sure it was a safe place. There was far too much of me there.

* * *

Marcus picked me up in the van. Em and Peter were already inside. The day was dull, the light sluggish, and the wind damp. The hedgerows were going to seed. I yawned.

"Should go blackberrying later. Take some back for Mrs. East."

Marcus's hands were tight on the wheel. He drove fast, accelerating out of corners so Em and Peter slid about in the back. He slowed down as we came to the manor.

"It wasn't like that yesterday," he said. The front gate was open, the sign about guard dogs lay on the ground.

"What were you doing out here yesterday?"

I'd been in the office. In the evening Marcus and I had gone to the cinema in Swindon and then for pizza, a proper date like he'd wanted. When I thought about breaking up with him, it was Darren I worried about, not just the job, but that he wouldn't think the same of me.

"I came past. On the way back from the Upham site." Marcus swung the wheel round and we went in, through the gates and over the gravel that spat under the wheels.

An empty quiet met us. The front door was bolted from the inside, the back door locked.

"Where was Darren yesterday?" Em asked.

"He was in the office with me," I said.

David had originally got in through the back, crawling in through a window that wasn't latched properly. It was latched now. I called out for him. Em jogged down to the lake and back. There was no sign. We went back to the front steps. I kept my face blank.

"He's got our numbers. He can call." Marcus was worrying a bit of crumbling stone with the toe of his boot. The tips of his ears were red.

"But what happened?" I said.

Em shrugged. Peter was perched on the steps in his black coat, like a crow. "Maybe he got what he came for."

"Meaning?"

He unfolded himself, turning his back on me to look at the house. He sounded bored.

"I mean the necklace, Andy. What else?"

* * *

David had our numbers. I sat on the front step at night waiting for the phone in the red box to ring. I didn't know what to do with the pain. Sometimes a car would drive up the lane, its headlights passing over me, the glow of red taillights fading on the skin of my hands. Mostly the phone stayed silent. On the few occasions it started ringing, as though pulled from a dream I would go over, swing open the door, pick up the receiver, and press it to my ear. And there was silence, not the silence of an empty line, but the silence of someone listening.

In mid-September, a few weeks before Peter left for Oxford, I saw the family, the ones who owned the manor. Work was being done to make it livable, and they'd come to inspect the progress. Darren was savage because they'd given the job to someone else.

"That's them, the Calcrafts." Marcus indicated the four people sitting at the next table in The Sun. The girl was complaining about the food. She was my age, give or take a year, and turning over a salad leaf with her fork.

"Iceberg," she said witheringly. "Iceberg?" She and her mother were fair. The men were heavier set, the son verging on fat. He looked a bit like Henry VIII, already jowly with a rosebud mouth and red-blond hair. He grinned, showing his teeth, and said something. The girl shrieked with laughter.

"Rob. Alice." The woman's eyes slid toward her husband, but he was looking down at his plate as though he couldn't hear them. The moment he finished eating, he stood up.

"I'll meet you at the car."

Alice watched him go, jaw set, eyes ablaze. Her mother murmured something about the pressures of work. The boy, Rob, caught my eye and I looked away. He said something else and both women laughed, his sister with enthusiasm and the mother as though she really shouldn't.

"Wicked child," she said, and Rob grinned again and looked straight at me.

When Marcus went to pay, I went to the ladies'. It was down a narrow corridor at the back of the pub. When I came out, Rob was blocking the corridor. I stepped left and so did he. Then right, so did he.

"I could dance like this all night," he said. He was so close that I could feel his breath on my face. "Made you look. Made you stare. Made you lose your underwear." He took a step nearer, cast a quick look back over his shoulder. "What is it, gorgeous? Why don't we scoot into the ladies' here and you tell me all about it before your gorilla comes looking."

I wanted to ask him about David so badly I almost took him up on it, but he made a mistake. He put his hand on my waist. Picking up his fingers, I bent the index finger back till he yelped and snatched his hand away. I pushed past.

"Well, you're no fun, are you?" he called after me.

* * *

It was getting colder but still I went out, not every evening, but some of them.

The phone rang.

"Hello?" I said. I wanted him to know it was me, but there was no answering voice, not even the sound of breathing, as though the caller at the other end had covered the mouthpiece with their hand.

One night it rang and rang. Each time it was the same.

"Hello? Hello?" I listened into the waiting silence, heard the receiver being placed back gently in its cradle. Only once the sound of a ragged breath, as though drawn by someone breaking the surface of the sea.

"Is it you? David, I—"

Then the dial tone, and then nothing.

The next morning the air tasted bitter with burning. The verge was soaked in dew. It seeped through my shoes, which left silky green footprints among the silvered grass. The glass in the door of the red phone box had cracked and blackened. I opened it. From inside, you could see that the roof was half-gone. The receiver lay among blackened coils on the floor, the unit was half torn off the wall, and everywhere the stink of petrol, the acrid smell of burning, but the fire long out. Water dripped down the ruined walls. A black puddle was forming.

Could have been vandals. Locally, there was hardly a bus shelter, a phone box, a parking meter left untouched. But I had my suspicions. Peter. Or Marcus. Or Peter. I kept them to myself where they smoldered in my chest, a damp, toxic fire giving off choking billows of smoke, still holding my peace when, at the end of the month, we waved him off to Oxford.

I might have spoken them to Em, but my mother died. On October 18, four months after she predicted the end of the world, she fell again, this time in front of a car.

It was a Friday. I took the call at Darren's office. What had she done now? There had been an accident. Yes, I would come.

Darren looked up from his desk. He was wearing reading glasses, crappy ones he bought for a couple of quid in Boots because he couldn't stand the idea of an eye test, being loomed over by someone in a white coat.

"Mum's been hit by a car."

I looked back down at the computer screen, at the columns of numbers I was doggedly inputting. I loved them then, or rather I appreciated that I loved them, loved the safety of the office, the boiling kettle and tinny radio that Darren turned off every time the DJ played a dance song. We went in Darren's Beamer. They'd taken her to PMH in Swindon. The Chiseldon road was closed so we went over Hackpen, across the Downs. Darren had sent word to one of the sites and we'd barely been there five minutes before Marcus jogged in.

I was invited into a little room. Darren went to get tea and I was left sitting with Marcus, surrounded by misted glass, a choice of women's mags and *AutoTrader*. A doctor came, a woman with streaks of gray in her hair and a no-nonsense expression. I had the sense she didn't like me, but maybe she just didn't like this part of her job.

My mother had been struck by a car and died in the ambulance. The driver said she had fallen into the road.

"How did she seem this morning?"

"I didn't see her. I went to work."

"In the last few days then? How was her speech?"

"I didn't speak to her."

The doctor squared her shoulders and tried again. "You live with your mother. When did you last speak to her?"

"I don't know." They thought it was shock.

Marcus at my side down the long hospital corridors. During the formal identification and the signing of papers, that night in his single bed at his mum's house, at the funeral director's, and later at the funeral, and for all that came after over the next three years. You have to love someone who stands by you like that, even if it isn't in the right amount—not as much as they deserve, but too much to do what's right by them. I was going under and I held on to him with a vice-like grip and he took it for love.

But even Marcus couldn't be there all the time, and he wasn't there on the morning the report from the coroner arrived, the report that showed a blood alcohol level of nil, signs of malnutrition, a tumor in the brain—significant in size, affecting speech, motor function, balance—and, in addition to the injuries that killed her, not relating to her cause of death but there nonetheless, old bone fractures, multiple historic bone fractures, fingers, wrist, collarbone, ribs, pelvis, dating back to childhood.

* * *

Marcus stepped up, half moved in, hell-bent on being nothing like his dad. Marcus to the rescue. Marcus getting on to the council so I could keep the house, getting the bills changed over, clearing out her stuff while I sat on the back step, chain-smoking and staring at the plowed fields. Marcus painting, fixing shelves, and buying plants. Marcus suggesting holidays. Traveling. Antidepressants. Once, he even suggested a baby. Marcus at a loss, because he had got what he had wanted, but it wasn't supposed to be like this. Me the problem in Marcus's life, the thing that needed to come right. Sympathy giving way to anger, giving way to coldness because I couldn't reward him for his efforts. Because everything else was going so well: managing some smaller projects for Darren, business booming, enough money coming in that he bought a terraced house in Swindon, renovated and sold it on at a profit. *Rinse and repeat, Andy, rinse and repeat!*

I worked for Darren, as and when. He made sure I had enough. When Em came round in the evenings, Marcus would cook and we'd drink beer or wine and no matter how hard I tried to stay up and make a good show of it, by nine-thirty I'd be done, wiped out, taking the stairs like a geriatric. After I'd gone to bed, I'd lie there and hear them talking as I drifted off, not the words, but the tone, the urgent concern.

Sometimes, I woke in the night and they were gone. Out drinking or clubbing. I didn't resent it. I'd pretend to be asleep when he came back and would go out early to the shops, make sure there was fresh bread, bacon, and eggs for breakfast, tomato juice, milk. I found condoms in his pocket once and put them back. I didn't begrudge Marcus that either, a girl he met in a club, an escape.

Peter had disappeared into his life at Oxford and when he came home, he told stories of quads and balls and punting. Em did an art foundation course in Swindon while temping part-time at Nationwide. Everyone expected her to go full-time the following September, but instead she surprised us by taking up a place at Camberwell to study textiles and renting a room in Peckham.

In some ways it was easier with her gone. One less person to hide from. I couldn't bear people that much, not for too long. Outside of work, I walked a lot, twenty miles at a stretch, sticking to the smaller footpaths, pack of twenty Embassy and a 20 cls of vodka in my pockets. I didn't drink in the house, smoked up only in the evenings, toeing a line Marcus had drawn. I couldn't see beyond it.

At best, in the fields, the spring of the earth giving under my heels or sheltering in a slate-roofed hut among the nettles as the rain fell, I would fall into a sort of animal daze, and sometimes an animal pleasure, at the breeze rattling through the beeches, at the spreading lichen in mint and peach and mustard on a fallen oak, at the red-tailed kite sailing over a wood.

As children, Peter and I had often played detectives. We'd searched for clues—the red scrap of cotton caught on a fence, a single sheet of newspaper folded up and tucked away in the drawer of an old desk found decaying in the Savernake. Now I wondered if we'd not missed the point, missed the fact that the world itself was readable: the formations of the clouds, the tiny spray of punctures in the cross-section of a rotting trunk, rain spattering the surface of the river, the slender ribs slowly emerging through the fur of the corpse of a fox. Were these not also clues of some kind, a kind of message?

At work I did the books. I added the figures. But what I found on the walks was a realm where there were no sums, no ledger of accounts. Outside of the human world, there is no bankruptcy. In the heart of the Savernake, among the old trees, trees that were older than the oldest standing building I'd ever seen, older than Peter's father's church, I sat with my head in my hands and I did not want to go back. What would have happened next I'll never know. If I would have found a way out by myself. If I would have survived the finding of it. If David had not come back. If we had not gone to the manor in the snow and played the game again.

CHAPTER 12

PRIVATE DETECTIVE

MY PRIVATE DETECTIVE HAD OFFICES NEAR FINSBURY PARK. Over the years, I had had a personal trainer, a colorist, a nutritionist, even—for one whole hour—a therapist. Why not a private detective? As I took the tube up to my appointment with Mr. Hutchinson, whose listed services included video surveillance, vehicle tracking, and honey-trapping, the visit had a feeling of inevitability about it. Too much TV, I supposed, too many films. One day wouldn't I also confront the serial killer in an abandoned building, defuse the bomb in the final seconds, untie the screaming girl from the railroad tracks? All still possible. But I would never see my mother again, not ever, not anywhere.

I had the little telephone box in a plastic carrier bag at my feet and nearly forgot it in the press to get out of the carriage. My head wasn't right. Lack of sleep. Unwelcome thoughts. Dredging up the past was no help to Peter, and it certainly wasn't helping me. But now that it had started, it wouldn't stop. In the middle of the night, just to do something, I'd called and left messages at the offices of a half-dozen private detectives suggested by Google. Mr. Hutchinson had been the first to call me back, on the dot of nine, offering to see me at twelve.

The website had shown an aerial photo of the Thames at night, but when I found the address and rang the doorbell, I found myself climbing a dingy, narrow staircase above a fried chicken shop. The beige carpet was tacky underfoot and the whole building, part of a row of three-story late Victorian terraces, seemed imbued with grease. A film of it shimmered on the walls as though the building was sweating it out.

By the time I got to the top, I was unsurprised when Mr. Hutchinson came to the door himself. Unbelievably, a half-eaten box of fried chicken sat on his desk next to a couple of laptops and a phone. The detective clearly outsourced the honey-trapping. Mr. Hutchinson was a slight man, hardly taller than me but a few years older, with a large forehead and bulbous, slightly hunted eyes. A door led off the office, and without looking I knew that behind it would be a single bed, a kitchenette, a bathroom with a fraying towel, a cracked bar of soap, and a single bottle of value shower gel.

"Thank you for fitting me in." I shook Hutchinson's hand. He invited me to call him Steven and to sit down.

"It's a missing person?"

I told him about Patricia's phone call. Old-school style, he made crabbed notes in a spiral notebook, taking down Peter's date of birth, address, email, and phone number.

"Corporate law?"

"Yes."

"And you and Mr. White are close? But not . . . ?"

"Peter is gay." He paused for a moment and then wrote that down too.

"Do you have the contact details for any of his colleagues?"

I did not. The interview went on. I told him about the wedding, that I believed Peter traveled a lot. I described my visit to Peter's apartment. In answer to his questions, I said that there was nothing that led me to believe Peter was suicidal, or had problems with drugs, or money, or a relationship. I told him the names of Peter's boyfriends, Anders the Norwegian, Karsten von Kloss who had been eaten by a cannibal, and by dredging my memory an assortment of first names—Matthew, Patrick, Juan—that could have belonged to anyone.

"Could he have broken the law?"

"I wouldn't have thought so."

"But you haven't called the police."

I hesitated and shifted in my chair. "I thought this might be quicker."

"In your opinion, as Mr. White's friend, where do you think he is?"

"Perhaps he's just gone away somewhere. Perhaps work got too much for him. I don't think . . . I don't think Peter's very happy. He's successful but—" I thought of how Peter had looked when I found him in the American Bar, the stillness as he had sat holding the whiskey tumbler with both hands. "People do that sometimes, don't they? They just walk out on everything all at once, because they don't know how to do it piece by piece. Your life doesn't want to let you go. If you think about it too much, it won't happen. You've got colleagues, projects, subscriptions, deliveries, memberships . . ."

Hutchinson nodded quickly. "And there's nothing else you can tell me about Mr. White, about Peter, that may help me find him?"

"You don't need to find him." Now the detective looked lost. "I mean I just want to be able to tell his mum he's okay, to know he's all right. It might not be that difficult. On TV, the police just look at people's phone records, or their email. I don't know if that's something you can do." My eyes fell on the box of chicken. I could see his teeth marks. He saw me looking and I felt something shift between us. Mr. Hutchinson swallowed.

"What's in the bag?"

"I found it at Peter's place." I was loath for him to see it, but I took it out and when he stretched out his hand, I gave the little telephone box to him.

"What's this about then?"

I was suddenly overcome by weariness, a tide of it. I could have lain down on his carpet, inhaled the chip fat, and never woken up.

"There was a phone box outside my house when I was growing up. We didn't have a phone, well, sometimes we did, but we were always getting cut off, so people would call me at the box at pre-arranged times, or on the off chance. It got burnt down. Like this. People were always vandalizing it."

"It used to take ages to get connected again after you'd been cut off, didn't it?"

"Yes." In my lap, I gripped the strap of my handbag more tightly. A suspicion took shape that there would be other elements of my childhood that Mr. Hutchinson was familiar with: empty cupboards, say, or lying at school about what you got for your birthday. I wished I had waited for one of the other detectives to call back, someone smoother with a fancier office, someone less like a forlorn hedgehog.

"Do you think it's relevant? The telephone box?"

"I suppose . . . I suppose Peter might have done it. I didn't want to think so at the time. But, there was a boy we both liked. It was all very many years ago."

"Teenage stuff then. Unrelated?"

"It was strange that it was there. Nothing else. There was an accident. Not then, a bit later. It's all tied up with this place, this manor we used to go to, a game we played. We all felt guilty afterward. It ruined a lot of things, friendships, trust." I swallowed quickly.

"So he might be upset, then." Hutchinson put the telephone box down on the table and I scooped it up quickly and put it back in the carrier bag. "Might be . . . dwelling on the past?"

"Do you usually find them? Missing persons, that is."

"Most of the time. The kids, teenagers I mean, they can't keep off Facebook or WhatsApp. Half the time, they post pictures of themselves in their mates' bedrooms. And then with adults, usually they're just evading their other half, living half a mile away with someone else. It's marital, most of it. And people don't make the effort, they want to use their bank cards." This had been his opportunity to inspire me with confidence. Instead, he sounded almost disappointed.

"Why do you do it?" The question slipped out. "Be a detective, I mean."

Mr. Hutchinson blinked slowly. "Why do you do your job?" When I didn't answer—any satisfactory kind of answer was evading me—he looked down and furrowed his brow. When he looked up, he said, "I like puzzles. Always have. Even though the answers are almost always the most obvious and boring thing you could imagine, there's a feeling when you're trying to solve a case, a certain feeling, especially when you're getting closer, that is. I used to be a chef at a Wetherspoon's. Nothing wrong with feeding people, especially when they've got a couple of pints inside them. This is better."

After we'd sat with that for a bit, I asked, "What will you do? To find Peter."

"As you say, I'll start with the phone. I know people at the providers. It could be very quick. I'll let you know as soon as I have anything. If we don't get anywhere, there are other steps we can take."

He cleared his throat and told me both his hourly and his day rate. I gave him my credit card details, which seemed to cheer him, and saw myself out, fleeing off down the stairs and then out into the street. Despite the difference in surroundings—the therapist had had sunny rooms in a villa in Chelsea—there was something similar about the two encounters, the stream of questions, the flood of weariness.

Only in the presence of the therapist lady, in her pleasant consulting room hung with tasteful abstract prints, with her fresh flowers on the coffee table, with her acronyms—PTSD, OCD, CBT, there were others—after the weariness had come the rage. Her theory, carefully laid out, made sense. She put forward that there were defenses, defense mechanisms, established in our vulnerable childhoods, necessary at the time, but unhelpful and restrictive in adulthood, needing, via the painstaking work of therapy, dismantling. But the nicer she had been, the gentler, the more it made me want to kill her.

The last thing she said to me was "People often make the mistake of thinking that children who have neglectful or abusive parents must love them less. It's more bearable."

I walked for a while. It was mizzling a bit. My wanderings took me into the park. The characters were eternal, familiar to everyone. The mothers with their prams. The man in a cheap suit staring vacantly at a flower bed from one of the benches. Teenagers dodging school, playing some kind of game. One had turned away, was trudging off toward the gates, shoulders hunched in misery. He was not playing anymore. The game was spoiled. What can I say? It struck me as familiar.

The mad man waving his hands as he raged at the pigeons. What language was he speaking? What was he saying—something about daughters? And her, why didn't she have a coat on? Why was she chasing that man, and plucking at his clothes? That yellow lady, yellow for her eyes, and skin, and teeth. When he shoved her, she fell, but was up again, quick as a flash, yelping until he turned and shook his fist at her and she slunk away.

I passed him further on. He had taken up a place on a bench, beer in hand. Tattoos were crawling up his arms, climbing up his neck. He sat at the center of a pool of shattered glass. When would I be finished with the likes of him?

Men were like dogs. Once you'd been bitten a couple of times, you just couldn't feel the same about them as a whole, not deep down, no matter how appealing some of them were.

I came out the other side of the park and kept going through quiet residential streets. Turning a corner I recognized a house. I had, I realized, rented a room in it for a couple of months. There, on the corner, was the shop where I bought cans of beer and two-for-a-fiver bottles of wine. There was the front garden with a low wall, the one I hid behind from the enraged cabbie I was doing a runner from, while he paced meters away. Between arriving in London and my current existence, there had been a few lives, short-lived, each one sealed off from the next by a slew of burned bridges.

On the next street was a church, redbrick and dumpy. The door was open and I went in. It was inferior to our church, our church being mine and Peter's. This one was brightly lit and had a carpet. I took a seat. There were chairs rather than pews. Peter and I would have scoffed at that. Not Peter's father though. The vicar said God was at home everywhere, even in the Methodist church where they served the elderly dinner on Fridays and which smelled of gravy.

Sitting there, I wondered when Peter lost his faith. While I knew these things happen gradually—the doubts, the whole things starting to feel like an ill-fitting suit you'd inherited from a relative—there must be a moment when the faith you have can no longer keep subdividing, the moment when the thing is actually gone. And in that moment, when the thing is gone, if your heart doesn't heave, if there wasn't a kind of grief that remained in spite of logic and reason.

It was all coming back: the hard pews, the ridiculous singing—Mr. Harris, a verse ahead of everyone else and twice as loud—Peter's father's sermons. The He with a capital H. Our Lord. His Son. The intoning. The sitting and standing, the kneeling and Amens. But I had paid attention. Children are all ears, aren't they?

I remember Peter's father in the church telling the story of Jesus and Pilate, and jesting Pilate asking Jesus what the truth was but then not staying for an answer, and so we never got to find out, not any of us, not ever. I was so disappointed and on our way back to the vicarage, hell-bent on my share of the roast dinner—chicken, chicken, let it be chicken!—I pestered the vicar, "But why didn't the disciples ask him instead? There he was on the cross, it's not like he was going anywhere. Why didn't they ask him?" With his hand on the gate, he turned. A watery smile. "Sometimes Andy, I think you are the only one who is listening." Which, of course, was no answer at all.

Nor was there anything in the Gospels that shed light on what Jesus would have said about Joe. I don't remember anywhere in the Bible Jesus meeting a truly wicked man. It was all tax collectors, moneylenders, and Pharisees. A savior for the poor, the meek, the oppressed, but what did he actually say?

In my pocket, my phone went on beeping and buzzing, work stuff.

Joe had been from the Midlands and drove a battered black Merc. Came and went as he liked, a fat wad of notes in his pockets, no job but always off on business. I was thirteen. Life had been chaotic before but I was used to it. My mum had an eight-octave emotional range and more black keys than most.

But then, thirteen and enter Joe. Fourteen and a half, exit Joe.

Interim: I started losing my hair, got a bald patch, but I parted my hair over it. Stopped talking back. No one could believe it. Stopped talking. Sometimes I wouldn't go to school. I'd go up the castle or wander the fields, ears open for the sound of the Merc's engine. No words. Never any words. Even now, here. The silence spread to Peter, neither one of us saying anything to one another, to anyone. But he knew, I don't know why I'm so sure. The vicar asking me once if Peter was all right. "He's having bad dreams. He woke his mother. You would tell me . . ."

A loss of control. Black dream hurtling toward something final, that was how it felt, the last days of Joe. Something final coming. But I woke up in time. Joe went out and didn't come back. One day, two. A week. A month.

"He won't come back, Andy."

I shook my head. Peter couldn't know for certain.

A winter spent biting my nails to the quick, cutting school to hang round the traveler camp or busing into Swindon. Spring made me a believer, bringing small flowers, rain, and rage. Rage made me vicious, sent me wild, climbing buildings and trees, at their apex I wanted to rattle the earth. No one was in my mind, there was no room for anything but rage. Rage taking me out to raves, into the backs of cars with boys, me and my rage. Only, I lost Peter. The rage took up Peter's space and when it was finally sapped, I looked around me and he was gone. There in body, as I took up my old place next to him at the desk in class, the same old Peter with a book in his hand and his effortless A grades, but with the door firmly closed, even the secret doors that only I knew about.

Outwardly, I accepted it. I took what was going. But I resented Peter, his withdrawal from me, his retreat into a fantasy of the halcyon future in which I played no part, the way he seemed to shy from me as though I were not only contaminated but dangerous. Gross insult upon a grievous injury.

We had met Joe at the pub. My mother and her mini-me, perching on the climbing frame that was for the under tens, bickering for shandy, slipping inside to down the last two inches of any pint that had a back turned on it. Out on the climbing frame in the dark with someone's fags and a lighter. A figure at the back door, a man watching and then later his arm around my mother. I lounged in the back of the car as he drove us home. Smirking when he told me to put the seat belt on. Looking up to see his eyes in the rearview mirror. At the house, my mother had turned and invited him in.

"That all right with you, young lady?"

And I had said that it was.

The world only really has one story for that girl. That's one of the reasons why you don't tell, don't report. Because among other concerns, it means being that girl. I won't be her for you. I can't even be her for myself. Beyond the walls I have erected, I sometimes hear her weeping. Sometimes I do not think it is her, I think it is my mother. I hear the weeping woman behind the wall. Sometimes it is the music I live by.

"Are you all right? Can I help at all?" I looked up. The vicar, of course. A kindly face, but vicars, I wanted to tell him, shouldn't have beards. Vicars should have nude pink faces. Once, on a Saturday afternoon walk, we had come across rutting donkeys in a field, Peter's mother had said, "Well really, Richard," in a disappointed way, and on the way back to the car I had noticed that the vicar, while pretending to stare into a field, was silently weeping with laughter. A vicar should, after taking you to a football match—and God only knew why because none of you liked football—and after listening to the crowd jeering insults and making monkey noises at a visiting black player, say in a tight voice in the silence on the way home, "Those were the men who crucified Christ." A vicar should be quite shy and get himself into such a state before giving a sermon, your son and his friend were forbidden on pain of death from occupying the bathroom on a Sunday morning

"I am all right," I told him. I sailed to my feet. The vicar was sorry. He hadn't meant to disturb me. I was welcome to stay. "It was a very long time ago," I told him, making for the doors.

I wanted to protect him, Richard White, that is. Protect him from ugliness, keep him innocent. I should have trusted him, but the thing is, of course, that to trust you have to be taught to trust. If I'd been capable of it, I wouldn't have needed to tell him anything.

Outside, it was raining again. As I left the church behind, I felt myself calming down. Once, I met Peter in a museum. After I'd come to London, but before I'd turned things around. By then, he was working in Geneva and on his way to becoming the Peter of recent years, the outward confidence, the nice clothes, stories that would begin, "After the club, Pierre took us all out on his boat on the lake . . ."

We'd meet when he was over. Sometimes I put on a front that everything was fine. Sometimes I didn't have the energy. Sometimes Peter gave me money and it felt like being paid off, the envelope of fifties thrust from his hand into mine and tucked away out of sight with undue haste. Like neither of us could bear being asked what it stood for.

The exhibition was entitled *The Secret Cabinet*. As we paused on the threshold a glance passed between us, something of the old spirit. We went in. Disappointingly, it was about sex, stuffed with lewd bits of pottery, classical erotica, and ancient sex toys that had once belonged in the private collections of Renaissance princes. But I had liked the idea, the idea of a secret place inside a palace where precious things were kept. That you could be the curator, that you could choose what you kept there, in the secret cabinet.

I was high, I think, that day. It made me garrulous. I tried to tell Peter what I was thinking. He cocked his head. "So what's inside?"

"Moments, words even. Do you remember the foal with the furry ears?" We had gone to one of the racing yards on race day to buy hash from a stable lad who was dealing. The foal had been a couple of months old. It had raced at me across the dark barn, stood shivering under my hands, its muzzle pressed into my armpit. Like it knew me, like it knew there was something special in me. I thought of David too. David in the little room under the eaves at the manor. Listening to wood pigeons with David on the mattress, the light pink as roses.

"There are some moments, Peter, don't you think? That are never quite over."

Peter was quiet. In his eyes was the memory of something awful. He had not understood.

I thought I knew what it was. I thought he was thinking about that morning at the manor, out on the drive in the snow. The body. The cold hands. As he tore his gaze from mine and stumbled away, it seemed like an admission of an accusation I hadn't been able to whisper, not even to myself.

* * *

I had every intention of going to the office and being productive for a few hours. Afterward, at home, I would treat myself to dinner in bed in my tights where I would lose myself in news websites, celebrity gossip, in the scroll, the Wiki trails, the image parade, the sly, beckoning click bait. But I didn't go to work and I didn't go home, not straightaway. Perhaps because it was a Friday, and the prospect of the whole weekend ahead unnerved me to a greater extent than I was willing to admit. I got close, as far as the bar two streets away, where I sat in a corner and ordered the first glass of wine, discussing my choice with the bartender as though I actually cared what it was. He promised me notes of passion fruit and kiwi, something slightly oily with an almost maritime finish. It could have been turpentine. I wanted a tunnel deeper and blacker than the screen could provide, no matter the consequences. I wanted escape, and my body, although part of what I wanted to escape, was also the means.

At five the bar began to fill. At the next table, a girl said something and her friends cried out that it was her, so her, to say what she had said. But even personality seemed to me a game, and she was being congratulated for getting it right, the performance of herself. I sat there drinking with the telephone box still in its plastic bag on the seat beside me. Sometime around the third glass of wine it came: the roar in the blood. A soaring feeling of excitement, the promise of change, the sense I was leaving behind what I knew. Strength. Power. Recklessness. A lurking knowledge, that alcohol didn't make everyone feel this way.

I got my phone out and went from app to app. By the time I realized I should eat, the kitchen was closed, so I ordered more wine and four or five packets of bar snacks, fancy ones with rosemary and glazing and sea salt, and a joker at the next table thought he'd ask me if I was enjoying those. Possibly he meant it in a friendly way, but I paused in the shoveling to stare into his eyes, so the smile slid right off his face. Then, at some point, I went on LinkedIn and sent a reckless message, before taking up a stool at the bar.

The lights were already flickering on and off in my head, my hand jerking every few minutes to my bag to make sure it was there. At some point, I had the sense to hand my card over and pay up. On the way home, weaving down the pavement, I called Peter and left a message, a long message my phone told me the next day, nearly an hour long, only by then I couldn't remember what I'd said.

CHAPTER 13

THE BODIES IN THE LIBRARY

TWINKLING LIGHTS WERE UP IN THE MARKET SQUARE. Christmas was a week or so off, the new millennium within touching distance.

"How's Marc?" Em was back from London. We were eating cake in The Polly. She'd cut her hair short and it suited her, made her look simultaneously older and more elfin. The waitress asked her where she got her earrings and seemed put out when Em told her a friend had made them.

"All right, I guess." Distant and barely speaking to me would have been more accurate. It had been worse since she left. Sometimes when he looked at me, it was like I was something he had spent a fortune on, and now wished he could take back to the shop. Em was quiet. I had the feeling she was measuring her words.

"You have to do something, Andy, get help. This is not fair. It's just not fair on . . . anyone."

I stared down at the crumbs on my plate.

"It's not healthy, not for either of you."

"I know I'm not much fun." It was difficult getting the words out.

"I'm sorry. I'm so, so sorry, Andy." Like it was her fault.

When we said goodbye, Em hugged me hard. Drawing apart, she held on tight to my wrists.

"Come to London. Stay with me. You can get a job up there easy. Get away from here."

And I would, of course, only not with Em.

* * *

When I turned, Marcus was in the doorway, his mouth a tight line. How long had he been there?

"We need another beater to come on the shoot tomorrow. Out on the Collingwood Estate. Darren says he doesn't need you in the office."

"I don't think—" It had snowed in the night. I tried to picture myself flushing a load of pheasants from their hiding places toward a row of shotguns. That morning, I'd only made it as far as the kitchen and a cup of tea, and from there looked out into the white day and the mist. The contours of the hills were fading in and out of sight as though struggling into being. I waited there, at first thinking and then not-thinking, with the sensation of being emptied, as though through the corridors of my vision something was passing out of me, expending itself in the snow. Now it was dark. Where had the day gone? The week, the month, the last three years? "Marcus, I'm not sure I'm up to it."

"You're coming," he said.

* * *

The alarm went off at six in the dark. Marcus had stayed at his mum's again. I pulled my clothes from off the chair next to the bed and struggled into them still under the bedclothes. When I heard the van, I got up and half fell down the stairs and out the front door into the snow. I took a handful and rubbed it across my face.

"You better have made tea." And he had, a thermos of it, and as we took the road to the shoot I poured myself a cup, spilling scalding drops on my thighs. The Collingwood Estate lay out past Hungerford and the road wound there through villages and hamlets and over hills where the tarmac was frosted, and then down among darkly wooded dells.

In the car park near the big house, we met the other beaters and then walked down to the river. The black water flowed clear and fast, and a lick of vapor was curling from it. The water was warmer than the air, and although the sky was clear there would be more snow. The guns were parked up by the house while the beaters, mostly old boys, had congregated round the game cart, a pickup with rails in the back to string up the birds. They were exchanging gossip while the dogs nosed about their feet. A pair of Labradors, sisters with fox-red coats and black-tipped ears, cried with excitement. It was their first season and as they danced and fretted, I felt a little of their joy seep into me, like a tiny drop of dye—yolk yellow—falling into a pool of white paint. Col, an old friend of Darren's who'd taken Marcus fishing and to shoots when he was a boy, offered me his hip flask.

"That's the one, one Marcus is talking to." A young man in tweeds was going round shaking hands with the guns, all of whom had paid upward of five hundred quid for the day's shoot.

"The one what?"

"Zack Allerton. His family owns the estate. He's got an older brother, Lawrence, but he's in banking. Not interested. So Zack's having a go at running the shooting and fishing. He's a DJ. Plays records in those London clubs, the ones the kids thrash about in like de-knackered bullocks while clutching bottles of water."

"How do you know about them, Col?"

"I saw it on *Panorama*."

By nine, I was standing on the perimeter of a field, holding my flag, a white triangle of fertilizer bag nailed to a stick. Marcus was a hundred meters to my left, Col further up on my right. The other beaters were on the other side of a small copse. The drive began and we advanced toward them over the sheep grazing and then through a small field of rotting maize stalks, waving our flags and driving the pheasants into the waiting guns. Dark birds with long tail feathers burst upward and sailed frantically in the direction of the river. The guns sounded, and I watched as a pheasant dropped out of the air mid-flight, like a switch had been flipped. They fell among the brush that bordered the river where it split into channels. The dogs hurtled in and out of the freezing water bringing back the bodies.

At lunch, the beaters perched on the veranda of the club hut. Most were retired country folk like Col, or dog breeders, but there were a few hobbyists like us, doing it for the fresh air and a couple of crisp twenties. The guns sat at picnic tables by the river. There was wine, beer, and whiskey for everyone, and Zack took around bowls of crisps and made sure people's glasses were topped up. He was just a few years older than us, but so polished he seemed ageless. I sat with my eyes closed, facing the sun. Mike, the gamekeeper, was conspiring with someone.

"We'll give him a brace," I heard him say in a low voice. "He kept quiet about the business with the mower, he deserves some birds."

Two women had arrived. They were talking some feet away by the picnic tables about the drive down from London and I amused myself by trying to picture their faces. They would be blond, of course, but whereas one—Priss, what kind of name was Priss?—was bursting with words, juicy with enthusiasm for the shoot, the day, the drive across the snowy country, the other sounded dry, had a voice that twitched with a permanent-sounding dissatisfaction. She would be dark, I decided, wasp-waisted, perhaps a bit wolfy around the face.

I opened my eyes. I'd been right the first time. Both blond, Priss taller and sandier, full-lipped and big-chested with narrow hips. The second woman I recognized as Alice Calcraft, the girl whose family owned the manor and who didn't rate iceberg lettuce. She was as slender as a weasel with small, even, white teeth and fine, fair hair, the kind of woman who would always be girlish. She caught my glance and then turned her back, like even a glance was common.

But then, I was never going to warm to Alice Calcraft. Because of ponies and skiing and posh school, and because for Alice to be nice to you, you had to disarm first. But mainly because, after she turned her back on me, she bent down to say something to the man sitting next to her brother at the picnic table—hair tickling his cheek, one hand on his shoulder—and this man, when he stood up, turned into David.

We did another drive, this one through the thickets by the river. I climbed over mossy fallen trees and through reed beds and brambles and patches of marsh, thrashing my flag about and banging it on the trunks of cricket willows, nose streaming. It was good to feel something as simple as fury. The guns fired overhead, and shot fell from the sky, pattering down through the trees. It sounded like summer rain on the roof of a tin shed. A small piece hit me on the forehead. I swore and rubbed the spot. The metal had been hot.

It was becoming overcast, the sky threatening to split open like a bag of flour. There would be one last drive. The beaters fanned out again and I took the furthest edge through a copse, pressing forward through tangles of ivy and briar. I heard a noise and turned expecting to see one of the dogs, but it was David. It had been over three years since we'd seen one another. If he was shocked, horrified, or delighted to see me, he didn't show it. If anything, he looked at me with weary recognition, like he was facing a familiar and unwelcome vision.

"Not like you to be waving the white flag." The guns were still firing, the shot raining among the trees, the sound of the pheasants breaking cover. "Listen, I wanted to—"

Only I didn't get to find out what David wanted. A gun fired close by, too close, and there was a shout of pain, and then another voice shouting, *Stop!* And then I was running, sure that it was Marcus I'd heard.

It had been one of the young ones. He hadn't shot a bird all day and there was one, so near, and he let off one barrel and missed, and then tracked it downward, firing again. There was blood when I got there, trickling down Marcus's wrist and spattering the ground. He was sitting on a log and his face was set and I did not know how bad it was, and I threatened to kill the boy, Alexander, so that his dad quickly led him away, Marcus calling after him saying he was all right.

I got his coat and shirt off; even I could see it wasn't much, but I kept checking. Even though Marcus was trying to calm me down and make me stop. It wasn't till David touched me, laid a hand on my shoulder and said evenly, "Come on, Andy, he's going to freeze to death. Let's get him to the doctor," that the earth steadied under my feet.

A green Land Rover was brought round and we helped Marcus into the back. Zack was at the wheel and soon we were joined by Priss, Alice, Rob, and finally David. Zack kept apologizing, stopping only long enough to introduce the others. I had my arm round Marcus's shoulders, one finger resting on his neck, warm and living.

"How do you three know each other then?" Rob was in the front. I could see his eyes on me in the rearview mirror. Alice had her head cocked to one side, listening.

"That summer I was on the lam and hiding out at your parents' house, Marcus and Andy were very good to me. Only I don't think they like me now because I disappeared without a word," David said.

"Is that why you were staring at me in the pub that time? I thought she wanted to rape and murder me," Rob said.

"You were half right."

"I'm flattered." His voice was amused. He clutched at his heart. "Anytime, Andy is it? Anytime. I promise I won't fight." And then quickly in response to the looks he was given, "Sorry. Inappropriate me. It's the tension, like when people laugh at funerals. Shock. I can't be held accountable for anything I say. Zack, you're a total prick. Maybe we should all have sex. How about a massive loan?"

The Land Rover bumped down the track. Behind us came the game cart. There were ninety birds, including eight partridges and a mallard, plus a rabbit that one of the dogs had stumbled over and brought in. As the light failed, I watched Col become a silhouette, a straight-backed figure swaying as the pickup lurched over the ruts, a silent Charon with his cargo of dead.

* * *

Zack took us to Accident and Emergency, and he fetched Mars bars and coffees and poured brandy into them from a hip flask and kept us entertained while Marcus waited to be seen, but it was Rob who invited us to the manor. He phoned Zack while the doctor, having checked the x-rays and given Marcus a shot of something, dug four lead pellets out of him. Afterward, I washed them off and slipped them into his pocket.

"Now you can tell everyone about that time you got shot."

"Back in 'Nam."

"Cheltenham." It was an old local joke.

When he was patched up, Marcus shook the doctor's hand and then walked gingerly back to the car with Zack and me dancing attendance.

"Rob wants you to come for dinner tomorrow." Tomorrow was a Friday, the seventeenth of December. "We're all staying at his place. He says you're to stay over, if you'd like, so it won't spoil the drinking. There's umpteen bedrooms and Priss has offered to cook." There was a slight hesitation in his stride. "He said to tell Andy that he's sorry for being rude to her and that he wants to make up. He said to invite your friends, Peter and Em. David would love to see them. He said to say that you're all welcome." Zack's voice was completely at ease, but his brow was slightly furrowed. It was a bit out of proportion in his book, I could see that.

"Get shot and win a weekend in a country house?" But before I could say anything else, Marcus cut in.

"What time?"

"Rob says eight."

"Fine. We're in."

Zack took me home first. As I got out he said, "We dress for dinner. Just for fun, really, and you can wear whatever you like, but just so you know."

"You sure you'll be up to it?" I said.

Marcus nodded. He had to go pick up the van, and then he was going to drop in on his mum.

Once inside, I moved from room to room, keyed up but with no idea quite what I should be doing. After a few minutes the phone rang.

"Is he all right?" It was Em and she was livid. News spread fast.

"Reckon so. They had to scrape a few bits of lead out of him."

"The whole thing is fucking stupid. It's not a sport. It serves him right. It fucking serves him right." It wasn't like her to be so angry.

"David was there."

"What?"

So I told her.

"And no explanation for the disappearing act?"

"Guess we'll find out."

"You want us to go then?" I heard her doorbell ring. She was home for another couple of weeks. Her parents were away visiting relatives in Salisbury. They'd taken Faye with them.

"Marcus is keen." It wasn't quite an answer. The doorbell went again.

"I best get that."

"Who is it?"

"Don't know, do I? Bit late for carol singers."

I had hoped for more chat, for questions—how had David seemed? How was it to see him again? The kind of teasing out Em was good at.

After a bit, I called the vicarage. The terms at Oxford were short, but Peter often stayed up to be close to the libraries. To the quads, and balls and punting. Or just away from home. But I was lucky and after a minute, Patricia succeeded in bringing him to the phone. After I'd told him, I listened carefully to hear what was in his voice, but he sounded flat. Perhaps it was just that Patricia was listening.

"Will you come then?"

"And Rob Calcraft invited me and Em? I mean by name."

"Yes." I thought about it and began wondering what other information David had offered up about us besides our names.

"If Rob's invited us, it's because he wants something. I'd think twice, Andy."

"You know him?"

"He was in the year above me. Left Oxford last year. Perverse sense of humor."

"So you won't come?"

Peter didn't answer straightaway. Outside, it had started snowing again. He would be in the front room, and from what he said next I knew the curtains were still open, and he was looking at the snow falling, on Patricia's flowers beds and on the lawn and the yew hedge. "If you're determined to, I suppose I will. It'll be sort of funny. The manor, a weekend party, the snow. Just like that night Mortimer died."

I can't say I felt any presentiment though, no shiver of apprehension or warning, although it struck me that neither of us had said anything about David. I had the TV on and the remnants of a tin of Roses on my lap, my fingers searching out any hazelnut caramels Marcus might have overlooked. There was a game show on. It involved people competing to win mystery prizes and then trying to hide their disappointment at what the prizes were.

And I fell asleep there, and when I woke up it was the middle of the night, and Marcus must have decided to stay at his mum's because the van wasn't there, and the bed was empty, and apart from the TV I was alone.

* * *

"Get in the back! Get in the back with us!"

I pulled open the sliding side door to the van. Peter and Em were huddled on the cushions inside, their faces ghoulish in the blue light of a battery lantern. In one hand, Peter was clutching a bottle of sloe gin. He was wearing a tuxedo that was too big in the shoulders, and

Em—underneath the blanket she had draped about her—was showing flashes of iridescent peacock green.

"We went to Sue Ryder. You should have come. We had our pick of golf-club Christmas-ball chic circa 1975. Peter wanted to wear his boring Oxford suit, but I forbade it."

Snow was falling again and turning to slush on the road. As we took the corners, I felt the rear wheels slipping and Em clutched at my arm, her eyes wide.

"You missed your chance. There was an amazing dress, green, floor-length, with sort of baubles on it, like a Christmas tree. We nearly bought it for you. But it was a tenner."

"A whole tenner."

"If it had been five ninety-nine—"

"Or even seven pound fifty."

"We love you seven pound fifty."

"Just not a tenner."

Em swung the bottle in my direction. "Have some of that."

"Look!" Marcus had slowed right down, and as we crawled up to lean over the front seats and look through the windscreen, I could smell Em's shampoo and the gin on Peter's breath and Marcus's aftershave over the van's usual reek of cigarette ash and oil. We were at the gates to the manor: pressing in on either side were the firs, and then before us was the snowy drive, and along its length someone had been out and stuck candles in brown paper bags which flickered, casting shadows on the ground. Fat flakes were lazing downward as though in no particular hurry. The sight reminded me of something, that is to say, I had a sense of déjà vu, but then Em was taking my hand and putting something in it and I couldn't locate it.

"I did bring you something." She had her mouth to my ear. Her palm was warm against mine. It was the necklace, the one from our games. I'd forgotten she even had it.

"Put it on."

I nodded and then I gave it back to her, turning so she could thread it round my neck. As we swayed up the drive, she struggled to fasten it, but as we ground to a halt the catch caught and at the same moment, my mind fastened on the connection I'd been trying to make: it was not a memory, but an imagining, that had struck me—because, of course, I had pictured the manor like this many times.

* * *

Zack's dogs were the first to greet us, their breath steaming, pink tongues lolling as they circled us, drawing tracks in the snow. Priss and Alice came next, and then Zack and Rob, each carrying a bottle of champagne and a handful of glasses, and behind them David. We stood on the steps, above the frozen fountain. Icicles hung from its tiers like crystal teeth. Priss was saying over and over again, "It's so warm, isn't it? Somehow the snow makes it warm," and Peter and Em were introduced to everyone and Marcus was asked about his wounds while Rob lined up nine champagne flutes on the stone balustrade.

David had bent down to fuss the dogs. They were working cockers, brown and white with ringlets curling from their ears. The little one, Goli, pressed her muzzle into his hands and he caressed her face with quick little strokes and she wagged not just her tail, but everything from the neck down while the other dog tried to nose her out of the way for a turn. I saw Peter watching and I wanted to give him a look, a look that said, *And to imagine we were once like that over him,* only I couldn't catch his eye.

"To living to tell the tale!" Zack raised his glass.

"To being able to bloody shoot straight," Rob added and scooped up a handful of snow and tossed it lightly at Marcus, only it missed and hit Peter. "Sorry, Peter. Nice to have another Balliol man here. How's it going? Final year, isn't it? Do people still not know what you're capable of?"

Peter showed his teeth. Not a smile but a chimp thing, a fear thing.

On his rare trips home, he told me about his studies and the libraries, about odd traditions and a little toy train that brought port and Stilton round the dining table. It had sounded so like the Oxford of his dreams, I had never questioned whether he was happy there. But now that I thought of it, he hadn't mentioned any friends and I felt an awful guilty pang at how blind I'd been. As though reading my mind, Priss raised her glass.

"To new friends," she announced firmly.

David straightened and took the glass Alice handed him. "And old ones," he said, and there was a moment's silence in which he looked lost and uncertain, eyes velvety.

"Oh Dave's being *ever so humble*," Rob said, stooping over like Uriah Heep. "Why don't you tell them where you were?"

"In prison," David said.

"For about two seconds," Alice said, then, "Let's go inside. I, for one, don't think it's warm at all, Priss. David, you can tell them about your criminal past over supper."

* * *

Darren had complained he'd lost the renovation work on the manor because the owners didn't want to pay for the job to be done properly. That would have involved damp coursing and pulling up floorboards and new pipes and electric. Rob and Alice's family had gone with an outfit from Devizes that he claimed would patch and plaster over the cracks on the cheap and Darren had been spitting blood. I couldn't say I was sad about it, because inside it looked like it was meant to look: the furniture uncloaked and more of it, pictures and mirrors on the freshly painted walls, and carpets unrolled across the shined-up floorboards. But it was still our manor. Something of the same smell remained.

We took our glasses into the dining room. A fire was burning in the hearth and the table was set with candles.

"Tell them, then," Priss said to David. "I've got to go check on the pheasants." Then with a wink, "I'd still count the silver before he goes, Rob."

"Well, it's quite simple," David said. "Someone called the police. I heard someone coming up the stairs and I thought it was one of you. Only it wasn't. It was Constable Stevens and his friend Constable Turnip, Turney, something like that. And after collecting up my things, they took me down to the station in Swindon. It wasn't any good denying who I was as they had my passport, and of course the headmaster of our school," he shot a glance at Rob, "had been kind enough to report the credit card thing in Britain as well as Italy, so of course I was arrested. And while Rob and Alice's parents were good enough to make sure I didn't get in trouble for the trespassing or breaking and entering, the credit card theft, the fraud thing, was a bit trickier."

He was pitching somewhere between rueful and apologetic with the usual humor. I wondered if only I saw it, the resentment at having to explain, his hatred of being pinned down and made to account for himself. But then perhaps that was David's way: to offer a glimpse of a second layer, a secret layer, and by doing so involve you in a private conversation with him. And I wondered if, under this layer, there was not another and in it David was bored, bored beyond measure, and alone, and in conversation with no one.

"Did you get sent down?" Marcus asked.

Rob burst out laughing. "You don't know him very well if you think that."

"Rob's family helped me out. His parents got their lawyer involved and Mr. Mackenzie, the headmaster, thought better of making an example of me. I mean, the whole thing put the school in a bad light, but he did have it in for me. Visited me while I was on remand and told me with a very sad face that it was for my own good, like he was sending me down the salt mines to save me from the gallows. He had it in his head I was going to the bad and the experience would turn me around."

"But then Dad's lawyer promised to paint the Italian jaunt in rather a lurid light. Underage drinking because David was a month off eighteen and Badger allowed us wine with dinner. An unmarried schoolmaster overly fond of Greek sculpture. You can imagine," Rob said.

"You were there too?" Peter asked.

"Missed the fun, though. The rest of us thought we were being daring by sneaking off for gelato in the cafe with the pretty waitress. When we came back, Dave had disappeared, having embarked on a career of international embezzlement." For a moment, Rob sounded bitter.

"You could have phoned us. We'd have visited you. Baked you a file inside a cake," Em said.

"Did one of you shop him? He can be insufferable. God knows I would if I had anything on him." Rob's eyes flitted between our faces. Peter didn't move a muscle, but in that moment I knew. Not Marcus then, Peter.

"It was someone from the village," David said quickly. "A dog walker, someone who'd spotted one of our wild orgies on the lawn."

"See. He always gets everything," Rob said.

"Seriously though. We weren't exactly careful, were we?" His eyes met mine for the briefest moment before I could look away. "I'm sorry. It's not an excuse but it already seemed very long ago. My hands were full trying to get myself out of the mess I'd created. By the time things had settled down and I could have got in touch, it seemed that ages had passed. It was only a month or two, I suppose. But it felt like thousands of years. It was unreal, the whole summer here, beautiful and magical and utterly unreal. I couldn't believe any of you were still alive."

* * *

The room was warm. There was a lot of wine, and the food was a long time in coming, so that when it arrived, the candlelight, reflected upon the table's polished surface, seemed to swim and ripple.

"It looks wonderful. The renovations, I mean." Em blushed a little.

"My parents spent a fortune on it and now they've toddled off to Paris so Alice and I have to come down and keep the home fires burning."

"Not exactly a hardship," Priss said.

"Alice doesn't like the country."

"That's not true, Rob."

"It is true, but David does, so you're making an effort. I, on the other hand, am just busy. But the country has its attractions, its areas of outstanding natural beauty. Now, Emma, wherever did you get that ravishing dress?"

He entwined his fingers, rested his chin on them, and batted his eyelashes at Em, and for all I had disliked him, he was the consummate host: opening bottles of wine, making sure people's plates were full, but above all keeping the awkwardness at bay with conversation, asking questions and involving everyone. Alice and Priss had gone to school together, now Priss and Rob were in finance at the same company. Rob had introduced Priss to Zack who was on the DJ circuit, part-owned a club, and had released a record—*Did awfully well in Luxembourg, didn't it, Zack? He's a god there. Has his own perfume range, Eau de Lucky Shit*—and now the shooting parties. Alice was thinking of doing a course.

"What kind of course?" I asked.

Alice shrugged. "One that takes illiterate people."

"Dyslexic, not illiterate, Al," Rob said swiftly. "My father thinks dyslexia's a made-up thing, but then as I often tell my sister, Dad's an arsehole. We're all lesser beings to him."

Alice gave her brother a quick, grateful smile.

"What about you?" Marcus had turned to David.

"I'm working at an auction house," and he named one of the famous fancy ones even I had heard of. "Just as a dogsbody really."

"But you're seeing if it's for you, aren't you?" Alice said. "Finding out which corner you might want to occupy before studying it. You know what the Japanese will pay for a rubbishy old oil painting. Then there's all the furniture and pottery and jewelry, carpets even. As long as you specialize, as long as you become the go-to person for something and know all the right people, it's a good line of work. Everyone says he has the eye for it."

Em burst out laughing. In the candlelight, she was truly the lady from a painting, poised and graceful, her shoulders and throat as white as snow. "I can see it now, David. Traveling up and down the country charming old ladies into parting with their treasures for a song. In a van with your name painted on the side. Perhaps one day you'll find the diamonds hidden in a box in someone's attic."

They knew about the diamonds, you could tell from their faces.

"David said you never found them. The ones that are supposed to be here somewhere," Alice said.

"Andy's wearing them," Em said, which made them all spin in my direction. "The ones we used for the game."

Rob leaned over to inspect them and for a second I felt his face close to the skin of my throat. "Fake," he said. "A gentleman can always tell."

A great oak root was burning in the hearth and above the conversation and chink of cutlery, one of the dogs would occasionally let out a deep groan. The talk circled the summer we had played the game, and then the real diamonds and Mortimer and the night they had been stolen—yes, so like tonight everyone agreed—and the rumors about Denford being a Nazi, or rather a fascist sympathizer, and what about the servants and couldn't it have been an insurance job, all subjects on which I had nothing to add, nor did I feel much like reminiscing.

"Are you still in the row of cottages, next door to the old lady you were always talking about?" David directed the question at me.

"Mrs. East moved in with her son Ian in Bicester. She had a fall."

"Are you still staying with your mum?"

Marcus touched my arm. "Andy's mum died. Car accident." And I tried to look the way you were supposed to look.

When we were done eating, we went into the library, the dogs padding after us. Priss inspected the fire proprietorially.

"I got it going while I was waiting for the crumble to come out of the oven." She bent over it, pushing the burning logs around with a poker so that streams of sparks shot up the chimney. "I love a fire." A blond lock had come free and she blew it away from her face. "David and Alice are moving in together. Her father has a flat in Victoria that he's letting them have." She crouched down further to stroke the little cocker, Goli, and gave me a sidelong glance. "It's short for Goliath. Except she's a girl of course." Then, to me, "Would you really have killed that boy if they hadn't taken him away? Zack says you had berserker eyes."

I took a cigarette from Peter and went to smoke it outside, my breath billowing like smoke. More snow had fallen and for as far as the eye could see the ground was pristine, luminous, and still beneath the moon, so that the courtyard and the rose garden seemed like a stage set.

After the wine at dinner, the cold air with the cigarette made my head spin. I took hold of Marcus to keep steady and he removed the cigarette from my hand and flicked it into a flower bed. David and Em were in the doorway watching us. As though I were an actress, and for the first time in a long time, I huddled in against Marcus and kissed him, feeling his body first tense in shock and then soften.

But I slept alone. I went up first and took the room with the window that looked over the courtyard, and before I threw off my clothes and the necklace and crawled into the icy bed, I know I locked the door. I heard the others come to bed and later slow footsteps in the corridor that seemed to reach my door and go no further, but I ceased to know what was dream and what was real and my sleep became seamless. And yet, when I awoke in the bright light of morning, the necklace was gone.

* * *

They were sitting round the kitchen table, all of them, drinking coffee and scarfing toast and eggs, and I had the unpleasant feeling that after I had gone to bed they'd all become the best of friends without me. It seemed horribly certain that I'd been the subject of conversation, of gentle mocking, at which Peter, Em, and Marcus had laughed, guiltily no doubt, but laughed none the less.

"Missing something?" Peter asked, and then, seeing my face. "Fuck, give her a coffee."

"Rob drank every last drop of brandy, didn't you, Rob? And now he's vile," Priss said.

"I am vile. Vile." And as though to prove it, Rob shot up, white-faced, and went outside. The dogs followed him out and when he came back in, wiping his lips, he said gravely, "I strongly advise you not to accept any kisses from Goli this morning."

"So who took them?" But I already had an idea. Em tiptoeing in on her little feet.

"We came up with it last night. You were in the right room, after all."

"I heard footsteps, but no one came in."

"It was this morning at six. I crept in. I was sure you were going to wake up, my heart was hammering so loud. I'm not surprised Mortimer had a heart attack."

"They want to play," David said. "We agreed last night, Em was to get the necklace and hide it if she could."

"And I did. I did everything just right. I went everywhere it says he went." Her face wrinkled. "It was ever so odd. I think it was the oddest thing I've ever done, like painting on the most giant of canvases. And it was so quiet." Seeing me soften, she said, "I mean, with all of us looking we might find the real ones. It's not impossible. It's as close as we'll ever get. With the snow and everything, don't you see?"

I did, and already I could see the appeal, but I didn't want to show that I was keen, that they had won, so instead I walked over to the door that Rob had left open and looked out.

"Just one thing missing," I said.

"What's that?"

"A corpse on that bench out there."

"Early days," said Rob. "Early days."

* * *

"Got any skates, Rob?" Priss asked, but the question wasn't meant seriously, for while the ice on the lake was thick enough—so thick that when I picked up a stone, a fist-sized rock, and launched it with all my strength at the cold rink, it merely bounced, skittered, and then slowed to a sliding halt out in the middle—there were ominous black patches, lacunae in the cloud of ice suggestive of the dark and freezing depths beneath. Goli wove her way down to the edge of the lake and rested one clawed paw and then the other on the ice, before creeping backward, hackles raised.

"Of course, you could give the game away, Em. They are your oldest friends after all," Alice was saying.

"No cheating," Marcus said.

"Are you quite sure about that?" Alice's voice had an edge to it and in response Marcus flushed.

"Maybe you want to check our bags when we leave, Alice. If you think we can't be trusted—"

Rob stepped between us.

"Calm down, Andy. Alice didn't mean anything. Let's all play nicely now." He turned to Zack. "I'm really not capable of doing this straight. I'll need a line of your coke. Chop, chop. There's a fellow."

"Didn't bring any, old chap."

"Liar!"

"Does the person that finds them get to keep them?" Priss asked. We all looked at Em.

"I think they should," David said carefully. "Finders keepers to make it more interesting."

"What if we find the real ones, Rob?"

"Finders keepers," said Rob. "Same if I find Zack's coke while searching for the necklace in his bag. Finders keepers start to finish. My money is on Peter, of course. We don't know what he's capable of, you see."

The tour had been for Priss and Zack, who didn't know the lay-out of the grounds.

"How do we start?"

In the end, we went back inside, to the room where I had slept.

"Can we have a clue, Em?"

She shook her head. "They're somewhere clever."

"You have to lie on the bed, Andy," Peter said.

So I did. I got up on the mattress and lay back feigning sleep while the others stood around me in a circle.

"Go on," Zack said.

So I raised by arms and stretched them out while miming a yawn, and then, rolling over, I reached out a hand for the bedside table, groped at its surface, drew myself up, and then howled, howled loud enough to shake the windowpanes.

"My necklace, it's gone. Someone has stolen my diamonds!"

* * *

On the first-floor landing, Peter and I barged at one another, grap-pling for the cupboard handles.

"No, you don't!" he cried. I shoved him with my hip. There was a brief scuffle.

Between gasps I said, "She's not put it somewhere she's used before. It's somewhere new."

"How can you tell?"

"She's too pleased with herself." This was true. Her face was inscru-table but there was a smile to Em's movements; the secret hiding place was giving her pleasure. Another thought occurred to me. "Anyway, what's up with Rob? What's with the *You don't know what he's capable of* shit?"

He backed away. "Because Rob is a fucking cunt, Andy."

In the laundry I found Priss elbow-deep in a box of washing powder and she raised her eyebrows at me. Alice I spotted through the window out in the rose garden walking with purpose toward the outbuildings. In the library, Em sat resplendent in one of the armchairs, a book in her hands, her feet resting on a tapestry-bedecked footstool.

"You've a hole in your sock," I told her. She did not look up, or meet my gaze, but her lips twitched.

I wandered, not quite aimlessly, occasionally spying one of the others in a passageway ahead or rooting through a set of drawers. Zack peered out at me from beneath a bed. From the tiny staircase window to the attic, I saw Rob falling down in the snow and then struggling up, even from a distance comically enraged, a murderous blue-anoraked ant, shaking his fists at the sky as he went down again.

I met David at the bottom of the stairs.

"No luck?" When I did not respond, he went on, "Always the quality of the silence with you. I mean anyone can do silence, but you really make them talk." As if he knew me, as though he could say always about me. I shrugged, not trusting my voice. "It's not so bad, is it? You're here. I'm here. All grown up. It isn't so bad, is it, Andy? What were we going to do? We were eighteen. We had nothing. No money. I was in trouble with the police. Half the time, I didn't know if you actually liked me or were just trying to—"

"Well, I'm glad to see you got your problems sorted. Found yourself an heiress and everything."

I heard someone coming up the stairs behind me and not wanting to be found there, I made to move off.

"So I'm damned to beasts?" he said.

"Yes, that's about it."

"Well fuck you too."

"You're her pet. Their pet."

"Good to see you've still got Marcus in a death grip."

* * *

Gradually, we drifted outside. I left through the library. Rob was there and drinking again.

"Em won't let me search her person," he said. "I'm giving up."

The others seemed, if anything, keener. I saw Priss and Zack kicking up piles of snow, the spray of crystals flying outward from their feet and landing with little thuds; Peter and David passing one another in the courtyard without speaking; Marcus heading toward the front of the manor.

"Think you'll find them in the fountain?"

He shrugged and I wondered how I'd pissed him off this time. We went on, an hour more, maybe longer. There would be more snow. The sun was visible only as a glare through thick white cloud. In the west it was hard to tell where the sky ended and the Downs began. The cold had seeped into my feet, but my cheeks were burning. I stamped and then took off toward the near edge of the lake.

Em had always been convinced the necklace was there, at the bottom among the reeds and mud. I imagined her, that morning, the stars still peeping out, tramping through the snow like a heroine from a Russian novel, standing at the lake's edge, sheltered from the wind by the roof of the little temple, while we slept in our beds.

I scanned the lake, registering the ice, the desiccated reeds, rotten or hollow, the churned snow from where we'd walked that morning. When I looked up, I saw David, almost directly opposite me on the other side of the lake. He was making with firm purpose toward the temple, moving eagerly, with quick sure steps, like a fox on its way to an unlocked chicken coop. The hood of his coat was pulled back and I could see a rim of forest green at his neck and the flush of color in his cheeks. My eyes moved back to the temple and then to David, from David to the temple. And then, of course, I knew where the necklace was, as though I had peered through a window into his mind. Somewhere clever? Who was cleverer than Athena, goddess of wisdom?

There was no way to catch him up, not even at a sprint, and at the prospect of defeat, I let out a bellow, so that David stopped and turned. Over at the house, I sensed the others pause in what they were doing. David was smiling at me across the lake. He was a hundred meters or so from the temple, and so was I, only the sheet of ice lay between me and the necklace. The stone I had thrown earlier was still lying out in the middle where white met black.

Marcus shouted as I took off running. The snow lay in drifts on the banks of the lake and at each stride I went in up to the knee, then I half stumbled, half leapt, out onto the frozen ice. My heels met the ungiving surface and I slid forward, waving my hands, until I reached a patch where the ice was rimed with frost and my shoes gained purchase. Managing to upright myself, I bounded forward, back in control and gathering speed. David was still frozen at the lake's far side but at the touch of my glance, he began to run and then we were both racing toward the temple and to where I was convinced the necklace was hidden.

The black patches lay ahead, but I was not thinking of them; I was not conscious of thinking of anything at all. It is odd to say it, but I was happy: my feet skimming over the ice, beneath me the dark depths of the lake, and then far down in the cold mud the slumbering fishes. I was aware of my body, flying forward, legs scissoring, my breath as it sawed in and out. The woods and hills were a blur. Yes, I was happy, possibly happier than I had been in years, even as I heard the ice crack and felt the faintest shift beneath my feet. My heart moved a little in my chest, and after that first lurch, I felt it beating against the bones of my rib cage and everything started going faster: my feet, the blurring at the edges of my vision, the air rushing into my lungs.

There was a second crack, somewhere behind me. It sounded

like a shot, not like the guns yesterday, but a pistol shot, and beneath my feet the ice dipped a little, just a small movement, and when I looked down a little water was rolling onto the ice, but I couldn't see the break. David was closer now, running flat out, his feet sending up flurries. We were converging, but I could not tell who would get there first. My feet were barely touching the surface. I was hurtling forward, now over the black ice. But I was always on thin ice, always waiting for the grasping embrace of the permanent cold, the always dark. At least now I was running.

My luck was in. The ice held, and then I was nearing the far bank. I was going to win. David had lost ground.

The bank ahead was steep. I jumped, landing in snow that was deep under a thin crust and I floundered, losing my footing, but pushing on, David only a few meters away. I might have still beaten him, but at my next step my foot kept on going and I felt my ankle roll over to one side and then a nauseating stab of pain. I struggled up, snow pouring from me, but my ankle wouldn't take my weight, so I could only hop and then hobble forward.

David trotted up the temple steps and over to the head of Athena. For a second, he looked puzzled. The necklace wasn't there. Not on the plinth, not around the statue's neck. His fingers traveled over her face, over the blind stone eyes, and then they nipped in and plucked something from the dark open mouth. The necklace came out black with leaf mold and dirt.

David turned to face me, rubbing the necklace between his palms. He was breathing hard too, and we stood there looking at one another.

"I won," he said.

"I guess you did."

"How was the ice?"

"A bit bouncy," I said.

His gaze fell on me gently, and he took a quick step forward, and then stopped to look over my shoulder. I turned and saw the others coming up the path, Marcus at the front and Rob bringing up the rear.

"He got there first?" Priss asked. I nodded.

"You nearly died out there on the ice and he still got there first?" Rob said. "Oh that's just priceless."

"Win some, lose some," I said.

"Spoken like a loser."

But I was glad of his prattle, and for the fuss Zack and Priss and Alice made of David. It made less of Marcus's silence. Em and Peter were not saying anything either.

"You both worked it out at the same time," Alice said. Her eyes flicked between us suspiciously.

"No, he was first."

"So how did you—"

"I kind of just knew. It was a good hiding place," I said.

"It was," Em said, but the look she gave me was strange. "But it's not—"

There was another crack, loud enough to cut her off. We all turned to look at the lake. It was snowing more heavily. The scene was beginning to look like a black-and-white TV with bad reception. Between the flying flakes, it was possible to see that out in the middle a large sheet of ice had broken into pieces, one was sinking beneath the water, and a black hole was visible, gaping wide, where I had stood only minutes before.

"You know, Andy, you are completely fucking insane. How do you feel when you look at that? You could have died," Rob said.

Priss, Zack, and Alice were looking at me curiously. Perhaps they thought I was capable of anything.

"Longing," Marcus said. "She feels longing."

* * *

In the boot room, I stripped off my outer layers and my wet socks. My ankle wasn't entirely good, but I couldn't really feel it. In the library, Zack built an enormous fire and while the others stood turning themselves before it, I took up a place in an armchair, jamming my bare feet beneath me. Away from the fire, the house was cold, but I was unbothered by it. My eyelids felt heavy and when I closed them for long moments, I found that I was still out on the ice, its frosted surface passing beneath my feet like a treadmill. Each time I felt the ice crack, I opened my eyes to see everything going on around me as before.

At one point a mug of coffee was thrust into my hand and then a ham sandwich.

I closed my eyes. The ice cracked. This time would I fall?

Peter and Marcus were at the window, looking out and discussing whether we should head back. "Must be four inches," Marcus said. "We should go."

"Up Burlip Hill?" Peter's voice was doubtful.

"No one's going anywhere. You have to stay. Besides there's a mad man out there. It's far too dangerous to set foot outside." Rob had come to stand beside them. "Yes, a mad man, a slobbering, ax-wielding, staggering cliché of homicidal mania, with a suitcase full of wrath and an encyclopedic knowledge of sex crimes."

"Are you sure?" Marcus asked.

"Oh, quite sure," Rob said, clapping him on the back. "He's practically family."

So we stayed, drinking steadily, first whiskey in the coffees, and then wine. Priss bustled in and out with the glasses and later there were canapés. "I got them from Marks," she said. "You just throw them in. What will you do with your prize, David?"

"Oh, I hadn't thought about it." David was by the fire and I saw him take the necklace from his pocket and hold it idly in one hand.

"It's only glass, isn't it, Em?"

"And if the necklace was real," she said, "what would we all do then?"

"What would that even mean? For it to be real?" I asked.

"It would mean you could exchange it for lots and lots of money," Alice said.

"Perhaps you should have them, Alice." And David held them out to her, dangling between finger and thumb in the firelight. I saw Priss smile innocently at the gesture.

"I don't take fake." Alice swung round and plopped down in a chair pouting, but David made no move toward her. I watched as he lay the necklace down on the mantelpiece. He did it deliberately; the necklace was unclasped and he laid it down in a line, adjusting it till it was quite straight.

The evening was a little subdued. Perhaps they were tired. Were they happy? Bored? I can hardly place my friends in the room, nor our hosts, nor Priss or Zack. In my memory, I can barely make them out. My attention was elsewhere.

Again, I was the first to go up. The bed was stone cold. I lay on top of it in my clothes, listening and waiting. The curtains were open and when I looked out it was upon a dream world, the velvet night, the nacreous glow of the moon. Beyond the pane, flakes of snow were rising on an updraft so that it gave me the peculiar feeling that time was running backward.

As I told the police, it was about one a.m. when I went back down. You forget how it is to move quietly, to creep. I was out of practice and my ankle was still throbbing from earlier. The whole house seemed to creak at my footfall. The dark was total, and once I had let go the bannister, I had to walk like the cartoon image of a sleepwalker, my arms stretched out before me. The door to the library was open and since there were embers still smoldering in the hearth, there was the merest murky, reddish glow by which I found my way to the fireplace. The necklace was there, on the mantelpiece where he had left it. My hand closed over it and a piece of the darkness detached itself, stepped forward. A hand closed over mine.

It was David, of course. We stood like that for a little bit. At least I can say that on this occasion he touched me first. His hand over

mine, mine clutching the necklace. But after that first touch, I have no defense. My mind went dead, like a phone line had been unplugged. Something else was taking over. He smelled the same, and his skin was warm and I could feel under my fingertips the stubble coming through. David put an arm around me and drew me in, chest to chest, cheek to cheek. A spreading shudder. Still holding the diamonds, I put my arms around his neck and kissed him. It had always been gentle between us, but it was not so gentle now. There wasn't any of me left that didn't want him. Still, I didn't let the necklace loose from my fist, not through any of it, not until the very end when I had to let it go, to press down both of my hands on the small of his back, such was the moment.

And, while it may sound like a stretch, for a time, that night with David in the library, I succeeded in finding what I had looked for that afternoon, that dark place on the other side of the ice. The great fall with no landing.

* * *

Peter was playing the piano. I could hear him from upstairs. A little jagged melody picked out with one hand, over and over, throbbing like a toothache.

There was a pot of coffee and some bacon sarnies on the side. I couldn't see Em or Marcus, but the others were there. David didn't look up as I came in.

"Morning, Andy," Rob said. He looked cheerful, buoyant, like he'd won the pools. No one else was smiling.

"Where's Em and Marcus?"

"Not sure. I suppose we should wait for them though, since it's traditional."

"Traditional for what? You've lost me, Rob," I said.

"I mean the gathering of the suspects before the great detective—Poirot, Marple, in this case me—reveals the guilty party, or parties."

"Someone steal the diamonds again?" They weren't on the mantelpiece. I threw a quick glance at the rug in front of the fire.

"No, we've got a new mystery. I'm calling it the bodies in the library."

With that, I knew what he was getting at and experienced a wave of horror, so like desire when you come to think of it, in the way it gripped you, made you feel like your organs were melting.

I poured out a coffee, the pot chattering against the rim of the cup. "Pete, where are Em and Marcus? We should get going."

"Marcus went to look for her." Peter was still picking out the little tune.

"Can you stop that? It's driving me nuts." His hands froze and then he set them down gently in his lap.

"Thing is, Andy," Rob went on, "yours truly passed out last night on the couch in the library. Not that you'd have known that, because you went up so early. Dave too, when I think about it. Anyway, so there was I passed out on the couch and then about one, maybe two, I wake up. It's pitch-black so I can't see anything, but I'm hearing these noises. Can you guess what it was? No? Don't want to take a guess, a wild stab in the dark?"

I heard the front door slam.

"Why don't you shut your fucking mouth?"

"Rob, what are you talking about?" Alice had gotten to her feet.

For a moment, the impish mask slipped and Rob looked almost sad. "Sorry, sis," he said. "But better you find out now than later. Better you know him for what he is."

David still didn't say anything. His eyes followed Rob. He didn't even look particularly surprised.

Turning back to me, Rob went on. "It was a couple, Andy. Two people. Fucking. At it. Hammer and tongs. On my parents' best Persian rug. Sixteen bedrooms to choose from—"

Marcus came in. He had his boots on and they were caked in snow.

"Shut up, Rob. Just shut up!" And I made a move toward him like I was going to cover his mouth with my hands and stop the words from coming out.

"Just in time, Marcus. We're reaching the denouement! I'm about to reveal . . . where's Em? She should be here for this too really. I'm just about to tell you how I caught Andy and David fucking last night."

"Em's outside." There was something wrong with Marcus's face. He didn't look right, or sound right for that matter. "Em's out there." He looked at each of us in appeal. "She's out in the snow. I'm pretty certain—" and his face collapsed, collapsed unbearably. "I think Em's dead."

* * *

She was not, as Mortimer had been, in the rose garden. She was at the end of the drive, near but not quite at the road. Later the police would ask how many sets of footprints there had been in the snow. Were there two? Or three? Or more even? I didn't know. I couldn't tell them. My gaze was fixed on the dark heap in the snow up by the gate. At some point, I started running. I got there first, but the others were there soon after, all apart from Marcus and Peter. I don't think Marcus ran at all. He was clutching Peter's arm and coming up over the snow like an old man afraid of falling and breaking every bone he had.

Em was lying on her back. Her coat was open. She had on her nightie—a Patti Smith T-shirt I knew she wore in bed—and her jeans and boots. I took up her hand, but there was no life in it.

"That's my coat," I said. "Why's she got my coat on?"

"I'm not a doctor," Zack was saying. His voice had a rising intonation as though one of us was insisting he was. "I'm not a doctor but I think she's dead."

But how could she be dead?

I heard myself saying her name, over and over. I heard myself crying. Not normal crying, something much worse. It was like coming apart.

Priss had called an ambulance straightaway, but it took a long time to come. There had been an accident on the M4 out by Junction 16 and all across the region, people were slipping over on pavements and breaking arms, elbows, collarbones, losing control of their cars and ending up beached on roundabouts or in ditches. When it finally swung up the drive in the wake of a police car, it felt like an insult. They confirmed what we knew. No signs of life.

"Aren't you going to do anything? Shock her or something? I mean it can't hurt, can it? Do something! Do something!" Marcus's face was liverish. He looked big and angry and I could see the police sizing him up. Peter moved to stand between him and the medics.

On TV, people would often seem dead for minutes—a week even, between episodes—only to revive at the last possible moment.

"She's not even hurt," I said. And it was true. Em had no injuries that I could see. Only when they moved her, there was a pink patch, not big, no pool of blood or anything, on one of the stone markers that bordered the drive.

"You need to all go inside now with my colleague." It was one of the police, a female officer. Another car was arriving, unmarked, with two men inside. Soon, they'd be joined by a photographer and the forensics officers. She turned to me. "Listen, love, you've only got your socks on. You'll catch your death."

But it was Em who had caught her death, caught the death I had called up, the one I had summoned from beneath the ice, and there was no bringing her back from it.

* * *

We were interviewed. First at the house, again at the station. I told the police how I knew Em and for how long, how we'd come to be there, and what we had been doing and how I knew all the others.

They wanted to know about the game and when I had last seen Em, and what time I'd gone to bed and where and with whom.

"You say it was about ten-thirty p.m.?"

"Maybe nearer eleven, but I was up in the night. I came downstairs."

"Time?"

"About one."

"And did you see Emma?"

"No."

"Why did you come downstairs?"

"I wanted the diamonds, the one we used for the game."

"The necklace David Graves had won."

"He had left them on the mantelpiece, but I wanted them."

"And did you see anyone?"

"I saw David."

"And how long were you downstairs."

"Perhaps an hour . . ."

I told them. It was all going to come out anyway.

"And you're in a relationship with Marcus Fisher?"

"Yes."

"And what about Emma?"

"What about her?"

"Was she in a relationship with anyone?"

"No."

"She had not fought with anyone? She wasn't angry with anyone as far as you knew? There wasn't a lover's quarrel?"

"No," I said. "Em wasn't in love with anyone."

A week or so later, I was called back. It was the same two detectives. They were interested in the footprints. It was like a puzzle, I could see that. They had photographs of the drive, color shots and some black and whites.

"Bit arty," I said. I felt ill, like a lifetime of eating rotten things had caught up with me. There was one of the house, a black and white.

The door was open. It looked like a maw. Black door and windows and everything bleached and unutterably sinister, like a lunatic park and all the love I'd ever felt for it was a knife twisting in my heart.

Some clever soul had painted each set of footprints a different color. Detectives Tailor and Vincent showed me various photos. There was one of the area around Em's body. You could just see Em's boot in the top corner. The snow was all mushed up from where we had kneeled over her. There were lots of pictures of the footprints in the snow leading to and from the house. One of the detectives, Vincent, seemed to think there was an extra set. Em had gone out, but not come back. Marcus has gone out once and found her, and then come back to fetch us, then he had gone out and eventually back again. The rest of us had gone out and back once. An extra set—boot prints. They were the same pair that Zack had been wearing, one of the pairs left by the door.

The other detective was less convinced. In places the tracks were obliterated, they crossed and disappeared and some could have been from the day before, and while new snow had fallen, it'd been an inch or two at most.

The cause of death had been confirmed. Em had died from a bleed on the brain caused by a blow to her head, this and hypothermia. It would have taken her a few hours to die. She would not have been in pain. But would she have known? Would Em, lying there, have known she was dying, known that she was alone?

I wanted to take a knife and cut the thought out of myself. To go further, to find the home of grief itself, the site where it was lodged and hack it out of my body before it killed me. In the middle of the night, I thought about joining Em, and the thought of being dead gave me comfort, gave me relief and allowed me to sleep. When I awoke it was to all the terror of a nightmare, but the thing you were scared of, already happened.

The detectives wanted to know what I thought she was doing out there.

"Was she leaving? Had she gone for another walk? Perhaps to meet someone? Or was it another game?" The necklace had been in Em's coat pocket. Detective Tailor slid it over the desk in a plastic Ziploc bag. I looked at it dully.

"She must have come and taken it from where I left it on the rug, after David and I had gone back up, after Rob had gone to bed."

What about this game? The detectives knew about Mortimer and the diamonds. It was odd, wasn't it? The parallel—that was the word Detective Vincent used, parallel. Who had started it, all this business with the necklace? And would I say I took it seriously, more seriously than the others, so much so that I had risked my life running over a half-frozen lake? He'd even dug out a statement I'd given to the Marlborough police when I was fifteen and they'd caught me climbing on top of the supermarket.

"You like games, don't you, Andrea? You said that was part of a game. But they have a tendency to get out of hand, don't they? Some games, that is."

"We used to play cops and robbers too," I said.

"And which were you?" he asked.

"I was always a detective. I thought they were the clever ones."

Detective Tailor went back to asking how much we'd all had to drink, whether there had been any drugs. If Em had argued with anyone, if anyone could have wanted to hurt her? Had we fallen out? Was she trying to walk home?

I couldn't help them. Even if I could, it wouldn't have brought Em back.

Detective Vincent caught me up on the steps outside. His demeanor was different outside the interview room, softer, like he'd been putting on a show and now it was over. A family was smoking furiously on the pavement: the parents, two older boys, and a small scowling creature who was eyeing the cigarettes jealously.

"My wife made me give up," Vincent said. "I don't know what it is about it that I miss. Do you mind if I ask you a question? It's not related. Your mum used to be mixed up with Joe Hind."

I nodded.

"Do you know where he is?"

"In hell, I hope."

"We found his car a few years ago burned out in a wood, but no sign of Joe for some time now. Wanted on a number of charges. A couple of them related to young women like yourself. Know anything about that? You all right?" Vincent put a hand out to steady me but too late. I fell against him.

"Is he dead?"

"You're all right. You're all right. There you go." Vincent glanced over at the family, but they were not looking at us. "No one knows where Hind went, and there were plenty of people interested."

My knees seemed trustworthy again and I let go of his arm.

"What's going to happen now?" My voice was small and childish.

"Go home. Have a cup of tea," Vincent said. He turned to go and then stopped. "No idea why she was wearing your coat, I suppose?"

"We always borrowed each other's clothes," I said.

"Look after yourself, Andrea," he called after me.

* * *

The inquest would take months and return an open verdict. I didn't go to the final hearing. I didn't see Zack or Priss or Rob again. Nor David. I thought he might show up but I was wrong again. The only one I saw was Alice. It was a few days after Christmas. She was sitting in her car in the car park behind Waitrose. The snow had all melted and lay in slushy pools full of floating, bloated fag ends.

Alice rolled down the window. We exchanged a few blunt words. I walked closer to the car but she rolled the window back up before I got there. I wished Marcus was there, the low voice and restraining hand. But Marcus was staying at his mum's.

She started the engine and I went and stood in front of the car. It was a neat little Volkswagen, all shiny and red, a gift no doubt. I felt like a shark circling a diving bell. There are times when anger makes you feel superhuman, capable of tearing metal. Alice revved the engine.

"Go on then," I mouthed.

Bless her, I could see she really wanted to. She had more than a touch of crazy. When I stepped aside, she drove off riding the clutch. A shitty driver in a car someone bought her. I wished her ill and then I stopped wishing her ill and started crying.

* * *

Marcus didn't come and he didn't phone. I had left a message with his mum, but something in her voice stopped me calling back. In the run-up to the funeral, I went to see Peter, calling on him at his parents' house as of old. We sat on the stone wall that enclosed the graveyard.

"Are they going to put her here?"

"I think so."

Grief was making ghouls of us. Peter's face was the color of a dead tooth. I was wearing the clothes I had slept in, the same clothes I had been wearing the day before.

"Have you seen Marcus?"

"Once," he said.

"How is he?"

"He's angry. He's not thinking straight."

"Should I go and see him?"

"I'd leave it a bit."

I nodded. There was something I wanted to ask him.

"Pete, at the manor that summer, were you and David . . . I mean were you fucking him?"

Peter got to his feet.

"No, Andy. Don't worry. You got there first."

I stayed sitting on the wall, the cold sinking into me, staring him in the eye.

"She was wearing my coat."

Peter gave me what I can only call a strange look.

"What would you have done if I'd said yes, Andy?" Then he walked quickly away before I could answer.

The millennium dawned. I slept through it. Back at work, I didn't see Marcus either. He was on-site, I was told, and he stayed there. But he came to the funeral. Peter was back at Oxford by then. He took the train down for the day, and during the service we stood, the three of us, in a line. I could feel Peter trembling on one side, Marcus as hard as wood on the other.

Songs from the old lady choir, all in tears, a eulogy from Em's younger sister, Faye, Peter's dad leading us out into the graveyard, the bit with the dirt. The startling stab of rage—that I was expected to say goodbye to her, now, with all these people watching, that I was expected to say goodbye to her forever, and then another stab, this time with Em herself. *Em, you prick, you total prick. What were you thinking? Look what you've done to me! And you're going to do it forever!*

Afterward there were sandwiches in the back of The Green Knight. People from school sliding looks over. *They were there. Say they don't know anything. That she was just wandering about out there on her own and fell over.*

Em's mum came over and hugged all three of us.

"You'll come by the house, won't you?"

I promised that I would. Knew I wouldn't.

"She'd made you all Christmas presents. She'd done tapes for you."

When we left, she came and hugged me again, crying, her round face wet and wobbling. "I think she was out there hiding them again, so you could have another go at that game. That would be like her, wouldn't it? Doing something nice for you all. What will we do without her, Andy? What will we do without our Em?"

I got in the van, into the back next to Peter, and Marcus drove us to the station at Great Bedwyn in silence.

As Peter slipped away, up the steps and onto the platform, I could see his eagerness to be off and I envied him. Back in Oxford no one had heard of Em, and its libraries and lecture halls and greens would be untainted by her and by the grief of those who had loved her, and at times he would, I imagined, be able to forget any of it had ever happened.

* * *

The darkness was coming in as we drove back in the rain, down the Roman road, through the ancient forest. I was in the passenger seat. At the lights in town, I stole a glance at Marcus and could see a tear flexing from the surface of his eyeball, until the light changed from red to green and he blinked and it broke. He didn't take me home, he drove on, taking the Swindon road to Chiseldon and then up to Barbury Castle.

The car park was empty. It would close in another hour if the caretaker could drag himself away from his cottage to padlock the gate. The windscreen misted up, obscuring the view of the winter wheat, the dun hedgerows, the bulk of the aerodrome and beside it the gray cracked tarmac of the runway from where Mrs. East's pilots had taken off on their wartime bombing missions. Beyond the mist, raindrops fell and ran together to create ripples of descending water. When the joint was rolled, I plucked it from his fingers and got out, briefly feeling the wet slap of the wind before I slid open the side door and got into the back. After a minute, I heard him open his door and get out on the driver's side. He was gone minutes and when he finally came in, his hair and face were wet with rain.

Marcus gave me a smile that was just a movement of the lips. I sparked up and we smoked, passing the joint to and fro, but that wasn't what we were there for. The rain fell on the roof and the radio, tuned as always to Radio One, played deeply inappropriate songs—Ricky Martin was "Livin' La Vida Loca." Britney Spears was "Born to Make You Happy."

When the spliff was halfway down, I pinched it out and, without meeting his eye, I crawled over to where he was sat, back against the wall panel, legs stretched out. I'd bought a black dress for the occasion and now I knelt in it before him, my knees either side of his thighs, his face at the height of my breasts. I stayed like that for a moment or two and then leaned in to press against him. His hands came up around me and I pushed against him and kissed him hard, and felt a quiver of triumph as he reacted, as his mouth opened and his grip tightened and I pulled back only long enough to pull my dress over my head.

All the sorrows and hurts were outside and couldn't get in for now. I felt them circling, pressing against the windows, but they could not reach me. In the past, I had struggled to want to fuck Marcus often enough or at appropriate times. It took drink or a spliff, a fight, another woman eyeing him. But I wanted him now, even though I knew it was the end. It was like burning the house you live in, when there is a storm raging outside in the middle of winter. Don't say you haven't wanted to, never had the inkling, the almost-knowledge that everything you love and hold dear is holding you back. Back from what? I was going to find out.

He got there. I felt him go, but there was still time, a little time. I held the dead weight of him, counting the seconds. A sudden and terrible comprehension of everything I was losing. My mouth was an inch from his ear. I wanted to say something, use words to hold him hostage. I knew the secret name he had given his bike when he was eleven. I'd seen his face, green with leaf light as we lay beneath the willow trees. But I wanted to keep those things safe too, sealed off from the present, so I said nothing.

Marcus had a few words for me.

"It's over. I don't want to see you."

I said I was sorry about David. I managed that.

"I used to be jealous of him, of what you had between you. God, I wished you'd fucked off with him all those years ago, instead of hanging round to poison everything. I don't want to worry about you or look after you anymore. I'm sick of it."

"I'm sick of you looking after me too." Like all the gratitude I had to feel, all the guilt for not getting better, had gone bad. Resentment, that between us he always got to be the noble one, the knight, and what that made me. For a glorious second, it felt that I was slipping my chains and riding off on the back of the dragon, but then it lurched back to feeling like I was in a film, that all that was keeping me from falling forever was Marcus's hand gripping mine, and his grip was slipping, and then I had that odd dreamlike sensation, like in the second before you wake up, when you are finally falling and it's such a relief.

"Well, hope you enjoyed the fuck, Marc. Are you glad you got it in before you told me you don't want to fucking see me anymore, your last-minute sightseeing?"

He didn't say anything to that.

"Em—"

"Don't fucking say anything about Em." Shouting in my face, spit flying. I got my dress on and opened the van door.

"It's not like it's ever any good with you anyway." And this was unfair and untrue. Or it was only true sometimes, and when it was, it was not Marcus's fault.

He did look at me then, ugly with hate, like I was a criminal, a robber who had stolen something precious from him and sent him a video of myself shitting all over it before destroying it forever.

Marcus blinked. When he opened his mouth, his voice came out hoarse. "And every day you get more and more like your mum."

He drove us back. I got out, floated down the path toward the house, like one of those cyclists who get back on their bikes after an accident, not realizing yet the bones they've broken. Inside, I sat down at the bottom of the stairs. I wanted to call Em. I wanted Em to come and hug me, and make me tea and tell me it would all be all right. I would want the same thing a thousand times. I want it now.

There was a knock a couple of minutes later. When I didn't open up, Marcus pushed the letterbox open with his fingers and peered through to confirm I was there. Then he told me to find a new job, to do it quick, and not make him get his uncle to sack me.

CHAPTER 14

GENTLEMEN'S CLUB

AFTER MY NIGHT AT THE BAR, THE INEVITABLE EPISODE. I woke curled around my laptop, next to the tail end of a ketchup sandwich and the burned-out telephone box. It went downhill from there. Episodes could begin innocuously enough. I would get the idea that I deserved a duvet day as reward for my long hours and professionalism, a bit of telly in bed with a bowl of ice cream, but they always ended the same way: binge-watching series or films while binge-eating whatever was in the house, first addressing the fridge and cupboards, eventually the freezer.

One screen was never enough, so I'd have the tablet open as well, usually the browser on the phone too, my eyes flickering from the show, to the news, to the shopping or social media site. Every half hour or so, I'd shuttle back to the kitchen to fetch something else to eat, occasionally ordering in or even venturing out to the corner shop. Only once I was a few hours deep in an episode, I couldn't stand to be looked at, wasn't able to even meet my own eyes in the mirror, so I tended to make do with what I had in the house, mashing up butter with icing sugar and spreading it on bread, or making my own cookie dough and eating it with my fingers from a bowl, the kind of food that I had resorted to when I lived with my mother and there were no other options.

The rules regarding what I watched during an episode were

strict. Art of any kind was forbidden, as were old movies, musicals, documentaries, love stories, and anything that gave significant screen time to children or animals. No, I watched action movies, watched them for the explosions, the moments when the whole screen was a consuming, raging fire, and for the fight scenes, in which bad men were eventually overcome with maximum force. The fights were like beautiful dances, rising toward climax, the body count swelling as Vin, or The Rock, Jason or Bruce, snapped and stabbed and choked, punching and ripping and slamming and gouging bad men toward unconsciousness or death, their faces flushed and contorted with the effort of it. The violence always justified. A wife murdered. A child held hostage. But the women and children merely ciphers, excuses for the violence unleashed. All the while on the second screen, I'd be clicking through the news, where there was neither climax nor heroes, only rolling horror leavened by celebrity thighs and sponsored lifestyle features about juicing.

Sometimes, the episodes rolled over from one day into the next, could gobble up a whole weekend, during which I'd become more and more agitated, feeling the presence of the mirrors in the house, even while I lay cocooned in bed with the curtains closed. I would want to stop, but at the crucial moment, I would either click or not click so the next episode or film would begin; I'd rarely remember falling asleep but, waking up next to the laptop's greedy eye, I knew if I so much as tapped a key, there would be another fourteen, sixteen hours of explosions and murders ahead while I ferried something or other to my mouth, waiting for it to end, implicated by all of it—the violence, the news, the shopping—moving further and further beyond rational thought, brain scrambled, as though computing that by staying there, via my avatar on the screen, I could defeat the bad men, overcome the terrible threat from the safety of my sticky crumb-infested bed, out of sight, tunneled into the sheets like an animal.

There was no pleasure in it, only a bone-deep, inarticulate panic, matched by the unwillingness or inability to end the whole episode because it would have meant, once the devices were all turned off, once the flat was quiet around me, that I would have been alone with my own thoughts.

* * *

The day after my meeting with Mr. Hutchinson, as my hero, armed with a hunting knife, stabbed and slashed and slit his way toward the enemy lair, sending up fountains of blood, the news featured a line of men kneeling in the desert awaiting execution; a herd of refugees with their saucer-eyed children, knee-deep in mud, corralled at a border by armed men in black; and a special report on the links between London-based financiers and Russian kleptocrats revealed by the leaked papers. I was mechanically eating cereal with peanut butter. A girl had gone missing. Her picture was everywhere, her face young and painfully open and now marked for death—she was missing, feared something-ed. By tea time she would be found something-ed. The hero of the film, no matter how hard he fought, was unable to save the girl with her shining eyes and plait done up with a pink bobble.

Rob was an unlikely savior, but he brought the episode to an end, quite swiftly around four o'clock. It was Rob Calcraft I had messaged at the bar. Rob from the manor; Rob who was once the kind of boy who would smirk when he was being told off, who would have been unable to stop no matter how much worse it made matters.

I'd invited him to connect with me and then written, *I need to talk to you.* I'd never bothered uploading a profile pic so I'd added, *It's Andy, remember? From Marlborough.*

The message I got back the next day went, *Oh I remember! Phone number?*

I hesitated, but only a little, then sent the digits across. Then nothing. I went back to my hero, who was fighting a bad man in the cockpit of a plane, eventually biting him on the face before strangling him with a parachute cord and throwing him out the back, the phone cradled in my lap. On another screen I searched for news of the man who'd come off the roof three nights before. His name was Ward Collier. He'd worked in the city and was engaged to be married before he'd jumped or fallen from the top of the multistory car park. The family was mystified.

After a short interval, long enough to suggest someone enjoying the tension but unable to really wait, my phone rang and I jumped like a bomb had gone off.

Rob, sounding much the same, insisted we meet at his club. It was one of the old ones, one of the last to finally admit women. He seemed surprised that I knew where it was but quickly recovered. Before he rang off, he asked me if he would recognize me.

"I think you'll know me, Rob."

"Will I? Will I indeed?"

His parting line contained the same mix of malice and bonhomie I remembered:

"I could always ask Alice to join us. Make it a proper reunion. Maybe I'll do that." And he hung up before I had a chance to say anything.

* * *

"What can I do for you, Andy?" The club, a pornographic spread of establishment clichés, was fairly empty. All the members off in their constituencies, or enduring family time, or visiting country houses. There were lots of oil paintings of prime ministers, viceroys, and generals through the ages in huge gilt frames, oak paneling, the works. How was it all still here? All still standing?

"What's your guess?"

"Money seems to be what women usually want from me these days, but you don't look very needy. All this time I've had it wrong. All these years, on the very rare occasions I've found myself at home during the day, and put the TV on and there was the usual trash on *Jerry Springer* or *Jeremy Kyle*, I found myself thinking of you and wishing you'd make an appearance." Our drinks arrived and we paused to let the waiter put down two little white napkins and set the tumblers upon them.

"What would have been the show's theme that day, do you think?"

"I'll admit to a weakness for the paternity test ones. You know, is daddy Cousin Wayne or is it Uncle Kev? But you left all that behind, didn't you?"

"You've googled me?"

"I have." And he looked all fake bashful and fluttered his eyelashes. It was after six. Beyond the tall windows the day was giving up the ghost. A short time before I'd been in bed in a stained T-shirt with a multipack of Hula Hoops, but I'd scrubbed up for Rob, and now I was glad. Our armchairs were leather. Beneath a portrait of the Light Brigade, a cheery little fire burned. Rob was fatter now, and receding a touch, but otherwise little different. In return for my glance, Rob leaned in and gave me a very direct, very appraising look.

"It's very good." His eyes had come to rest on my face, like a surgeon admiring a particularly nice bit of work. "All utterly unexpected. If a little—"

"A little?

"Homogenous? Are you forty yet? Not quite. Well, it's the new thirty, I hear. And fifty is the new twenty. And eighty is the new three, since you're back wearing nappies being fed with a spoon. You know we sold the manor? It's a care home now, a warehouse for the decrepit."

"How are you, Rob?"

"Married. Divorced. Two children, a boy and a girl. Nearing the top of the queue for VP at work. Girlfriends, houses, cars, school fees, skiing holidays."

"Well done, you."

Rob curled his lip, upended his glass, and waved the empty at the waiter. I wondered how many he'd had before I arrived. "I'm so bored I could weep. And I don't like weeping so sometimes I behave badly to be less bored."

"Drink and women?"

"And rudeness. My ex-wife said it was the rudeness that was worst of all. That has to be a British thing, doesn't it? A wife who will overlook you fucking her . . . well, no need to be specific, is there? But ultimately can't bear the tone you take with waiters."

"Poor old Rob."

He closed his eyes. "Just don't be boring. Please don't be boring. I suppose you want to talk about David, or that friend of yours, that lovely girl who died."

* * *

Rob held up the telephone box on the palm of his hand. His hands were surprisingly childish, soft-looking and small with pink, plump fingertips.

"And you found this in Peter's flat? Perhaps he's become an artist. It's rather Banksian, isn't it? I can see a whole series of them: a cricket bat with a dog turd on it, a giant dildo sculpted from Kendal Mint Cake, the corpse of a corgi wearing a diamond tiara. It's too easy. Come on, you do one."

"Last time I saw him, he said he'd seen David."

"And this," he indicated the box, "is relevant to Dave how?" Rob put the telephone box down on the table and wiped his hands on his napkin. I told him about the phone box outside my house, about the fire. How I was certain it was Peter who'd torched it.

"Because?"

"Because I had an affair with David that summer. Because he liked him."

Rob raised an eyebrow. "Are you sure he's not just in a dark room somewhere, ketamined to the eyeballs, having the jolly old chem-sex time of his life?"

I shook my head.

"I was at the same college as your friend Peter. I was a year ahead of him so we didn't have tutorials together, never knew him well, but he stuck out. Odd, self-conscious, even the way he spoke, like it was still the 1920s. Always trying to insert himself, not a good drinker. Rumors about him wandering around talking to himself at night like a nutter. And then there was this one time when, well . . ."

My throat thickened. "What happened?"

"If he'd taken it in good spirit, it'd probably have been different for him." Rob stood up and went to the long windows. Outside, Saint James Street was quiet, the day graying into evening. He tapped on the glass, and as if in response, the streetlights came on. Looking down at his hand, for a moment his face became foolish with delight.

"Did you see that?"

"I did."

"Little victories."

"What did you do to Peter? Bugger him? Made him lick your boots?"

Rob managed to look shocked for a moment. "It wasn't me, Andy. I just happened to be there. He used to walk about nights, your friend Peter. Some of the lads bumped into him coming back from a few drinks. Chased him about a bit, had a go at stripping him off."

Dimly, I recalled something similar happening in one of the books Peter had lent me as a teenager. A gay character turning the tables on a bunch of oafs, something about a fountain.

"They put him in the bins, Andy. Headfirst, I'm afraid. One of the big black ones on wheels at the back of the kitchen. He absolutely lost his shit. Shouting. Screaming that we didn't know what he was capable of. Kept saying that. Then he started crying. Don't look at me like that."

"Do you know where David is? Where Peter might have seen him?"

"No, not a clue. Could be on the moon, for all I know. Takes me back, being invited to talk about the complex mystery of Dave to one of his admirers."

A ruddy-faced man in a charcoal stripe swept into the room and came over to say hello. Rob introduced me as a great friend of his sister's. When he finally pushed off, Rob turned back to me and said, "But of course, you're going to stay and have dinner with me." And then, "I'll tell you everything." He stopped. "Or will I? How about this? I will if you will. We can make a game of it."

* * *

The game was we got a question each. Lying was cheating. Rob took my arm as we went into the dining room and tucked my chair in behind me. The menu was all Dover sole and Chateaubriand. We ordered, the wine came, and Rob hunched forward in his chair.

"You go first."

"Why did you invite us that weekend?"

"Wasn't the greatest idea, was it? Not since it ended with a dead girl in my garden and the house being crawled over by police. Let me see—" He closed his eyes, opened them, and shrugged. "Honestly, I suppose I thought your presence might prize my sister's fingers loose from Dave. Call it a hunch. He's always been suspiciously vague about his time on the run. And then, at the shoot, it was obvious there was something between you. He'd been funny about coming. Not my idea of an ideal brother-in-law. I thought I'd gotten rid after school, but no, a couple of years later he saunters in on my sister's arm. Guess who it is?

"This was after all the business about him nicking the credit cards had died down. I think that's how it started with Alice. Everyone was sick of him. I certainly was. He was on remand awaiting trial. No one else was going to step in, and he knew it—so he went to Alice. She'd have been what? Sixteen? But Alice knew a thing or two, even then, and she worked on my parents and some of the other students' parents and a teacher here and there. You know, the right whisper in the right ear? *Can't see a promising young man go to prison for a foolish mistake.* Golden boy had got himself off the hook again. I don't know what happened to him after he was released. But I'm certain they were seeing one another on the quiet. When he reappeared, Alice said they'd just bumped into each other at Portobello Market. But they'd been biding their time. I'm sure of it."

"You never liked him. Did you all bully him?"

Rob looked genuinely hurt. "He was my best friend! Yet in Italy, he dumped me and went off on his adventures without a word. Honestly, if you think that, you never knew him at all. Far too cunning for that. Good at making friends. So amenable, so subtle. No deep, dark, painful secrets in David's past, not one. Admittedly, not entirely easy being a scholarship boy, but hardly a Dickensian struggle. Nice parents by the look of it—saw them quite a few times. Mild mannered, mousey. They seemed to be a bit in awe of him. Like they'd have preferred something from Argos. And in the beginning never really standing out, just another little boy. But who gets to be nature-table monitor? Who gets whisked away to a private Serengeti hunting lodge at Easter with Rafe Fithern's family?" He paused for a moment. "My turn to ask a question now."

I waited expectantly. We were having salmon to start. Rob looked to the heavens, swallowed, and pointed at me with his knife.

"Tell me about your transformation. No, that's not really a question, is it? Okay, tell me this. How does a hard-faced scrubber like yourself end up at Oliver March's outfit? Last time we met, you weren't exactly full of social graces."

So I sketched out for him my career trajectory, skipping over the first few years, of course. When I finished, he smiled.

"Pulled yourself up by your bootstraps. Maggie would be proud."

I shrugged. "Evening courses were next to free when I did them. Night school. All those people coming in after work to do A-Levels or bookkeeping or what they used to call computer programming. Doing Access courses so they could go to uni, which they could also do part-time, which was also free. But I was used to working—at school I had to keep up with Peter."

"Funny, you liking him so much. I didn't get the feeling he liked you a huge amount."

"What do you mean?" A cold tingling in my flesh, almost like pins and needles. I could accept we had grown apart, even that I had alienated Peter. That we mistrusted, as well as loved, one another. But the thought of Peter not liking me was hard to bear. "Give me examples."

Rob shrugged. "Just a feeling."

For someone unwilling to talk about David, Rob didn't need a huge amount of prompting. He was bitchy and unguarded. David the manipulator, David the professional mirror, so plausible, such a void.

"I know I say I'm bored, but I wasn't then, not when we were at school. I truly wasn't. Lessons were dull, but there were all those rules to be broken, and there was getting caught and getting away with it. Fun. And then the grown-up world looming on the horizon. Everything we weren't allowed, soon to be ours. It was an optimistic feeling. Soon we would be given the keys to the city. Only when you get there? What's inside? Girls, and he was good with them as well, of course. Nothing was ever enough for David. It all came too easy. Maybe that's what attracted him to Alice. She wasn't nice to anyone. I mean I love my sister. I really do. I didn't want to see her hurt. But what do they say? High maintenance. Touchy. Having people treat her like she was thick because of the dyslexia, watching our father trample all over our mother her whole life. I think perhaps David liked that. I've no idea what she saw in him. Maybe she liked having rescued him."

"What happened afterward, after that weekend?"

"After the police had finished with us? We went back to London. Hunkered down. Got on with it. I mean, we hadn't known her well. Well, I suppose David had a bit. But I didn't see that much of Alice and David. I hoped she'd straight-out chuck him, but they limped on for a bit. I think there was some trouble about the job at Christie's. Left under a cloud, shall we say. I'm not sure of the details. I expect he was up to something shady. Alice chucked him, or he chucked Alice a few months later. It did occur to me that he might be with you."

"No."

"Not a dicky bird? I heard you, you know. The bodies in the library! I woke up and, of course it was dark and I was still pissed as a fart, head already thumping, longing for a glass of water and my bed, only there are these two people clearly banging the life out of one another. So I just lay there trying to work out who the hell it was. It didn't sound like you. Although it didn't sound much like him either. Very romantic, very touching. I must say it made me feel a bit lonely, and horny of course. Which is why, after you'd sloped off, I had the crazy idea of going off to find your friend Em. I had the notion that if I knocked on her door and told her, I don't know, that I couldn't sleep? That I was feeling a little sad? Well, I thought she might invite me in for a cuddle, or at least invite me in and let me lay out my sorrows, after which . . ."

"And did you?"

"I did, but as I told the police, she wasn't there, or wasn't answering. It wasn't Rob's night, I told myself. But then it wasn't Em's night either, was it? It sort of ruined things for everyone, didn't it? Zack babbling about getting rid of his half a gram of coke before the police came, like that was the most important thing. He and Priss didn't last. Alice was all right once she got clear. Sad little interlude, echoing down the years. Shame because it shouldn't have ended like that. That game, the diamonds. Because it was beautiful, wasn't it? I remember you running out over the ice and my heart just went with you. The wildest thing with your hair flying . . ."

For a moment Rob seemed lost in reverie. The waiter came and bore our plates away. After he was gone, Rob turned to me.

"I held her hand, you know, while we waited for the ambulance.

And she was like a stopped clock. That laugh she had . . ." His eyes were wet, and he rubbed them with the back of a hand. "What really happened to her? To your friend Em?"

I realized it was the question I had been waiting for him to ask. Perhaps I had come here so Rob would ask precisely this question.

"She fell?" I said.

"Really, do you think so?"

"Why would anyone hurt her?"

"And yet, Peter goes missing and you're here asking questions about something that happened nearly twenty years ago."

"The telephone box. And he said he'd seen David."

"Tenuous, Andy. Very tenuous. Have you ever thought it was you they were after?"

"She was wearing my coat." I hadn't expected to say the words. They just came out. It had always stayed with me, that Em had been wearing my coat, that and the sad little melody Peter had been playing on the piano.

"What about that Marcus of yours? You'd just cheated on him. Maybe I wasn't the only one to hear you. You didn't look that different, not from behind anyway."

I shook my head. "Punch someone out in the pub, yes. Start a fight on a football pitch . . . but no. Marc, I pushed him at times. Four years we were together and if he was ever going to hit me, he'd have done it. I wanted to know if he could, to find out so I could feel safe, but no. Not once. He wanted to see himself as a white knight, a good guy. It was everything to him."

"Or maybe Em and David had been at it all those years ago too, ever think of that? They might have had a bone to pick with one another. And your friend Peter didn't have the best mental health, I would say."

I stared down at my plate. Eventually Rob tried to lift the mood. "In all honesty, it probably was an accident, Andy. I'm sure Peter will turn up. You'll see."

I ate my way through a steak and a tarte au citron, putting my hand over my glass every time Rob tried to fill it with wine. I kept up the questions about David and in return he asked me inappropriate questions, to which I gave boring, bland answers because the truth was boring and bland.

"You got domesticated. Is it only outwardly? Secretly are you someone else?" When I looked at my watch for the third time, Rob put his hand on top of mine. "Not too late for us, Andy."

With my other hand, I reached over and bent his finger back. But gently.

"Alice might know," Rob said. "Alice acts like she knows something. But then she always does. I'll have a word. If I ask her, she'll meet you. She's in the Cotswolds. You'll probably have to go down."

* * *

In the vestibule, I waited while my coat was brought.

"Would you like me to call a cab?"

"I think I'll walk."

The cloakroom attendant looked dubious. "It's still raining. Norfolk's flooded, Chepstow too. Even worse on the Continent." He was in his early sixties, with an honest, affable face. Glancing around to see that no one was in earshot, he leaned forward. "Tell you what, we've stacks of umbrellas, hundreds of the things. People leave them behind all the time. Just wander off home without them. Some have been here decades. I'll fetch you one."

He came back with a rather fine navy blue affair with a wooden handle.

"You know, you could sell them off on eBay."

"I couldn't do that," he said, and blushed as though I'd suggested something indecent. It was a gift, I realized. He'd been inspired to give me a gift, and I regretted what I'd said.

After that, I felt obliged to walk a little. Instead of Green Park, I headed for the station at Saint James, which took me across the park where Peter and I had fallen out only a few weeks before. The rain pitter-pattered on the canopy above my head and as I crossed the Mall, passing cars splashed through puddles, sending up waves that spilled over onto the pavement.

The clouds were so low they seemed to touch the trees. Visibility was poor. I saw myself moving down the wet pathways as though through a stranger's eyes, and I was a dark shape, an indistinct human figure hurrying along with an obscure purpose. I wondered what it was, beyond finding Peter, or finding out what had happened all those years ago. Didn't we all have a purpose really, bundled up inside us like a secret?

I hadn't lied to Rob, but I had not told him the whole truth, if there was such a thing. My progress had been less linear than I let on. London keeps no accounts. Two streets away from home, there's a blank slate and you can start again. I imagine it's harder now, but once it was the same with jobs. When I came to London, companies were computerizing their payroll systems. I knew the software from working for Darren. It was simple, but people were scared of it. The temp agencies I signed up to practically threw their arms around me. In those first years, I lost count of the desks I sat at, the rooms I stayed in.

Scraps of the lives I ghosted: a bedsit room in Earl's Court, the orange shower curtain getting stuck in the fridge door, the Chilean with the guitar singing "Eleanor Rigby" late at night in the next-door room; a basement flat in Finsbury Park, barelegged women on the Seven Sisters Road cadging cigarettes on winter mornings; Brixton, Tufnell Park, Mornington Crescent, Clapham North, Bounds Green; a month's rent as deposit and a month in advance, a current CV, a jar of ten-pence pieces for the hall phone, a packet of Marlboro Lights, extra-long Rizla, Coco Pops two meals a day; Friday nights given to the dance floor, the teeth grind, sweat drenched with my top tied round my waist, going back to parties in Tower Hamlets one week and Chelsea the next; walking back on Sunday morning, the city empty, baked beans in a caf, the tea like treacle, phone numbers thrown in the Thames from London Bridge.

"Is Peter there, Mrs. White?"

"Is that Andrea? I'm sorry he's not, dear. He's spending Christmas in New York. How are you? London, isn't it? Rather you than me, dear."

"Do you have a number for him?"

"I don't, but he calls us every Sunday after Evensong."

"I've a new number. Can you pass it on?"

"A new number? Another?" Her voice rising a little. "Are you all right, dear? Richard and I worry about you, you know, you and Peter. The world's just so very big, isn't it? But I suppose you like it. London, all the shows and exhibitions, so much to offer a young person . . . You will wear a warm coat, won't you? Don't be going out without one."

Two cans of Stella and a £1 pizza for tea. London with everything to offer and nothing to spare. Unrelenting in its teachings, the bank letting you go over your overdraft, then charging you 16 quid for it, so when your rent fell you went over again and they charged you again. Caught and fined when you jumped the barrier on the underground because you were a quid short of the fare and you didn't want to be late and lose another job.

Life a national insurance number, a golden reference from Uncle Darren, and the long weekends spent in dark clubs, the black-haired, blank-faced girl dancing on the podium; weekends spent like coins thumbed hard into slots machines, which paid out with blaring jingles and a dazzle of lights, three-day comedowns, strangers' bodies, the grasped-for moments of self-forgetting always just beyond reach. Moving from one circle of people to the next. Two weeks is how long it takes to shrug a friend, unless you owe them money, of course.

I owed everybody money. I didn't wear a warm coat. I was a knife, a blade. I cut. I was cut. I didn't know the difference. A new address, a new agency, a new SIM card. A set of friends abandoned. Another adopted. Rinse and repeat.

Coke and pills, drinks, a smoke, a vally, then a fit of some kind on the bathroom floor of a stranger's house. Like the old lady who swallowed a fly, I wriggled and jiggled. Em was standing in the doorway, in a black dress, holding a black phone. "Not possible, Andy," she said into the receiver. "Not possible."

But it wasn't even that that did it. I missed her. Peter too, but Em most of all. I'd have kept at it if I got to see her again. Truth is, I only ever followed in my mother's footsteps as far as the foothills of the Appetites. Never scaled her heights. It wasn't in me. It wasn't moral strength. I just didn't have the stamina.

So I shaped up. Got serious. I stuck at jobs, invested carefully in the right kind of friendships. But still, always something holding me back from going all in. A sense of loyalty to the past perhaps. I was a good sixth-best friend. The kind of friend, it turned out, who you invited to your child's christening but didn't ask to be your child's godmother, the kind of friend who—when life became a juggling act between work, parenthood, and aging family members—got squeezed out.

I reached the station and took the Circle Line west. Others were on their way out, all done up, made up, turned out for the evening, their faces fresh and full of anticipation. I no longer feared an episode; the odd spell was broken for now. Idly, I thought how funny it was that Rob had asked me about my transformation. Transformation. Such a magic word. It made me think of the stories Peter and I had read as children, in which frogs became princes, ugly ducklings swans, scullery girls elegant ladies; from there my thoughts skipped to makeover shows, then to the articles I was partial to, the ones about women who, via weight loss or surgery or both, remade themselves entirely. Grown-up versions of Cinderella. I had spent most of my life waiting for the magic transformation, the transfiguring, unlocking moment. I suppose everybody did in one way or another—children waiting to become adults, the young to be transformed by love. *Tonight Matthew . . . I'm going to be . . .* How strange that Rob thought it had already happened, when I knew I was still waiting.

CHAPTER 15

TRANSFORMATION/ FORGETTING

IN SELFRIDGES, I GOT TRAPPED IN A DRESS. IT WAS TOO small, and trying to get it off over my head, I found myself stuck, sat there in my bra and pants, my hearing muffled by the layers of material swathing my head as I wriggled this way and that, the dress cutting cruelly into my armpits and the teeth of the zipper biting my side. I couldn't get it off and I couldn't get it back on, and suddenly it seemed a realistic possibility that I would have a panic attack there in the fancy changing rooms, would either have to call for help or stagger out of the cubicle waving my arms like the animated carcass of a headless chicken.

My chest tightened, but I held on and found, instead of panic, a limpness, the animal-who-has-given-up limpness, and I rested my head against the wall and let my toes dig into the soft carpeting, listening to the sounds of the women coming and going, complimenting one another, complaining that sizes were wrong, and whispering about prices.

Friends shopping together. Mothers and daughters. Laughter.

"You've my hips, that's the problem."

"But what will *she* be wearing? God forbid we turn up looking like twins."

The outfit I was trying to buy was for Alice. The summons had arrived; I would see her Friday. Today was Thursday. I had taken both days off, much to Oliver's surprise. It was satisfying to use up some leave. The more I had banked, the more uneasy it made me—all those empty days stacking up, waiting to be filled.

My phone rang, but I couldn't reach it. I sat there listening as it went to voicemail, sweat beading my lip.

When clothes became important, going shopping used to mean nicking. I went with Em to Swindon on the bus. It was best to wait till the shops were about to close and the staff had their eyes on the clock.

"You ready?"

"Yup."

I went in first. Flicking glances at the security guards, drawing the eye with my curled lip, boots, and shifty truculent look.

"Can I help you?" The sales assistant fixed me with a stare and bared her teeth.

"Just browsing."

In the corner of my eye, I saw Em moving swiftly toward the lingerie section, a small, polite smile on her face. I ducked half out of sight behind a pillar clutching a couple of tops. The sales assistant shared a meaningful nod with the security guard.

Em would have to find the right sizes: 34B for her, 34D for me, plus the knickers. I grabbed up a few more items, hanging them over my arm and heading toward the changing rooms.

"No more than six, Madam."

Turning, I glimpsed Em making for the exit. I waited till she was safely through, then dumped my haul on the desk.

"I won't bother then."

Later on, we'd glory over the spoils back in Em's bedroom, swigging from a bottle of whatever we'd managed to get our hands on. Diamond White. Cooking sherry. Mad Dog 20/20. There was a certain amount of necessity to my thieving. Em did it for me, to be close to me.

I missed her again. I missed her all afresh. If she had lived, what would she have become? An artist like she hoped, an art teacher like she expected? I saw her in a plastic apron leading the potato painting. I saw her with kids of her own.

Fuck! The dress tore loudly. I got it off, panting, and threw on the next one, stumbling out into the shared space with the big mirrors. Not a teenage face anymore, not a teenage body.

From what Rob had told me, Alice was rich and married and had two children. I had brought up an aerial view of her house on Maps; it seemed large, not quite large enough to have what you would call grounds, but there was a wide drive, and a substantial lawn bordered on all three sides by fields. It was not on a par with the manor, but even without seeing it up close, I could tell it was worth a couple of mil.

The last time I'd seen Alice I was tempting her to run me over in a car park. What did I want to say to her now? Was this dress going to say it? Or did I need a cashmere knit, designer jeans, and a handbag that cost a couple of grand?

I see your house and husband and family and raise you—with what?

I switched this way and that, wondering how many times in my life I had stood like this, presenting myself to the mirror. Legs. Arse. Stomach. Tits. Those worrying upper arms. There was something archetypal about it. All those women, all across the world—women in Paris and Moscow, Lagos and Sydney—women throughout time—at the court of Louis XIV, in Weimar Berlin, in sixties San Francisco—and all of them, having that moment, the moment of self-appraisal before their reflection. If the clothes parsed the right code, if they accentuated what you had, if they disguised what you lacked: beauty, money, class, confidence, youth.

I wondered how many women had felt as I was now feeling, and then I wondered if Alice had ever felt like this, and then if Alice had loved David and how badly she had been hurt by what we'd done, whether it had stopped her sleeping and made her heartsick; if I had broken something she valued and made her feel small and not said sorry.

* * *

After I made my purchases, I went down to the brightly lit displays and cosmetic stands on the ground floor. Handbags were set on pedestals like statuary. One was encrusted with diamonds and had its own security guard.

The message on my phone was from Mr. Hutchinson. His contact at the phone company was on leave, but he should have something for me the following day. In the meantime, he would look into Peter's credit rating, try and turn up more about his employment record, and make a few calls.

The light filtering in from outside was weak; I lingered in front of a makeup stand, painting my lips and making fish faces in the mirror. The makeup girl sidled over.

"Just looking," I said, before she could get anything out.

"Well, let me know if you need any help." She gave me the once-over and I must have passed, because she swooped down on someone else, getting them up in the chair and bringing out the makeup brushes. On impulse, I put the lipstick in my pocket. In the mirror, a look flitted across my face, alert and predatory. In my head, Peter said, *In a society that worships individuality and elevates consumer commodities to the highest form of personal expression, appropriating the means to make such an expression possible can only be a virtue, dear Andy.*

And Em, *Have it! Forty fucking quid? Serves them right.*

A ripple ran through me, a quickening, and I tore my eyes from the mirror and strode off. Just before I got to the automatic doors, I slowed down and flipped over the price tag on a black leather wallet, a display of unhurried innocence. Once outside, I took off feeling both foolish and alive. The rain ran down my neck. My heels clicked merrily along the pavement as I dodged the tourists and shoppers, nipping across the road in front of a big red bus so that the driver blared his horn.

It made me aware of how dormant I was most of the time. How my life—my job, my screens—made it easy to be occupied every waking moment, hurrying, distracted, and equally, on some level almost entirely asleep, comforted by dreams of effortless transformation.

But I was not Cinderella. Instead, there was another story Peter and I had often found in the books of our childhood. It came in different disguises. It was the one about the traveler who arrives at an island, or a castle, or a secret door into the side of a mountain. There, welcomed, the traveler stays, perhaps against their instincts. Often they eat or drink—strange fruit, or wine from a goblet. There is always something they should be doing, an important task for them to fulfill, but they forget it, they are waylaid, and if they ever remember, their companions, if there are any, distract them with promises, or songs, or riddles to ponder.

Often the traveler sleeps, sometimes they dream, always they are nagged by the sense that there is something they are forgetting, something they must do. Their true love is waiting, or their aged parents. There is a sick child they must bring herbs to, a kingdom for them to inherit. But they do nothing; they are paralyzed. And when they wake, if they ever get away, once back in the world they find that centuries have passed, that they are too late, too late for everything, and that all that they loved, everything that truly mattered, is lost forever.

To sleep on? Or to wake? This was the question facing me. To sleep, or to wake and face the reckoning, to find out what had been lost.

CHAPTER 16

NO WONDER ALICE

THE HOUSE WAS COTSWOLD STONE WITH CLIMBING ROSES IN beds at the front that were not yet in bud. I'd made a deal with the cabby. He would wait down the road, out of sight, but within reach if I had to flee. Alice must have heard us. As I got out, she was already standing in the open doorway. A smile on her face, barefoot, in jeans and a pale knit. Unlike her brother, Alice had kept off the booze and out of the sun. She had not put on weight or cut off her hair.

"Andy." Her tone was familiar, fond even. Nearing, I noted the delicate fan of lines at the outer corner of each eye, but she stepped back as I came in so there was no cheek to kiss or hand to shake. "I've got the kettle on." Already she was walking away from me and with barely a hesitation I crossed the threshold and followed her inside.

The air was fragrant with baking; the whole rear of the house was taken up by a huge open-plan kitchen and living room and some little cakes were cooling on a wire rack. Through the glass wall that ran the length of the room, you could see the garden and beyond it a patchwork of fields and, in the nearest, a handful of sodden-looking sheep. We were a little over an hour's drive from the manor, but the countryside here was flatter and on a smaller scale. There was a stream further away; you couldn't quite see it, only the long and lovely willows bordering its banks.

I had what Alice was having, so we both had green tea and a little cake that fell into ruins the moment I touched it. Alice offered me a conspiratorial smile.

"I'm not much of a baker. Usually I buy. The boys are just as happy. It doesn't even touch the sides. I swear you could throw a load of fat and sugar in a trough and it'd be all the same to them. These are gluten free, no dairy either."

"How old?"

"Nine and six."

There was a bit more of that. Alice's husband commuted to London for work. Her eldest boy boarded but came home at weekends. The younger one was at the school in the village and Alice would pick him up later. "He likes to walk back. He's convinced there's a troll living under the bridge. He tries to feed it cheese. So what can I help you with? Rob was very mysterious. Childish man, my brother. I don't blame his ex-wife for divorcing him. Childishness is fine until you have kids of your own."

I told her; she dabbed at the crumbs on her plate with a fingertip, nodding as though I had confirmed her suspicions.

"I thought this would be about David."

"It's Peter I'm looking for, only he did say he'd seen him, David that is."

"Peter who played piano."

"He did." And I remembered again the stuttering melody—all sharps, all discord—that Peter had been playing on the morning we found Em. Alice cocked her head on one side and looked at me as though she knew where my thoughts had led.

"So what you'd like is for me to tell you where David is because you hope that will lead you to your friend." A pause. "Did you see much of him? Peter, I mean, before he disappeared."

"Now and again."

"But how often?"

"Couple of times a year, or so."

"And yet you're both in London."

I said something about it being normal not to see old friends all the time. About my work and his work being so busy. Late nights. Weekends. "We were friends as children. He was my oldest friend." And I told her a few things about us, old stories, the slowworm through the letterbox, the games, the looking out for one another. Alice listened carefully.

"I thought he didn't like you very much. Perhaps he doesn't like his parents either. Or perhaps you've made this all up."

"No."

"No? None of you seemed prone to telling the truth. All that sneaking around. Em and Marcus. You and David. Peter, your dearest, bestest old friend looking like he hated you when he wasn't whispering to David in corners."

First Rob, now Alice saying Peter didn't like me. I bit my lip. If I lost my temper, she'd have won. Besides, wasn't it true that once you knew someone through and through, and they knew you through and through, love was always mixed with antipathy? Antipathy because you knew the worst of them, all their flaws, even the things they hid from themselves. Even more antipathy because the reverse was true. Didn't they understand that?

Something else occurred to me.

"What do you mean Em and Marcus? You hate me for what happened. David and I—"

Alice shrugged. "People move on, Andy. I am sure you, yourself, have moved on. I wasn't happy at the time. When someone cheats on you, it's a blow, isn't it? That suggestion that you're not enough, lacking in some way. You must know yourself. Your friend Em was in love with Marcus. Always talking to each other with their eyes."

"We were all close. After my mum died, I went to pieces. They looked after—"

"I saw them kissing. That first night. You'd gone to bed and they were beneath my window. In the moonlight. Her shivering in that ridiculous dress. They were arguing, but then they kissed and made up. I swear it."

There were lambs in the field too. One of them was jumping for no reason, jumping and twirling its little tail. Em and Marcus.

Of course. Not possible. Of course. Pushed together. Marcus leaning on Em, confiding in her, despairing even. Em trying to comfort him—

"You really didn't know?" Alice leaned back, not displeased by whatever my face revealed. "Well, I wouldn't take it personally. People want variety, or the risk of getting caught, or just a bit of validation. So I don't hate you, no more than I love David. There'd be something wrong with me if I did, after all these years."

"Now you're going to say I did you a favor."

"Why not? It would be true. David and I weren't together very long. It suited for a bit. Rob was always talking about him and he was charming. Nice-looking and charming, and just that little bit lost, and he listened—none of the men I knew ever actually listened to you—and he knew how to be entertaining. No, he wasn't a bad man, but what else do you call someone who causes destruction wherever they go? That poor teacher at school. I doubt he ever taught again. And when you think about it, really think about it, what was he? Good with waiters. Charming to strangers. But it's like a card trick. If you're there watching all the time, in the end you're going to see how it's done. A man of no substance, my father would have said. Or did say in fact.

"I found all that charm a bore, and maybe that's why he liked me, for a time. I was never enthralled. All that childishness you went in for, diamonds and hidden treasures and going on about how magical the manor was when it was a great, rotting, freezing money pit. Playing games then, and playing games now. I invited you down because Rob made me curious. How you'd changed. But I don't see it. And it was all a cheat anyway."

"What was a cheat?"

"'That game. It was fixed.'

Alice reached out and took two more of the virtuous cakes from the rack. Without asking, she dropped one on my plate and ripped the paper casing from her own.

"I watched Em hide them. That morning, I snuck out of bed and watched her from the window, trailing about the grounds, leaving her footprints all over the place for us to follow. I wanted to win. I'm embarrassed to admit it now, rummaging around in all that snow like an idiot. Anyway, I was sure she'd hidden them somewhere out the front of the house; I couldn't quite see where, not from where I was, but there was a difference in her step afterward; she wasn't looking anymore for a spot to hide it, just leaving clues for us to follow. But you got to find them, you and David and not me, and it was funny, funny because I would swear she didn't even stop at the temple, just swished straight through, kicked the snow about, and went on."

The house was very quiet, not a ticking clock or a radio or a little dog for company.

"It bothered me, it did. When we were interviewed, I even wondered if I should tell the police about it. That there had been cheating in this silly game. Because someone must have moved them. And how was it you both suddenly knew they were in the statue? Ridiculous!" For all her accusations of childishness, Alice's cheeks burned red.

"Maybe it wasn't cheating. Maybe we found the real ones." At that, Alice laughed in my face. It was all I could do to keep my voice steady. "Do you know where David is, Alice?"

"I wondered why he liked you. That first night Em was apologizing for how rude you were, poor Andy this, poor Andy that. But I could see you just didn't care if you were liked. Maybe that was it. David was always so careful to not ruffle anyone's feathers. Had to have people on his side."

"I was used to it. My mother never liked me."

"Were you nice to her?"

"No."

Alice sighed, "At least you've tried to grow up, Andy. Or Andrea, I should say. Much better."

I did not believe Alice knew anything that would help me find Peter; and even if she did, she would not tell me. With her, it did all seem ridiculous, and yes, childish. And yet what I said next surprised me.

"Perhaps childish is right. Perhaps you mean we believed in magic too long. I don't know, Alice. My mother drank. She was odd and often angry. It was like living on the slopes of an active volcano. People who do are prone to religion, to wishing, to magical thinking. Sometimes I was not her daughter but the enemy. Later she brought home a man, a bad man, Alice. If I hadn't believed in magic, I'd have died. Sometimes believing in magic is all children have."

It'd been a long time since I had spoken on the subject of my mother or Joe to anyone. With friends, it never seemed the right time. With lovers it was even trickier. At the beginning of a relationship, when things were going well, there was the fear it would color how the person looked at you. At the end, it felt manipulative, a plea for exculpation, at worst an attempt to handcuff someone to you through pity.

Alice got up and took our plates to the dishwasher. I watched her steadily. When she turned, she acknowledged what I'd said with the smallest of nods. Her face betrayed neither sympathy nor disbelief, for which I felt a small, seeping gratitude.

Our eyes met and I realized Alice was wavering, was on the verge of telling me something.

"I lied to the police for David. I said he was with me from two a.m. After he was with you. But he wasn't. I didn't see him till breakfast. He had that criminal record, didn't he? Not only the theft, but the assault would have been there, buried among the paperwork."

"The assault?"

"The teacher. They called him Badger. David blacked his eyes. He had to go to the hospital. Or that's what he said at first. Then he withdrew it and said David had stolen his jacket when he was out having supper. Then later he changed his story again. Unreliable. Rob and his friends were always doing impressions of him, a funny, pathetic little man. David once said, and he wasn't joking, that he loved him. Badger, that is, loving David. And he ruined him, didn't he? I've always thought what happened to your friend was an accident. I mean, David wasn't dangerous. Not physically, not in that way. I don't think so . . ." Alice's brow furrowed. "But then I don't know what he was like really. Did any of us? Still, I lied for him and I'm afraid I kept it hanging over him. After the way he'd treated me. But I got tired of it in the end, dragging him about. April was the end of it. I dumped him. He got the boot from his job for conspiring with one of the dealers to rig an auction. He didn't want what he was supposed to want, what he said he wanted—to do well, move in the right circles, get on. Or he wanted something else more. What can you do with someone like that? If I were you, I'd forget all this. Peter will turn up again, or he won't, but it won't be your fault." She looked at the clock. "Time to fetch Tim from school. Sorry I couldn't help more."

At the door, Alice turned to me. Her face was unreadable. "I have that bag too," she said, and she reached out and gently touched the strap.

* * *

It was a while since I had been in the countryside. The wind blew the rain right into my face. I heard a car driving up behind me and slowing down. A small hole opened in my chest, but the moment of horror was quickly resolved when I turned to see the grinning cabby raise an acknowledging hand.

His wife was on the phone and he had her on speaker while we navigated the narrow lanes.

"I've got a customer with me, Davina. Say hello!"

An Indian takeaway was agreed upon. There was a debate over a chicken balti or a rogan josh.

"Two naans."

"One naan, Alan. We'll share it."

"But I never quite get half, do I, my darling?"

"That's the price of love, babe."

I wondered if Alan had ever had an affair with Davina's best friend.

We ground to a halt. Ahead of us, the lane was flooded. We sat in the car looking at the water. Alan wanted my opinion if we should drive through it.

"Depends how deep it is," I said.

"If I knew that, I wouldn't be asking."

"Is there a way round?"

"Yes, but it takes ages. Not that I'd charge you, mind."

I pulled off my shoes and got out. The road was cold and wet. The puddle was twelve feet across, but at its deepest it was only up to my calves. I gave the cabby the thumbs-up and went and got back in.

From the glove box, he pulled out a tea towel and handed it to me in the back seat.

"There was me thinking you were a town mouse."

And I wanted to do nothing more than to go home with them, with this nice man to his cheerful wife, to watch telly and eat a curry.

* * *

On the train, Hutchinson called. Floods were causing havoc everywhere. We had been late leaving and another service had been canceled, so the carriages were packed. Darkness was falling and the windows were occluded with steam. It was hard to tell how fast we were going. It could have been walking pace or a hundred miles an hour.

I struggled down the aisle and into an unoccupied space just in front of a toilet.

"What did you find out?"

"Well, his phone hasn't been turned on for two weeks. But if he hasn't been seen in nearly four that's good news, isn't it?"

"I suppose so."

"But it was switched off before that too. Like he was switching it off for a few days and then turning it on for a few minutes at a time. He did that three times, before it went off completely."

"Can you tell where he was?"

"London. Then the last time he made a call, just before it was switched off, he was out west, not far from Heathrow."

"So maybe he's abroad."

"Could be."

"Those last five calls, they were all to the same number. Shall I phone it? I can pretend to be a telemarketer if need be, just find out who they are for starters. If it's his job, they might even be able to tell us where he is."

I agreed, while trying to maneuver myself out of the way of a lady with a pram.

"Hang on a minute. There's someone trying to get past."

"You not at work then?"

"No, I—" The woman smiled apologetically at me. One of the handles was caught on my coat. "I've . . . I've been following my own leads. Speaking to old friends."

"So we're an investigative team, are we?" His voice was jovial. Hutchinson told me what else he'd achieved. Via Facebook he'd gotten hold of Karsten von Kloss and Anders. He was proud of himself, gabbling about the average person's total lack of interest in his own privacy. "Fortunately for us! I messaged both of them, asking if I could give them a ring. Made myself out to be a concerned friend. That was right, wasn't it?"

Before he rang off, he asked if he could bill me for two days' work and assured me we'd speak again in the next day or so. He sounded pleased, excited even, and I felt an answering optimism all the way home.

I had lots to think about: whether my boyfriend had been cheating on me with my best friend. Whether Peter had, in fact, not been my friend at all. Forced to look at them, my own feelings were not unmixed. Peter had been my one constant, since I was very small, and yet that summer he was leaving me, eagerly, off to a life I wouldn't have a part in. Peter had had the loving parents and the bright future, and in the beginning hadn't that been part of David's appeal? That Peter had wanted him?

Then there was the possibility—and perhaps this was the least strange thing I'd learned from Alice—that we had actually found Mortimer's diamonds. But if so, why hadn't Em said anything? It was unbelievable. And yet. I leaned against the window and closed my eyes. The truth will set you free.

What was it Hutchinson had said? *A feeling, a certain feeling . . .*

But Hutchinson didn't get back to me, and when I called him there was no answer, and when I went to his office above the chicken shop, no one came to the bell, and the young men behind the deep-fat fryers said they hadn't seen him, the man from upstairs, not for days.

* * *

Without Hutchinson, I was at a loss. I checked my credit card, but he hadn't even billed it. Like Peter, he was gone, and I was torn between fear that something awful had happened to him and the conviction that he was an opportunist, a fraud, a failure who had never been any kind of real detective at all.

In the end, I phoned Patricia and told her it was time to report Peter missing to the police. It was what you were supposed to do, after all. After delivering the news, I hung up and watched two films in a row that left no discernible trace in my mind whatsoever. There were explosions. That's literally all I can tell you. But films with explosions weren't enough. On YouTube, I hunted for footage of molten lava, volcanic eruptions, showers of magma. From a drone, I looked down on Plosky Tolbachik in Russia, Marum Crater on the island of Vanuatu, on Nyiragongo Volcano, Congo. I saw uninhabitable landscapes of roiling fire, flowing lava rivers that destroyed everything in their path, and I couldn't look away.

Back at work, as ever, there was much to be done, the never-diminishing list of tasks. But I couldn't feel it anymore, the hounding urgency. It was like my job had gone the way of other games, crazes we had indulged in at school, like marbles or cat's cradle, until the day we suddenly didn't. I sat at my desk and did nothing. Sometimes I signed off without reading what I was signing off on. At night, I watched the volcanoes, waiting to see what would come next. Something was coming free, underneath the surface, somewhere under my skin, away, out of sight, because how else can you explain it? The quickness with which I responded to Alice's email, the fact that within nine hours of receiving it, I was on a plane.

The email came at about eleven in the morning. It'd been two weeks since I'd seen her. I paused before opening it, wondering if Alice was perverse enough to send me a thank-you note. The message took less than twenty seconds to read. There was an attachment. Around me, my colleagues tapped at their keyboards with lowered eyes. The air-conditioning droned. My skin prickled all over, like I was being stung by a swarm of microscopic bees. I clicked, and the file opened to show a color scan of a cutting from a newspaper. The writing wasn't in English—a Romance language. Spanish? No, Italian—but there was a picture, a photograph underneath the headline. It took a few seconds before I saw what Alice was getting at.

Standing to the right, only just in the frame, was David. His arms were folded, his head inclined to hear what the dark-haired man standing next to him was saying. At the photograph's focal point was a painting, a grand Renaissance job showing something biblical in an ornate gold frame. There were a number of other people in the shot and if I hadn't been looking, I wouldn't have noticed David among them, although I might have taken note of the man he was in conversation with. Extreme wealth announces itself. Or maybe it was the incline of David's head, the suggestion of deference before power.

David was not bald yet, despite Mrs. East's prophesying. His hair was shorter and perhaps a little darker, and he was more solid. Unlike the dark-haired man, he was not wearing a blazer, only a light blue shirt. I looked at the photo for quite some time, carefully, as though memorizing it, as though it would vanish the second I looked away, and then at some point I went back and reread Alice's email.

A friend had sent her the clipping. It was from a Florentine newspaper, from the previous summer, and, recognizing David, she had passed it on to Alice, who was now sharing it with me. The article, as far as she could translate it, was about an art fair, and the purchase of a recently rediscovered painting by a Russian oligarch via a local art and antiques dealership, Galleria Vittorio Buono. On balance, Alice thought I probably shouldn't try and find David, because of sleeping dogs and all that, but of course it was up to me. She signed off by saying that it had been interesting to see me and that she wished me well.

There was no subtext, no clue other than the unexpected gesture itself. It occurred to me that I had never known Alice, that I had constructed her, made her into what I wanted her to be. By the gesture, she had become someone else and escaped me entirely.

CHAPTER 17

APOCALYPSE IV

HUTCHINSON PHONED JUST AS WE WERE BEING CALLED TO board the flight to Florence.

"Where've you been?"

"I'm sorry. I'm sorry. It was my mother. She's very old and I had to go to Bournemouth." He said something about a care home, a broken hip, a missing power of attorney. His voice was breathless, as though he'd just run up a flight of stairs.

"Two weeks and you couldn't leave a message?"

"I'm sorry." A voice came over the PA system asking for priority boarders. "Where are you?"

"At Luton. I'm going to see someone. Listen, did you ever call that number? The one you said Peter phoned a bunch of times before he stopped using his mobile?" There was a moment's silence in which I thought we'd been cut off. "Hello? Mr. Hutchinson? Are you still there?"

"Sorry. No. I mean, yes, I called it, but nothing doing. A dead end. Who are you going to see? Is it about Peter?"

I was nearing the front of the queue. "I have to go."

"Where are you going? Please—"

But the lady in the uniform wanted to see my boarding card and passport, so I said I'd call him when I was back and cut him off.

It was the last flight of the day. The earth dropped away and with it came a feeling of unrealness, of unreality. We flew into evening and evening embraced us, the light fading gently, the clouds flowing over the wings like a movie signal for a dream sequence. I turned the little reading light on while around me my fellow passengers napped or read or fingered coins in anticipation of the snack trolley.

I liked people this way, and experienced a shadowy feeling of fellowship with them; like this, I was surprised by how much I suddenly loved them and wished them well, and yet if my neighbor had turned to me and attempted conversation, I would have shrunk from it. I loved my neighbor, but I feared him too.

My thoughts drifted, my gaze resting on the soft, white backs of the clouds. Something had been playing on my mind ever since my visit to the Cotswolds.

The game that weekend had not been fixed. If Alice was right and Em had not hidden the necklace in the temple but somewhere else, then where had the ones David found come from? I took out my notebook and under the reading light's beam, I wrote *DIAMONDS REAL?* Then I stuffed my notebook in the seat pocket in disgust at my childishness, before once again hauling it out.

If the diamonds had been real, it would have given someone a reason, a reason to hurt Em. Who would've known? Em, because she hid the fake ones? David, because he'd held them in his hands and discerned a difference?

How far was David prepared to go to get what he wanted? Not just with the diamonds, but with everything? It was a question I was determined to have answered.

I had chosen to believe Em's death was an accident. If, at certain unguarded moments, other possibilities had occurred to me, it was not David I fought to keep myself from imagining in the scenario in which someone walked with Em, or followed Em, or was followed by Em, out of the manor and down the snowy drive on the night she died.

* * *

Florence was under water. Algorithms had given continental weather events a low priority in my newsfeed, making me wonder what else I was missing. On the plane, the in-flight magazine had featured an article about the poet Dante and his *Divine Comedy*. In hell, there were circles where souls were tethered in realms according to their earthly failings: one for the lustful, one for the gluttonous, and so on. This made me think of the Internet and how, the more you clicked on something—porn, or shoes, conspiracy theories, or the gruesome reports of violent crimes—the more you saw of it, until it became nearly all you saw, and that real life might be in some way similar, that there were circles you could find yourself in and from which it might take a great effort to break free.

Rainwater ran in streams, pooling around the drains. In the streets, it roared beneath the pavements. The departure board showed a series of delayed flights and ranks of stranded travelers were standing gazing up at it, mouths open in horror like bystanders in a painting of the Crucifixion. I booked a hotel via an app, something mid-priced and central with good reviews, but some streets were closed and the taxi driver was forced to drive round in circles until he found a way through.

When I struggled in, the staff seemed surprised to see me. The lobby was empty and the young man on duty slid fearful glances over my shoulder, as though at any moment a monster would loom out of the darkness and menace us through the rain-smeared glass. In the room, the Wi-Fi wasn't working and I quickly gave up trying to figure out the telly. I slipped into bed.

At some point during the night, air-raid sirens started howling, and the alarm entered my dreams. It was too late. I was too late. I had slept too long. I dreamed that on waking I would discover that something terrible had happened while I slept for which I was culpable, so that even asleep, I pretended to sleep, and awoke later than I intended, already drained. I reached the breakfast room as they were putting the cereal and cold cuts away. The chef hadn't come in and the bakery hadn't delivered.

Parts of the city were being evacuated on account of the flooding. But the hotel was on a rise. Would it remain open? A young woman was now behind the desk; she grimaced and opened her hands. "My father hasn't seen this since 1966. Then the river came over the top. It was a catastrophe for Florence. If the Arno breaks its banks . . ."

Reluctantly she drew my route for me on a map, while I eavesdropped on a group of game old English ladies. Their leader was instructing a tour guide to find them a boat. "Ruth rowed for Cambridge! And we do so want to see the Spanish Chapel."

I went out. It was crepuscular, the rain slant and chill. The few people I saw seemed to have pressing errands. I saw a family, mum, dad, and two kids, climbing into a car packed to the gunnels with their possessions. They had a bichon frise too, and in her arms, the little girl carried a cage with sawdust in it, a hamster wheel, and a little plastic house in which, I presumed, a small creature was huddling. Then there were no more people.

Traffic lights reflected on the surface of black puddles that lapped at drains, rippling the colors. Rain seeped under my cuffs and ran down my neck, and my feet grew so wet I stopped going around the puddles and started plowing straight through them. The map disintegrated further each time I looked at it, the puddles deepened until turning a corner, I found that the whole street was flooded, and I was wading through water that got deeper as I went on.

It didn't occur to me to turn back.

A greenish river flowed past, leaves and paper coffee cups and plastic bags riding the current, the surface in patches marbled with oil. The sky was wadded with low-hanging clouds, and in front of the houses, at the top of the steps that led up from the street, sandbags had been placed in front of the doors. From somewhere above the city, the sirens were wailing again.

An upturned chair raced past, its legs pointing to heaven. I plowed on, the water eddying about my legs.

Galleria Vittorio Buono, the gallery named in Alice's article, was where it was supposed to be, but still further from the center than I had imagined, sandwiched between a shop with women's clothes in the window and a stationer's. There was no sign of anyone as I climbed the steps to ring the bell. No sound came, so I hammered on the door fit to wake the dead. While I waited for a response, I turned to watch the water racing past. Somewhere a church bell had started tolling. My mind was curiously quiet. It occurred to me that if the waters rose any further, it might be risky to try to go back, but I wasn't particularly concerned about this, or about anything else, so that when I heard footsteps approaching and then the door open behind me, I felt neither fear nor excitement, only a certain inevitability. Still, it was a moment before I was able to turn and face whoever it was who had opened the door.

* * *

I watched David recognize me, and then I pushed past him through the doorway, our shoulders brushing.

"What are you doing here?"

We were in a white-walled room. There were empty spaces on the walls where paintings had hung. They lay resting in their frames against the wall. More were stacked against a desk.

"Perhaps I need something to go over the mantelpiece."

"The city's being evacuated."

I took off my plastic cape and draped it over a chair. "You're still here."

"There's the stock. I was moving it upstairs."

"Do you think the water will really come that high? I mean up the steps and inside?"

We turned as one to the window and to the newly born river running down the street. The sky was dark; it only promised more rain.

I snuck a glance at David. He was wearing glasses and seemed generally more solid, not only heavier but thicker about the neck and forearms, his features more definite but with a loss of tightness about the jaw. He reached for the light and then swiftly let fall his hand.

"I keep forgetting the power's out. Oh shit. Oh shit." Beneath the door a thin stream was seeping serpentine across the floor. "I've got to get the paintings upstairs. Will you help?"

And as though I were a friend who had popped in for a coffee, I found myself roped in. It took almost an hour. The stairs were narrow and twisty and led up to three rooms: a tiny bathroom, a storeroom, and a third space, long and narrow, in which there were bookshelves, a table, and a camp bed on which a twisted sheet and a woolen blanket were encoiled.

The stairs were too narrow for two, and several times I found myself halting at their foot, the corners of a frame digging into my arms, waiting for David to come down or to indicate that I should come up, and in the moment's hesitation before one of us hurried forward every question hung.

The water was coming. In the little bathroom, along with the sliver of soap and a disposable razor, was a tired-out little towel. The photograph Alice had sent me—the huge painting, the rich, powerful man—suggested a greater enterprise than this. I picked up the towel and laid it in front of the door, but it did nothing. In the galley kitchen behind the wooden desk there was a tea towel and half a kitchen roll. I put them down and found myself laughing breathlessly. Beyond the window, the glaucous waters were frothing and gobbling. A stream was flowing in under the door and making for the Turkish rug. Then the last of the paintings was upstairs, David came down, and we rolled the rug up together and put it on the desk, and there was nothing more to be done.

"They said it would end. They said there would be some slight flooding, a little flooding . . ."

"But it won't come up the stairs. You're just going to have some water damage down here." To my own ears, I did not sound convinced. "You don't have any sandbags, do you?"

"No. No, I don't have sandbags." The rain had got up, was slapping at the window. David stood there frozen, as though seized by indecision. When he turned again it was to look at me properly.

"Will you risk going back?"

"Don't you want to know why I'm here?"

"I'm sure you're going to tell me. The desk isn't going to fit up the stairs, is it?"

"No."

"I'm staying," he said. "Do what you want. You always did."

And with that he turned and sloshed away through the floodwater, and for a second I suddenly thought he would elude me, throw open the door and be carried off on the current, but then I heard his footsteps on the stairs, achingly slow, and then the sound of him settling in a chair. After a moment, I followed him up.

Since he had taken the chair, the only space remaining was the camp bed, so I perched on it, feet flat on the floor, our knees a foot apart. David was wearing trainers, and he took them off and stripped and wrung out his socks and laid them on the edge of the table.

"I don't have any candles or anything."

I had the light on my phone, but the battery was low and it occurred to me that it was actually possible that we would need to call for help. I could hear the water everywhere and once or twice the building seemed to move ever so slightly. Beyond the window, I thought I saw a tree, a whole tree, uprooted and afloat, sail past with a Smart car in its branches.

"So."

But I did not know how to begin.

"Will the paintings be safe now?"

"Well, if they aren't, then neither are we." But he seemed anxious and his eyes slid to the one he'd kept with him, an indistinct pencil drawing in a small, wooden frame. David took it up and held it in his knees as though the floods were already lapping at it.

"Why have you come, Andy?"

"The apocalypse was always my thing, remember?"

"It was, wasn't it? Really, what are you doing here? If you don't tell me I'm going to have a panic attack. Things are not going well. You've come at the worst—"

"You can't hazard a guess?"

I felt him peering at me.

"Divorce? Your therapist sent you. I don't know. I don't know."

And this time, when I answered him my voice didn't come out as I intended it to at all. Not strong or accusing, but small, almost pleading.

"I'm looking for Peter."

* * *

I told David about the wedding, and Patricia's phone calls, how I had visited Rob and Alice, about the clipping from the newspaper.

"Ah yes, Mr. Domnikov. He never actually paid for that painting, you know. I really thought I had him on the hook. Michele's convinced I've lost my touch."

"At the wedding Peter said he'd seen you. Did you see him?"

"Yes."

"Where?

"In Rome. At the art fair. I saw him from the corner of my eye. I thought, that man looks a bit like Peter. Then he was gone. It was busy. It's one of the times you can make real money. Russians, Arabs, the super rich. For them, a few hundred grand on a painting is nothing. Lots of business gets done at these things. Not just art." David ran a hand through his hair.

"Did you talk to him?"

"Briefly. Later on." He stood up for a moment and looked out the window. "Andy, I don't have him here. He's not hiding in the attic or under the bed. You should probably go, you know, if you can." He stopped. "I don't know where he is."

"What happened?"

"He came to my hotel. We had a drink, a few drinks. Reminisced over old times."

"I'd like to hear about those old times."

"Would you, Andy? Would you indeed?"

"Do you know where he's gone? Why he's gone? Did he seem troubled?"

"We all have our troubles, Andy. Perhaps I was too busy thinking of my own to notice. Besides, he was always troubled. It was only because everyone was looking at you that it wasn't so noticeable, when you look back."

"Do you look back often?"

"I'm allergic to the past. To the past and to kiwi fruit, oddly enough. What about you?"

"Of late."

"Any thoughts you'd like to share?"

So I told him everything I'd discovered since Peter's disappearance. I expected him to laugh at me. But when I finished, when I had recounted what Alice had said, and my theory that there were two sets of diamonds, that we could have found the real ones, Mortimer's diamonds, David said nothing for a while. I watched him very carefully, but he showed no signs of guilt or discovery. When he finally spoke, he sounded older and sadder.

"Imagine that," he said. "Imagine that, holding the real thing in your hands, Andy, and not knowing it for what it was."

* * *

I went downstairs. The water was to my knees. In the streets it would be to my waist. In the falling dark, all the colors were bleaching. I heard David come down, and suddenly I knew I was playing an old game, threatening to do something dangerous in the hope that someone would stop me.

"Stay. I'm happy to see you. I am. It's just the timing." He laughed suddenly, without mirth. "It's always the same."

So I went back up and we resumed our positions.

"Why are you holding that picture like that?"

David looked down at the drawing. "When you were hammering on the door, you know, I thought it was the police. Michele's having a few problems. I work for him. There's no Vittorio. It's just a name with the right sound. Anyway, he's finally sold the wrong picture to the wrong person. It's all over for him in this business, for me too by extension. In this country. Anywhere, above a certain level."

"Fakes?"

"It's not binary, Andy. When something is five hundred or so years old . . . back then, each painter had whole studios of apprentices and everyone copying one another. Authenticity is on a scale." He screwed up his face, like the false notes in his voice were hurting his ears.

"And this picture?"

"Mine. I sold all the others I had to get it. It's just a little sketch. I've always thought it's by Montocci. There's a painting he did in the chapel of San Clemente. It's of the war in heaven. I'm sure this is a study for one of the figures. It's always been my favorite. I was certain I could get it authenticated. But not now. I doubt it's worth a bean now. You can go see it, the original, it's not far from here. Well, you probably can't right now."

The house was making strange noises, creaking noises, like it was being squeezed in a fist.

"I hope you have it insured."

David put his head in his hands and groaned. "Can we talk about something else?"

At that moment, I very much wanted to ask David if he'd ever loved me. Because it was suddenly clear to me that I had once loved David. The way he moved, everything that belonged to him. It had been many years since I had seen him, and I was not the same person. Still, his voice moved me, stirred in me the restless girl I'd once been. I was unable to stop myself remembering certain things.

"Was it you who called the telephone box? After you disappeared that summer, I used to wait outside. Someone called it, kept calling it, but they never said anything."

"No. It wasn't me. It seemed for the best, Andy. I thought I could walk away from it and always have it, that summer at the manor, like a jewel in my pocket. And it solved certain problems in the end." David had taken his glasses off. "What was I going to do about you? What were we going to do? Move in with one another, play happy families. Get a Barratt home. We were teenagers. It wouldn't have lasted and then it would have been ruined. If we'd been a bit older, a bit wiser . . . I was out of my depth and I didn't like it. Being on remand was awful, Andy. Being locked up. I still dream about it. The sounds, the smells, the taste of the food. When I got out, I was determined to play by the rules. To keep my head down, to secure some kind of future for myself, money, position, all that. I equated it with freedom, what Rob and Alice and their friends had, but in the end it wasn't."

"Was it Peter who called the police?"

"He denied it, but it had to be one of you. The police knew exactly who I was. They even knew where Badger's credit cards were. That weekend we were all at the manor again, the weekend Em died, I asked him. I was pretty harsh with him but he said no. I thought he was lying. I thought about it a lot at the time, after I was arrested. Wondering if it'd been him, or Marcus, Em even. Or you. I was never sure it was about me, you know, what happened between us. That it wasn't somehow all about you and Peter. But in the end he was the most likely candidate."

"Because he was jealous. Because of what we were doing."

"Maybe. Peter thought he was in love with me. You have to remember I went to public school, to a boys-only school. I was used to it. Crushes. Finding a chocolate bar under your pillow, all that. Peter was a virgin, wasn't he? He just wanted to be liked, to be allowed to be himself."

"You didn't sleep with him?"

"No. You knew that."

"I wondered if you'd lied."

David nodded. "A few meaningful looks, a kiss . . . I've not ever been what you'd call a strict heterosexual. I allowed myself to think it was harmless. That I wasn't misleading him, that I was just being friendly. Offering an ear. We all need someone to tell our secrets to. But he told me something . . . And I think he regretted it and that's why he got rid of me. That's why he called the police. In case I told you. I wanted very much to tell you in the end. When I saw him in Rome, I asked him. A few drinks in, I asked him if he'd been making it up—this incredible story—and he said he had. We all lie, don't we? Especially at that age. But I still wonder."

I could feel my younger self very close by, crowding in.

"What was the story?"

But I already knew. I had known then. Peter had told David that I'd been abused by Joe, hoping to ruin things between us. But I was only half right.

"Peter always said you must never know. But if it's lies, there's no reason not to tell you." Still, David seemed to hesitate. "Peter said he had killed someone, that he had . . . been involved in a murder. I know. Peter, right? Ridiculous. It was after we'd taken those pills. You'd gone. You wanted to see your mum, so I asked Peter about your mum, and that's how it started. We were sitting out on the ridge, high as kites. Some of it didn't make sense. He was sort of rambling. It was still light. I could see his face. I can remember how it looked now. He swore that he had killed a man called Joe one night out on the Downs because he was hurting you. That he'd had help. He wouldn't tell me who—I think that was what made it so convincing, that he was too frightened to say who. Only that he had just wanted to scare Joe away and something had gone wrong and Joe had died."

* * *

The end of the world was Italian this time. David found a packet of cigarettes and half a bottle of grappa that burned on the way down and then sat in the stomach burning. There had been a murder, but not Em. Joe. I didn't doubt David was telling the truth. But what about Peter? We filled the little room with smoke. I wrapped myself in the blanket. I had been losing possession of myself for some time, possibly from the moment I had answered Patricia's phone call on the train, but it had not been a steady journey. Now I had the sense of hurtling descent. Beneath the shiny life I'd built were ruins, and now I was among them. The blanket was brown and scratchy and I drew it around my back and tightly over my crossed legs.

"What was I like?"

"Wild. A menace."

"Self-destructive you mean."

"Perhaps, but wild too. There is a difference."

"And what is the difference?"

"I don't know. I suppose animals have that wildness, young animals, children. I don't know. Lovely when you were sad, lovely when you were happy. And moving, and still. Always suffering. It spoke to me that, but isn't it a sickness, to love a thing for suffering?" He looked down at the drawing again. "Peter said your mother broke your heart."

"She sided with him."

"With Joe?"

"Yes, and then she died and I was still so angry with her. And now in my dreams, she is a child, a child crying at night, from inside the wall, calling my name, and I don't go to her."

It seemed possible to say anything. The sound of the water. The sound of the rain and the wind.

"When he came to you in Rome, what did he want? Did he say anything about Em?"

"Not really. He didn't seem to have an agenda. He wanted to talk about you. At least he told me that you were in London, about your job. He didn't seem to rate his own work very highly. His firm were doing business in the 'stans, Russia, the Baltic States. That's why he was there."

"What did you make of him?"

"Hard to say. He came in armor. In command of himself, but not exactly at peace. Once Peter . . ." David stopped and tried again. "We talked, but all the time I felt him taking me to pieces. Not as interesting as he remembered. Not as good-looking, or clever. What had I made of myself? Not much, it seemed. Before he left he said . . . How did he put it? *You never read any of those books I gave you, did you?*"

* * *

We finished the cigarettes and the grappa. My stomach was rumbling. David thought that downstairs, in the little kitchen, there were bread rolls. It was dark and the water sloshed beneath us, although while we were talking the rain had stopped. At the top of the stairs, he took off his trousers. When he came back, dripping all over the floor, I handed him the blanket and drew the sheet over myself. Along with the rolls he had a jar of Nutella.

"I meant to stop eating this. Because of the palm oil. They're fucking the orangutans for it."

We ate the rolls, a little stale, covered in chocolate spread, in the flooded city, and then—after a little—we slept. David sat in the chair and at times, as I rose up out of my shallow dreams, I could feel his wakefulness, sharp in the darkness.

* * *

In the morning my phone was dead. Nearly a grand's worth and it couldn't last twenty-four hours. I had the charger in my bag, along with my wallet and passport, but there was no power. David was up and moving about.

"I think we should go."

"Go where?"

"I'll take you back to your hotel. It seems to have gone down a little bit. At least, it's not moving so fast."

"And the paintings?"

"If they get looted it'll have to be Michele's lookout. I think half of Florence is built on sand. What happens if the buildings come down?"

I struggled up off the camp bed to look out the window. Stretching as far as I could see was a greenish lake, moving gently as it lapped at the steps up to the houses, its surface reflecting the white sky. The floodwaters were still inside but had retreated down the stairs, leaving a coating of grime. The air smelled brackish, like a sofa left out to rot in the rain.

With some difficulty, David opened the door to the street. Litter and leaves floated like the silent survivors of a seaborne disaster. There was no breeze, no sounds. I followed David, stepping gingerly into the cold flood, wondering at the things that lay beneath the surface, feeling my way down the steps and into the street.

David knew a better way back. We sloshed through the flood. In the next street, the water deepened and David reluctantly took my hand. In a small square, we climbed the stone steps at the foot of a statue to rest. He was wearing a blue backpack and took it off, feeling it all over with his hands for dampness.

"Who's the statue of?" I asked.

"Garibaldi."

"Nice of them to memorialize a man for inventing a biscuit," I said. "It would be nice, wouldn't it, if they replaced all the statues of royalty and generals with people who'd done small, harmless things? The creator of the foot spa, the reclining armchair, the first person to make a lemon drizzle cake. What?"

David was staring at me. It made me want to put my hands over my face.

"I haven't seen you in such a long time. Let me look."

We sat on the cold, damp steps and the flood slipped past softly. As the current flowed, it bore time with it, but time in reverse, so that the years ran away; I felt them sluicing from me. I closed my eyes for a moment. The flood said *shhhhhh!* The sound seemed to bounce off the buildings, was magnified.

"What's that?" I had seen movement, a dark shape struggling in the current at the opposite side of the square. David got to his feet and I followed him. At first I thought it was a dog, but it wasn't. It was a deer, with fledgling antlers. Eyes rolling, hooves breaking the surface. Soon it was gone.

"I came to see you, a few months after Em had died, in the summer. I thought we might . . . But you weren't there. I saw Marcus though. Last person I wanted to see, of course. He looked right through me. Turned his back and practically ran. He looked bad."

"Alice said he and Em were seeing each other."

"You believe her?"

"In a strange way, I'd like to. Wouldn't have to feel so guilty then. Where were you that night, David? Alice said she didn't see you till morning."

"I didn't hurt Em. I didn't—"

"I didn't say—"

"I sat in an empty room on the top floor. The one we used to meet in. Panicking mainly. I was supposed to be with Alice, to be climbing the greasy pole at Christie's. But it all ran away with me. I wanted you so much. It was a shitty thing to do, what we did. But I would do it again. I could see that I couldn't, or wouldn't, keep in line. I couldn't trust myself. Where was it going to end? I didn't hurt Em, but I can't say I haven't hurt people. They have expectations."

"Like truthfulness?"

"Perhaps. But most people also want to be lied to, not just now and then, but all the time."

"Did you put that schoolteacher in the hospital?"

David sighed. "A case in point, Andy. You have an older man, an authority figure—although let's face it, it's Badger we're talking about, so not that much authority—with an interest in boys and power over them. I mean, I was on a scholarship but not actually that bright when it came down to it, so dependent on standout marks in certain subjects. Badger got me through. I mean by the end he was for all intents and purposes writing my essays for me, and in return I played my role, carefully oblivious to his true interest in me, reciprocating a romantic friendship, you know . . . two outsiders. Sharing in his admirations. It wasn't physical.

"It all came to a head in Rome. I don't think he could forgive me for growing up. I was less amenable. I think I'd awoken to the fact that he couldn't actually take my exams for me and I was going to fail them. He found this obscene cartoon. Of him. Rob had drawn it but I'd written on it. There was an ugly scene. Drink had been taken. And I just thought, well, there was no need for any of it. Not for him, not for school or exams or anything. He tried to stop me leaving. We were tussling over the door handle. I won and the door hit him in the face. Obviously it's an extreme example, but most relationships require a degree of complicity, don't they?"

"Once or twice I have had a similar thought, but about life."

"What's that?"

"I mean, you don't decide on the conditions. The body you live in. That you breathe and eat and shit. That you sleep. That you sicken and die. That even if you succeed, whatever that means, or have a comfortable life, there are others who suffer."

"None of us signed up for it, so why do we have to play along?"

"Something like that."

We sat at Garibaldi's feet on the steps. A breeze rippled the surface of the flood. It was possible to imagine unseen spirits listening.

"I saw an installation once," David said. "The artist had created a virtual reality game. There were headsets. You were supposed to control the game with your brain waves. Only afterward you found out, you couldn't. It was what the artist called a dark game, purporting to have one set of rules but operating under another, lying to and undermining the player. It won a prize."

"Alice said you didn't want the thing you were supposed to want. What do you want?"

"I used to want to prove my parents wrong. Loads of people are like that, aren't they? Mum and Dad's greatest concerns were safety, security, respectability. It was like honor to them, to be respectable. They kept great long lists in their minds. Tiny debts. Little duties, that kind of thing. Careful people, very loving in their way, but no talent for happiness. I wanted to show them life was wilder and grander and just bigger than that. Instead, every time I got in trouble I confirmed all their beliefs about the world. But then you get a bit older and think, if I spend my life dedicated to pointing out the shortcomings of your philosophy, I'll not have lived for myself. Not really. So the short answer is that I'm not sure anymore. And you, Andy? What do you want, I mean?"

"Change. For a very long time now. But I can't see. I lie there in the dark and there's this terror. I have to jump. I have to jump. But there's nothing. Just blackness. Or ads. The Tampax ad. The gravy ad. The car ad. As if someone has stolen my dreams."

* * *

A little further on there were people again. A man in a red jumper carrying a computer monitor. A short-haired woman with dangly earrings. In a crowd, I would not have noticed them, but after the deserted streets, I found them fascinating, was unable to look away. Finally, as the street climbed, we left the flood behind. Where the waters had retreated, the street and walls were filthy with silt and reeked of sewage. The army was out. Soldiers were positioned on street corners and at intersections. As we neared the hotel, I wondered if David was preparing words to say goodbye, and my empty stomach gave a little flip.

We got to within two hundred meters of the hotel, but they weren't letting anyone past. To deter looters and because it was not safe. Two young soldiers, both with machine guns, were standing at the intersection turning people back. One had a Brando mouth and liquid, thickly lashed eyes, the other the face of a good-natured clown. David spoke to them in Italian. Their youth made him older. I could see how he would look in ten years, twenty; and then he laughed at something one had said, and there was the David I had known.

"There's no way through. A problem with the gas mains. They said to try again tomorrow. Or next week. They said Florence is tired of tourists and is taking a holiday. The Venus in the Uffizi is sick of being gawped at and had a word with Neptune. But there's good news too. Two streets over, my Venus and I should find coffee."

We went in the direction of the train station, to where there was a small kiosk and a man making espresso over a gas burner. I sat on a red plastic stool feeling dumb with tiredness. Florence was in a basin and far away I could make out the contours of hills through the clouds over the red rooftops. David came back with drinks and a huge bag of paprika crisps.

"A third coffee, a third milk, a third sugar. He says fifteen, twenty minutes' walk that way, it's a totally different story; there's power for starters. You can charge your phone up. See what you want to do. Well, that's one option."

"There are others?"

"There's something I'd quite like to show you, Andy, now that I think of it. Of course, it may not be possible. Besides"—David, while not looking at me, allowed himself a small smile—"you probably want to get on."

* * *

We went back into the water, away from the people. The day had brightened and light reflected back from the surface of the waters, bobbed in ripples on the facades of the great buildings. David pointed out a statue, a crumbling old tower, a terra-cotta rondel with a man's face in profile. From a high open window, music poured. Hip-hop. Grandmaster Flash? Something old school, exuberant, and utterly incongruous among the Renaissance palaces.

"Batteries or generator?"

"No idea."

A helicopter circled. The water, gray brown now, was to my knees. I was more interested in what David was taking me to see than I'd been interested in anything in a long time. We turned off down a narrow street and then into an even smaller lane, where the houses were tall and set no more than five meters apart. Above, the sky was reduced to a scrap of blue and white. It was colder here and dank. We came to a chapel, a tiny thing in dark stone no wider than the house I'd grown up in. The flood had reached only to the top step.

"Here we are," David said.

"Is it open?"

"The priest is particular about it."

The door was only latched. David pushed it open and we stepped inside, into the dark interior, where it was colder still, raising goose bumps on the skin of my neck. Little light fell through the windows and with the power out, the electric twinkle of LED candles didn't do much to pierce the gloom.

David took off his backpack and put it down on a pew. There was a huge painting behind the altar and I moved closer to see it better.

"It is the one I was telling you about. *The War in Heaven* by Montocci. He was a student of Michelangelo's. It shows the Archangel Michael leading the angels against the rebel forces of Satan."

"And the dragon?"

"That's Satan." Crushed beneath the archangel's boot, he had rather a comical, terrified look. Black wings, a red and lolling tongue. Michael, looking like a haughty teenager, was about to stick a sword in him. Around them a host of angels did battle among dark crags, the clouds billowing and roiling crimson and gray as though filled with fire.

From his backpack David brought out a rectangle enshrouded within layers of plastic. After unwrapping it, he called me over, and I found myself looking at the drawing from the night before, still in its frame. Now I could look more closely, I saw that the figure had wings. The face, even in sketch, was expressive.

"Look here." David was indicating part of the painting, where a small barefoot figure stood poised on a crag, fierce faced, wings spread out. It was undoubtedly the same figure. In the angel's hand was a spear.

"Don't you see it?"

"What?"

"She's a girl. A heresy. Angels are always 'he' in the Bible. I mean they're all very androgynous, but this one is unmistakably a girl. You asked how you were back then. How I saw you. And I suppose this is my best answer. Can you not see the resemblance?"

And I supposed that in a way, I could.

* * *

We spent the night in an IKEA out by the airport. It was dark by the time we got there. With no mapping app to guide us, we had been wandering, lost, for what seemed like an eternity through a bleak industrial area. While we were above the flood level, there were no passing cars. In my shoes, my wet socks chafed my feet. Following the sound of an engine, we arrived at the depot where we found a security guard and another man in overalls both standing over the open bonnet of a pallet truck. I sat down on the curb, blank with exhaustion, while David spoke to them. He came back with a torch. A bribe had changed hands.

"We can stay. You can plug your phone in. The power's on, but they don't want us using the lights."

"My legs are so tired."

"That's what I told them. I said, *la donna*'s legs are tired. We'll find somewhere to sleep."

We passed a long row of tills, then climbed a set of stairs. On the next level there were the model rooms, the kitchens and living rooms, bathrooms and bedrooms, built to show off the stock, so you could imagine your life improved by it. The light from the torch played over the cushions and cutlery holders, the bunk beds, the clever storage solutions. It was as if all human wishes for comfort had manifested themselves in one place, and the result was alarming, as though touched by unreliable magic, so that you knew anything you took away from here would come to possess you.

I sat on a bed, too weary to think. David took off my shoes and socks. He held my feet in his hands. They were white and wet as fish.

"Can you find somewhere to charge my phone?"

"Sure."

I watched the torchlight bobbing away across the vast hall. When he came back, David switched off the torch and sat on the bed next to mine. He was eating the paprika crisps, rustling and crunching in the darkness.

"Hey. Hey. I want some."

"You're too tired to eat, Andy."

"I'm not!"

David got up and shuffled round to the other side of the bed. I felt the mattress give as he lay down. The crisps were in the middle and we reached for them in turn.

"I lost my nerve," I said.

"What's that?"

"Like that day I couldn't get up on the roof. But with everything." It was true. Not only in work and relationships, but in all matters, I played it safe—but the consequence was not a feeling of safety. I thought of the episodes, the panicked hours in front of the screen with the curtains drawn and door bolted, and I saw in my mind's eye a fly trapped in a jam jar. And then, I remembered how it had felt, with David, waist-deep in the floodwaters, the sensation of lightness and freedom.

After a while David said, "Once, when I was about eight, we took the ferry to France and then we drove to Spain. It was the one time I ever remember my parents taking a risk, venturing into the unknown. God knows what inspired them. We had everything in the car including the kitchen sink, but Dad had underestimated the distances. I don't think he even knew there were mountains in Spain. We drove and drove and drove. My mother went to sleep in the back and I was allowed to sit up front. We ended up driving over the Pyrenees. I'd never seen mountains and they went up and up, like something out of a fairy tale. It felt like it was just the two of us, alone in the whole world.

"It was summer, but at some point it started snowing. These fat flakes falling in the darkness. I tried to stay awake. I wanted to be awake when the snow stopped falling. Other people want families or houses, maybe I do too. Not having to worry about money, now that's a thing. You know that. All the other things I wanted, glory and success, the kind of success that means you can say fuck you to everyone. I've given up on it. I kept on, but that wasn't it anymore. That's not what I am after; I'm holding out for that very tiny moment. The moment when the snowing stops."

When he spoke again, his voice was lower so I had to lean in to hear him.

"I'm not special, talented, or even particularly good at anything. Once it was like a terrible secret I had to conceal at all costs. Over the years, I did think of you, Andy. I had daydreams in which we saw one another again, and I was always climbing down the steps of my private jet. I wanted to see you, but on my terms. I wanted my life to be something I could show off. Pride, I suppose. But you're here now and I can't think of a thing to impress you with, and it doesn't seem to matter."

"And what did I do? In these daydreams?"

The bag rustled. I heard David chomping on the crisps. "They were fantasies, Andy. You forgave me everything and then you took your clothes off."

There had been the people I wanted to talk to, and people I wanted to touch. But with David it was both—one would lead to the next and back again, like a tidal river. I'd had one and now I wanted the other.

I remembered now why I'd never thought he'd hurt Em. Why once, being touched by David had been my greatest good. I put my hand out and laid it flat against his chest. After a moment, he moved closer but turned away. I shifted so that I could put my arm around him and lie pressed against his back. For a moment my lips touched the cotton of his shirt. He smelled the same.

I let my thoughts drift. It seemed quite possible that I would fall asleep.

After a while, David turned onto his back and I moved till I was lying with my face against his chest, one leg resting over his.

My stupid body was so happy. It had nerve for this, it seemed. Idly, I wondered what it would cost me this time and why lying down with David was different from lying down with anyone else. It was a mystery, a real one, and as I brought my fingertips to his face, as David's arms came to hold me, I had the random and startling thought that everyone had them, one or two surprising and inexplicable things in their life, and that in such cases, should one show the doggedness of the detective of a certain kind, something might be revealed, a key of some sort.

* * *

I woke at first light and my first thought was that I would get myself a bedside table just like this one for the flat. David was sleeping, and I crept about among the furniture, trying to find my phone. When I found it, I had the urge to stuff it down the back of a sofa and be done with it forever. Instead, I turned it on reluctantly. Oliver had sent a string of increasingly irate texts and Hutchinson had called eleven times. There was also a message from a caller who'd withheld their number. I perched on the wing of an armchair and listened to the recording, waiting for the message. For the first few moments . . . nothing. Silence, an open line, and then, Peter's voice.

"Andy, it's me. Please stop looking for me. Please. I'm fine. I just need some time. I'm in the States but I'll be back in a few weeks. I'll be in touch, okay?"

I heard a faint sound in the background, faint but discernible. There was no mistaking it. Peter heard it too, because his voice changed, unmasked itself. "Please Andy. I got your message. None of it was your fault. I've done something. It's a good thing but you mustn't look for me anymore. Don't . . . don't come here."

But I had always looked after Peter. In my way. I couldn't hear his warning, only registered the fact that Peter was scared. Peter was being threatened, and my heart roared, blocking out all reason.

It was bells I heard. Church bells pealing, and among them that one booming flat. I would have known them anywhere. Clever Peter, but not clever enough.

David opened his eyes as I was putting on my coat. Once I had liked waking him up, liked watching him swim back to me.

"Popping out for a packet of cigarettes, Andy?"

"Off to see a man about a dog."

"Don't go—"

"Peter called. He's gone home. But there's something wrong."

A pause. "I suppose it is your turn. To disappear." I sat down for a moment and took up his hand. "I didn't call it, but I remember it. I wish I had, you know, if it makes any difference," David said.

"What?"

"The number. The red phone box. 4203417."

CHAPTER 18

HOMECOMING

AT THE AIRPORT, THE FLOODS HAD BEEN CLEARED FROM THE runways and planes were leaving again. The London flights were booked out, so I bought a seat on the next plane to Bristol. Once past security, I scurried to the gate to make it in time. As the flight attendant performed the pantomime with the life vest, my eyes were already closing. When I awoke, we were coming down through thick clouds.

On the aircraft steps, I noticed it had finally stopped raining. I had been wearing the same clothes for two days. My socks and shoes had dried, but I smelled of river water, and when I closed my eyes, gritty from lack of sleep, I saw the deer swimming across the square, the pink of its panting tongue; I saw David sitting on the chair in the dark, his eyes closed, holding the drawing on his lap.

I took the airport bus, then the train east to Swindon. There was a cab waiting in the taxi rank. As we drew away, I sat bolt upright in it, watching the familiar streets unfurl. The sun was breaking through as we took the road to Marlborough. The Downs were green, spring green. Beside the road, in the verges, the may, the elderflower, the cow parsley, all of it waiting for a single touch of sun to break into froths of white flowers.

We came down the steep hill into town. Here it all was, the wide market square, the town hall and tearooms. In my neck, I could feel my pulse throbbing. The fear of being seen, of being judged. My eyes flitted from passerby to passerby, from the small line of shoppers waiting for the bus, to the teenagers clustered round the bench outside the bank. What could they say to hurt me now?

One of the teenagers turned to throw his cigarette butt into the street and over his shoulder I caught a glimpse of a small face, thick dark hair. I could feel the daggers in her eyes even after we passed. In truth, I didn't need to come here to meet her. I took her with me everywhere. I told her again, what I'd been trying to tell her for years. *You did the best you could with the tools you had at the time. We did the best . . .*

The Sun had changed its name and become a restaurant. There was a Pizza Express. The Tudor Rose was no more. Waitrose and The Polly were as busy as ever.

My phone rang and I picked up without checking to see who it was, hoping it would be Peter again, but it wasn't; it was Hutchinson.

"Where are you?" He sounded odd, like he had a cold or something, a rattle in the chest as he drew breath.

"Back in England."

"In London? Can we meet? I might have found something out. It's urgent. I can come to you. Wherever you are."

The driver asked if we should go left or right.

"Right, up Church Lane. You're looking for the vicarage." I pointed up the hill and then turned back to the phone. "I'm not sure when I'm going to be back in London. I'll call you later, but, the thing is, I think . . . I think I know where Peter is."

"I have to see you—"

I hung up quickly, cutting him off, because we were pulling up alongside a yew tree hedge, the same hedge where Peter and I had once liked to hide in order to spy rapturously upon his parents.

"Target One is hanging out the washing."

"Target Two is boiling the kettle and helping himself to biscuits."

But Peter wasn't there now. I paid up and got out, then waited while the driver turned around and drove away. Beyond the hedge were the lawn and planted borders, as immaculate as ever. I wondered if Patricia still did them or if they got someone in. The vicarage looked no different, no different at all. I went up the path toward the front door, climbed the steps, and let fall the heavy knocker, just as I'd always done.

Patricia was not smiling when she came to the door. Her hands were floury.

"I'm in the middle of making a cake."

"What kind of cake?"

"A Victoria sponge, dear. But it won't be ready for a while yet."

"I came because I think I know where—"

"Peter called, dear. He's in America. I told him he had to call you to apologize. All that trouble you've been put to."

We looked at one another, as ever each taking the other's measure. Underneath the apron, she had on a blue dress and pearls. Her hair was set in a wave. Her eyes, a duller blue now, fell on the creases in my trousers, the stain on my coat. It made me feel like an evacuee, standing there in my rumpled clothes, hoping to be taken in. And there had been a time when I'd wanted to be taken in, had my eye firmly set on the spare bedroom and a permanent place at the dinner table.

"He's not in the States. He's here. Least he was."

Even the window cleaner got offered a cup of tea. As though reading my mind, Patricia said, "I'd invite you in, but I'm going out and Richard's with a parishioner." I hadn't slept. My eyes started burning.

"Did he say where he was? What he's been playing at?"

Patricia cleared her throat. "He's been staying with some lay brothers in California. I think"—her voice went up at least an octave—"he didn't say, not exactly, but I think he's been having a spiritual crisis."

"Lay brothers?"

"They're unordained. Committed to the religious life but not priests themselves."

"Oh, you're bloody clueless. Do you have any idea who Peter actually is?"

"The cake is going to burn. It's had over twenty minutes. I really must . . ."

And, because she clearly wasn't going to offer me a lift either, I turned tail and trudged off. I went down the hill toward the market square. If The Sun hadn't gone gastro, I'd have gone for a pint or eight. Instead, I took a room over the Castle & Ball, where I had a shower and lay down on the bed. But I couldn't sleep. I was burning. The anger was like petrol, and I lay there, sipping on it, fueling the fire, so that it grew, obliterating the hurt. Long ago, I had felt like this almost all the time. Anger had been my daily bread, but I had been capable of joy too. When I had shut one out, I had excluded the other.

I replayed Peter's message. The bells, distant as they were, belonged to Saint Helen's. I recognized them, as Peter had known I would, and that was why he had told me not to come here. He was *here*, or had been, I was sure of it. But if he wasn't with his parents, where else could he be? With whom? And whichever way I looked at it, I could only think of one name.

* * *

Marcus was married. He had a blond wife, Lisa, and two kids, a boy and a girl. Meeting Marcus was something I wanted to avoid, but I had wanted to see him, and as soon as technology made it possible, the spying began. I knew roughly where he lived, and with whom. I'd scrutinized his wedding pictures so often, I'm surprised they didn't feel me there on the day, an invisible presence hanging over them like a giant, hungry eye.

His son made his debut as a red-faced lump; within a few months he was a gap-toothed smiler in a Fireman Sam onesie. Marcus's daughter was the image of him. In the latest photo, she was clutching a cuddly pink pig, her little face a rictus of delight. There was a lovely one from last summer of them all together at a barbecue. Lisa had the boy on her lap. She had a solid body, a mum's body. Marcus was wearing a faded red T-shirt, paint-spattered shorts, and wielding tongs over the coals. Less hair, more muscle, a working man's tan. His eyes were narrowed against the smoke, but he was smiling. The little girl was standing between her parents, ketchup spread over her face like war paint. At her feet, the pig lay in a heap like a slaughtered foe.

The Facebook account was Lisa's. Marcus didn't have one as far as I knew. Her account was set to public, which I took to be a sign of a trusting nature, or ignorance. My own account was under the name Ay Cee. I didn't have a profile picture or any friends. It was just an eye. Lots of people were like Lisa, and I liked to roam, looking at pictures of random Christmas office parties, following seams of outrage, throwing in names of old teachers and classmates and seeing what was thrown back.

I lay on the bed in the room at the Castle & Ball cradling my phone, tapping on the screen with a finger. The window was open and from outside I could hear the traffic passing down the square, voices rising from the pavement outside where the smokers gathered. I felt that if I listened hard enough, I would hear us; piling out of the van to get fags and Coke at the shop, bickering over whose turn it was to pay. Not mine. Probably Marcus's. Maybe Em's, treating us with her earnings from the tearooms.

As though I'd summoned her, Em appeared, in an album of photos called "School Days—Saint John's 89–96."

Em is twelve. She stands among the choir wearing a toga made from a sheet while Joseph, decked out in a Technicolor dreamcoat run up by the teachers in the home ec department, belts out the song about having a dream.

The stage lights shine on Em's face. Her mouth is open in a perfect O, her hair parted in the middle, falling in two straight curtains.

Memory is not the analog photograph that fades. Memory is

a house, a castle with many rooms. Some of the rooms are deeper inside, honeycombed away. Each has a thousand keys—an image, a smell, a sound. Behind each door is a thousand other doors.

On the bed, in the room over the pub, I made like Mrs. East, time traveling, reentering the past in reverie.

Joseph is Tony Salter from the sixth form, who we all followed about that year. This year, the musical is the school's Christmas production.

Under cover of darkness, Em and I go out and cut down armfuls of mistletoe from the oaks in the paddock by her house. We smuggle it into school in carrier bags, waiting for our moment, stalking Tony Salter from football practice to his math class, to the ten minutes he spends wrapped up in the stage curtains with Amanda Walker at break.

I volunteer as a stagehand so Em and I can share glances. The dress rehearsal is a triumph. Afterward, the boys change in the music room. The school is largely empty, the corridors in shadows. Tinsel has been stapled to the noticeboards. By the office, there's a particle board manger and models of the holy family, the animals, shepherds, and kings. Carl Whitefoot earns himself a two-day suspension for his creative rearrangement involving empty beer cans, dog-ends, and multiple counts of bestiality.

Tony Salter in Levi jeans and a white T-shirt, channeling James Dean at all times, makes his way to the boys' bogs. We follow, but stop some feet distant beyond the evil-smelling miasma. Em's hand is warm in mine. Can we hear Tony Salter peeing? We hear the door open and immediately stop laughing. It is him! He is coming! As Tony rounds the corner we leap out, garlanded in mistletoe, decked in mistletoe, brandishing bouquets of mistletoe.

"Bloody hell!" Tony says. "Bloody hell, ladies."

We block his path, quivering. He sighs and casts a quick look in either direction. And then, as though he is doing something noble for his country, he bends his beautiful head to kiss, first Em, and then me, on the cheek.

CHAPTER 19

AILING KNIGHT-AT-ARMS

I DON'T KNOW IF IT WAS MARCUS OR DARREN I WAS HOPING for when I went to the site. Which of them was the lesser evil. Darren probably. As I walked over, I imagined him looking up from his invoices, wearing a pair of reading glasses he'd bought from the supermarket. *Look what the cat dragged in,* he'd say. Then later, *You always were a sharp one.* There had been calls, over the years. More at the beginning. "Can you say I left in September if anyone asks? No, September of this year . . ." But we hadn't spoken for the best part of a decade. The last time? Five years ago? Six? A project gone well. A raise. Dinner with Oliver, wined and dined, a car called to take me home. I'd dialed Darren's mobile from the back seat. It was later than was polite, but the warm feeling—progress, recognition, achievement—was departing, and I needed to summon it back. He picked up after three rings.

"Who's this?" Unmistakably Darren.

"It's Andy. How are you? I just—"

"Who?"

"Andy." There was the longest pause. "Can you hear me, Darren? It's Andy. I know it's late but—"

"You've got the wrong number."

"No, I—" But he was gone.

The site office was in the same place, but the mobiles had been replaced by a smart brick building. I stood outside watching through the window as a woman I didn't recognize answered the phone and tapped away at a computer, the sting I'd felt for weeks after Darren hung up on me warming my cheeks. In the end, I forced myself through the doors and asked for him. The receptionist was in her late twenties with ironed hair and bracelets that jangled against the keyboard.

"Mr. Fisher isn't here."

"When's he back?"

"I mean he doesn't come in anymore. He retired. Two, three years ago, I think."

"And Marcus?" Marcus had gone to see a supplier in Devizes. He might be back after lunch.

"Is it business? Can I take a message?"

"No. I used to work here. Just came by to say hello. Well, there is something. Where can I find Darren? Is he still—" And I gave Darren's last address. She shook her head. It took a bit of doing to get her to tell me where he was. I labored how good Darren had been to me, how he'd given me my start. It was funny, now that I thought about it. The interest Darren had taken, the support he'd offered to his nephew's scrap of a girlfriend.

"He's not been well," she said. "He's . . . well, he's in a home."

"But he's only sixty-five!" She didn't have anything to say to that. "Where is it then?"

"It's a new place. Well, not exactly. You know the old manor, out by the new golf course? It was redeveloped a few years ago and it's a residential home now. Not by us. Mr. Fisher wouldn't put in a bid, Marcus, that is. Not Darren. He was already . . ."

"Right." I walked to the door, then walked back. I wrote down my number. "Give this to Marcus. Tell him Andy came by. Tell him I need to talk to him."

"Andy?"

"Andy."

* * *

It was dry again, the clouds a vast white wall. I had nothing else to do, so I walked there, taking the Ridgeway as I had so often in the past. The track was muddy and rutted by dirt bikes, the puddles chalky so you couldn't tell their depth. For a time, I forgot where I was going and why, losing myself in picking a path forward, here and there climbing up the slippery grassy banks to avoid soaking my shoes. There was hardly a breeze.

Reaching the ridge, I passed the copse I had always known to myself as Crow Wood. The trees were in leaf and on their branches the black birds were tied like bows.

A memory—my earliest? Throwing crusts to the birds in the garden. "Where do they all come from? How are they always there? Is it the same ones always?" Another time. "Where does the world go at night?" My mother held me against her chest and we looked out the window, over the fields, waiting for the fox to come. The love was harder to remember than the hurt, but I stayed with it.

A crow loosed itself from a tree, ribboning upward. It was not the same crow always. The adult knew it. But another self watched the crow in flight and knew its black eyes had seen the stones set at Avebury, the Roman legions marching, the invading Viking hordes. Seen every love and sorrow and tasted every death. All around, the Downs rose and fell. A little breeze blew, rippling the spring wheat. It was good for wheat up here; the rain filtered down through the chalk hills, deep into the earth. Of all that I had loved and cut myself off from, this had cost me the most dearly.

Forty minutes on, I reached the stile. A nettle lashed my wrist as I clambered over. This time of year, they were at their most vicious. I plucked a dock, spat on it, and rubbed it over the row of welts. There, on the tender skin, the stings burned, but by the time I reached the manor, the pain would be gone and I'd have forgotten all about it. Cuts scabbed, became scars and faded. Even broken bones knitted.

I wished that the harms done to the parts of the self Peter's father would have had no trouble naming—the soul, the spirit—could be made visible, so you could know when they too had healed.

* * *

There was nothing to mark where Em had died, only a sign a bit further on asking visitors to sign in at reception. The firs were gone, replaced by a neat fence, and where the outbuildings had stood, cars were parked on a stretch of tarmac. The staff parking was half-full, the rest almost empty. I surveyed the grounds. The lawn had been reseeded and the borders planted with low-maintenance shrubs. There was a smooth path, wide enough for wheelchairs, curving around the lawn, and benches were placed beside it at discreet intervals. The specter of Health & Safety hung over the manor. The windows and roof had been replaced, the pear tree cut down.

I made my way toward the main entrance and then stopped. I wanted to know what they had done to the lake. Turning back, I followed the path at the far end of the car park, leaving the manor behind. Ahead, the lawn rose to meet the wood. The day was still, my feet upon the path the only sound.

The lake was still there, but it had a fence around it too. Water rippled behind a small colony of ducks making their way toward a gravel bank. The temple stood where it had always stood, its white pillars catching the light. There was a figure there, on a bench, seemingly occupied with staring down at the surface. Something about their posture was familiar. I walked the last couple of hundred meters to the temple, to where Darren was sitting, rubbing his hands together, eyes fixed upon the lake.

"Hello, Darren," I said. When he didn't look up, I took a seat next to him. "How's it going?"

He looked over. "Not too bad, thanks. Yourself?" He hadn't stopped rubbing his hands, drawing one over the other as though washing them. The big blunt nails were clean. Even in my day, Darren hadn't worked on the sites, but it'd never stopped him getting his hands dirty.

"Could be worse. Least it's stopped raining."

Darren's eyes had settled once more on the gently rippling water. You could just make out the temple and two blurred dark marks. A mallard glided across the reflection, breaking it into blocks of light and color.

"Don't suppose you've seen Peter, have you?"

"You'd have to ask at the site. They've got all the paperwork."

"Right. Right." Darren was hunched forward. He'd put on weight, but he seemed smaller, shelled, like a pea from its jacket. "Peter's disappeared. I'm looking for him."

"Trouble with the tax man, I 'spect."

"Wanting an arm and a leg as usual." It was one of Darren's sayings and when I gave it back to him, he lifted his eyes to mine and gave me a small culpable smile. "How's business then?"

"Coming along."

"Whoever it was did a good job on this place. Was it the Devizes lot?"

Darren shifted in his seat. There was something wrong with how he was dressed. I realized what it was. He had a polo shirt on under his jumper and someone had done the top button up. Darren had always worn his shirts open at the neck. I reached over and undid it, but he didn't react. It hurt to think that someone was dressing him. Opticians, doctors, hairdressers, he'd never been able to stand being fussed over.

"What is this place?" Darren asked.

"It's a care home, Darren." He nodded. "Right." Then, "Why am I here?"

"Problem with the old memory, I think." Points of light trembled on the lake.

"Don't mind me asking something, do you?

"Not at all."

"What is this place?"

I got up quickly, feeling something hard in my throat. I went to the stone head of Athena and ran my hands over her face. She had no diamonds for me today.

"We used to come out here when we were kids and muck about. Remember, when it was empty? Me, Marcus, Peter, and Em. There was someone else too, a boy, David. I think you turned a blind eye. I reckoned it was because we were Marcus's mates. But then I didn't know about you and Peter. It was you, wasn't it? Peter came to you about Joe."

"Little Peter?"

"The vicar's boy."

"'That skinny little fairy. 'Uncle Darren,' he says, 'you've got to help me.' Never would have agreed if I'd known what was coming. The guy came at me with a tire iron. If it wasn't for the kid . . . The grit in him. You just never know, do you?"

"No," I said. "You never know."

We walked back to the manor then. I took Darren's arm. He didn't seem to mind. The greenhouses were gone, but they'd replanted the kitchen garden. Onions and potato tops were coming through. We came across a bit of brickwork that needed repointing. Darren scratched at the mortar with his thumb.

"I'll send someone to see to that."

At the front door, there was a buzzer and I waited for a moment, looking into the camera till I heard the door unlock. At the desk, a Filipina care worker in a white uniform wanted to know where his nephew had got to.

"His nephew? Marcus was here?"

"Not Marcus. Another one. He took him for a walk, for fresh air."

I signed us back in. It was overly warm inside, thickly carpeted and with a pervasive smell of kitchens. The interior had been completely remodeled, and I experienced a dizzying sensation. Had the piano once stood over there? Or in the other corner? The shape of the room had changed to accommodate a lift, and where the great staircase had been, there was a smaller set of stairs, boxed in with doors at the foot and glass walls going up.

"Lunch is nearly ready. Darren has it in his room." She directed me through another set of doors. A sign read LANCELOT WING. I tapped in the code she'd given me. The library was now a sitting room. A flat screen hung on the wall but they'd kept most of the books. In various armchairs, the old and the very old were sat. None reading. One talking to no one. A woman, younger than the rest, was at the window. I had paused in the doorway, and she turned and cast me a furious look.

Outside each of the resident's rooms, a pinboard displayed photographs and sometimes a few lines of text. *I'm Terry. I like football and motorbikes. I was born in Liddington. I was in the infantry in the war, then worked at Lloyds. My glasses are probably in my pocket!* It was the photos that got you, the smiling wedding picture, the one of Terry valiantly digging sandcastles with a little girl on a windswept beach, then the ancient in an armchair wearing a party hat, a badge that said 80 TODAY!, and a mystified expression.

We arrived at Darren's door. Darren went in, but I lingered for a moment. Someone had tried. There were lots of snaps: Darren at school in his football kit, with a mustache and his arm around Marcus's mum, wearing trunks on a Spanish beach in the early '80s, next to the bride and groom at Marcus's wedding, in front of a shiny new Beamer with his dogs. A laminated note read, *I'm Darren. I have early onset Alzheimer's. I like watching sport. Sometimes, if I am confused, I get angry. If possible, I like to do things for myself.*

Too right, I thought.

Darren's room was large and bright with an en suite. He was sitting in the armchair and as I came in, he looked up.

"Andy," he said, and my heart flooded to the brim with love.

"Yes, Darren?"

"You figured out that program yet?"

"I did."

"That's my girl."

I picked up the remote control and flipped through the channels. There wasn't much on but I found some golf in the end, one of the opens. I sat with him and we watched it together for a bit. I could hear the trolley coming down the hall.

There was a notebook on the side. A pen lay next to it. I picked it up and flipped through. Each page was divided into three columns, one for the time and date, the second for the visitor's name, and the third for a message. It went back over a year. Marcus came Saturday mornings. His messages were to the point. *Me and Darren went to the game. Went to mum's for lunch.* There were other visitors too—Marcus's mother, whose lengthy entries in rounded hand screamed guilt; Brian, one of the site managers; a couple of names I didn't recognize.

The last entry had today's date. Mr. & Mrs. Wilde. Took Darren to a historic point of interest. Not a soul about. The time, 12, was underlined.

I knew the handwriting as well as I knew my own. It was a message from Peter.

Mr. & Mrs. Wilde. That was us, of course. And a historic point of interest was Saint Helen's. That was how the vicar had always described it. *At the heart of community, and a historic point of interest . . .*

Twelve. It was past twelve now. But there were two twelve o'clocks in a day, and I thought I knew which one Peter was referring to.

CHAPTER 20

CHURCH

NOT A SOUL ABOUT! NOT A SOUL ABOUT!

At half past eleven, I crept out of the Castle & Ball and made my way down to the river. On the footbridge I stopped, listening to the Kennet, but heard nothing but the running water, the willows stirring, and distant traffic on the market square. A footpath led through a kissing gate into a field, and from there to a muddy paddock that bordered the far end of the graveyard. I hid for a while in a hedge, trying to keep my feet in and my breathing quiet. In the dark, I could hear horses cropping the grass, but the moon, sidling over three stunted oaks, was the only watcher.

I climbed up and over the crumbling wall, slipping over the top, and down into long weeds, fighting the urge to laugh, as I so often had during my childhood games with Peter, in the face of all the terrors—vampire bats, marsh monsters, enemy agents—we had conjured. Of course, this was real, but then my games with Peter had always felt real. The laughter was a fountain, coming from somewhere deep, and for a moment I gave into it, with my back against a crooked headstone, one hand over my mouth. Through my clothes, I felt the scratch of lichen, the chisel cuts upon the stone. Everything would be absurd to those safe within the ground. Then the laughing fit abated, like a bell that had ceased to chime, and I crept forward, over the dead, avoiding the path, until I reached the darker shadows of the yew trees on the east side of the church.

Not a soul about! When I was sure, I checked my phone, hiding the screen under my jumper and peering down the neck hole to obscure the light. It was time. The vestry door was unlocked and I pushed it open a crack and made my way in. To the left were the choir stalls and the altar, to the right the aisle and pews, leading to the font. At the pulpit I waited, inhaling the familiar smells, enveloped by a hush accumulated over a thousand years. A pew creaked.

"That you, Peter?" I tiptoed forward, ready to flee if I was wrong.

"Here." He spoke barely above a whisper. I moved closer, but it was so dark I couldn't make him out, could only shuffle forward with my arms outstretched, until a hand caught my wrist. Peter drew me down until I was sitting beside him on the hard pew, knees pressed against the tapestry cushion hanging from the back of the row in front. I put out my hand and found Peter's cheek, giddy with relief, with victory.

"*Found you.*" Peter's cheek was cold. When he didn't reply, I said, "Not in the States then? Not having a spiritual crisis with the lay brothers?"

"Forgive her. I think she heard about them on Radio Four."

"They know you're here then?"

"I shouldn't have come, but I wanted to see them. To explain." He sounded tired, like someone at the end of a long, hard-fought race they hadn't won.

"What's going on, Peter? What is it you have to explain? What have you done?"

* * *

What Peter—tight-lipped Peter—had done was talk. Or more accurately, he had downloaded files, financial statements, client information, and internal memos from the company he worked for, from the corporate service provider with the half-foreign name. Like me, Peter had been playing detective. In his case, he'd been matching offshore accounts with shell corporations, detailing transactions, logging the money as it flowed upstream and downstream, from the Gulf and China, from Russia and Mexico, from the hands of politicians, public officials, and oligarchs into shell corporations in tax havens. Corruption. Bribery. Tax evasion. Money laundering. Money siphoned from aid projects, environmental protection projects, public services. Profits from illegal deals, from violated trade sanctions, the vast sums of the arms and drug trades. Then he'd leaked it, drip by drip and then finally in a gushing flood, to a pair of journalists from the *Guardian*.

"In the beginning, it was like a secret vice. Seeing it in the news, knowing it was me. Watching the people around me getting rattled."

"So you're hiding from the police? Or your colleagues?"

"Actually, it's the Russians. Mafia clients of ours. Predictably they aren't too keen on having their dirty laundry exposed. It's not that they're worse than anyone else, only the Russians are prepared to do something about it. To stop the leaks, I mean. They throw people off buildings. Everyone knows it. There were four suicides after the leaks broke. A fixer working for one of our brokers came off a multistory car park. They always say it's suicide, but I don't believe it. It doesn't add up."

"The broker, was his name Ward Collier? I was there. I saw it."

"Collier worked for a rival fund. I don't know how he was involved . . ." Peter swallowed. His voice was hoarse. "Andy, my phone was tapped. I was followed. After the wedding, I went home and someone had been in my flat. Then there were two men in a black car. I saw them twice. Once outside my building, then the same car with the same men waiting for me in a side street at my work. I knew. I just knew. Did anyone follow you here?"

"How could anyone follow me? No one knows I'm here."

"You hired a fucking private detective."

"Yes, but he . . . he's a bit useless. Maybe that's unfair." I thought quickly. "He might know I'm here. We spoke on the phone yesterday.

I can't remember what I said. But still, I don't think he'd have broadcast—"

"Small? A bit gnomish? With a beard?"

"Yes." I thought of Mr. Hutchinson and his hunted eyes with a sudden pang.

"Last seen being bundled into a black SUV. One of the journalists I've been working with saw it happen. Somehow your detective had gotten hold of their phone number. It was a number only I knew. He called to arrange a meeting. Only before he could meet them, he got shoved into a car as he came out of the underground. Leo said it happened so fast they couldn't do anything to stop it. Which means if your detective called you, whoever did it was probably listening."

"I'm sorry—"

"They'd have come anyway, Andy. Hiding with my mum and dad, it's hardly Cuba, is it?"

An owl hooted from somewhere in the graveyard and I shivered, remembering a school project on early Britain, how we'd learned the invading Vikings had imitated owls, calling to one another in the darkness as they crept up on the Anglo-Saxons bent on murder and pillage.

"I thought this was about the past. I thought this was about Em's death, about David and the diamonds. At the wedding, you wanted to talk. I went to see all of them, Rob and Alice. I went to Italy and found David because you'd said you'd seen him."

"Did you really?"

"Yes."

"And how was that? How was it seeing David?" When I did not immediately reply, he read my silence. "Really? Still? When I saw him, I said your name. The ripples, Andy. You should have seen them. I actually felt sorry for him. And you with that young man at the wedding. I'd seen that look on your face before. It preyed on my mind, after seeing David in Rome. That I had wronged you both. Telling myself I was doing the right thing, protecting you. But knowing it was a lie. That I was jealous. That I hated you. I went back that night. The day we met David. All the way there on my bike. I was thinking that maybe this was it. That everything was finally going to begin. But when I arrived, you were already there, and it was like you had stolen it from me."

"So you called the police?"

"Yes. In the end, I called the police. I put on a funny voice and told them a young man called David Graves who was wanted for stealing credit cards was hiding out at the manor."

"I went to your flat. I found the telephone box."

"Oh that? When I saw the men at my work, I hid in a shop, one of those tourist shops. In the end I had to get something. So I bought it, then I got pissed and took a lighter to it. Reliving the past, you might say. All the mistakes."

"It got me thinking too, Peter. About Em, whether it was really an accident." I told him what Alice had said about the game being fixed. About Em and Marcus. The possibility that we had found the real diamonds. I steeled myself for anything he might tell me. I took his hand but it lay loose in mine. "We were so close once. It was never the same afterward. But maybe it didn't begin then. David told me—"

"You thought I did it?"

"I don't know."

Peter gave a cold little laugh. "Funny, Andy, for a time I wondered if it was you. You were . . . possessive. Marcus and Em. I saw them, out in the courtyard. It occurred to me you might have too. You were so unpredictable then. When you ran out onto the ice, it was spiteful. That's what I thought. Spiteful, to try to harm yourself in front of people who loved you. It made me wonder, but if it's any consolation, I did think it was an accident. In the end. Stupid and tragic and pointless."

Knowing I'd suspected Peter made it no easier. It made sense in a way. The violence that had always been in me, like a virus I had caught, from my mother, from Joe. But not in Peter, which was why he'd always been such an easy target. How could I ever have thought it was him? I said as much.

"You're wrong, Andy, I'm afraid. It's in all of us, given the right circumstances. But no, I would never have hurt Em." He stopped. "It was so long ago, but speaking about it is still the hardest thing."

"Tell me," I said.

And he did.

* * *

It was Joe that Peter had hurt. He had gone to Darren, waiting, ankle-deep in mud by a digger on a half-built cul-de-sac, school bag over his shoulder, till Darren had finished what he was doing and come over.

"We went for a drive in his car, over the Downs, and I told him about Joe, what Joe was doing, how I wanted his help to get rid of him, make him go away and never come back. He thought it was funny at first, that I wanted to step up and protect my little girlfriend. He liked that. Said he'd look into it."

Only he hadn't, or nothing had happened, so Peter went back. Kept on at him, backed him into a corner.

"He liked being looked up to, Darren. Liked to be thought a hard man. And I was calling him on it, wasn't I? Calling him on everything he liked to think about himself."

So Darren had agreed, only he had insisted Peter went along for the ride.

"We were going to threaten him. Tell him Darren was going to fit him up and fuck him up. There was a vague idea about planting drugs on him, or say that he'd nicked some of Darren's gear, equipment from the site. But it wasn't thought through, not beyond the threats."

They had followed Joe, followed the beat-up black Merc one night after it left my house. Tailgating him across the Downs, till he pulled into the car park at the top of Hackpen Hill.

"I was so scared, but Darren made me get out. I had to say it while he stood there with his arms folded, like a ref. All part of his plan to make a man out of me, no doubt."

And Joe hadn't said anything, hadn't laughed or told them to fuck off, only reached inside his car and came out with a tire iron. Went for Darren first.

"Never seen violence like that in anyone, Andy. It was like a vicious dog being let off a chain. He had Darren on the ground in seconds; all he could do was put his arms up to protect himself."

The Downs are quiet at night. Peter had stood there, frozen. But no one was coming. No one was ever going to come, so Peter had scrambled round the side of Darren's car. Perhaps Joe thought he was running away, or perhaps he was just enjoying himself too much to notice.

There had been a hammer on the back seat. Darren's car was always chock-full of crap, tools and papers and empty sweet wrappers.

Peter hit Joe from behind. He was tall for his age and wild with fear, and so the hammer had a lot of swing behind it. Joe must have seen something from the corner of his eye, because he turned, just slightly, and the first blow caved in his cheekbone. The second he took to his skull, same side, just above the temple. And that was how it ended. All the films have it wrong, the action movies, the endlessly climactic fights, the antagonist who keeps coming back for more. Peter said Joe went into convulsions, just for a minute, maybe less. Then he died.

They put Joe in the boot of Darren's car, then they drove the Merc along the Ridgeway and onto a farm track. It was winter, and muddy, but the Downs are chalk, so they'd managed to get it into a copse without getting bogged. Torched it with petrol siphoned from the tank, hoping that when it was found it would be taken for the work of joyriders. Only it wasn't found. The farmer had no business up there till spring, and the dirt bikes would churn up the mud, obliterating the tire tracks.

"And Joe?"

"Under Darren's patio? I don't know. Concreted away somewhere. He said we could never tell you, Andy. That if the police came, or anyone else, you couldn't know, so you wouldn't have to lie. They wouldn't come to us. It would be you and your mum. I wish I could have told you. I can't tell you how much I wanted to. How hard it was to be alone with you because at any moment it might come spilling out.

"But I'm not sorry. Not after I'd seen the way he was. I'm so sorry, Andy, that it happened to you. I'm still so sorry. But I wish it hadn't happened, that I hadn't killed him. I used to try and pretend. But I'd wake in the mornings and there it would be. This horrible, soiling, secret weight. Tons of it. The terror that I would be caught. What it would do to my parents. Having to sit there in church and listen to the sermons. Damned for who I was. Damned for what I'd done."

I pressed Peter's hand to my lips. I didn't have any words.

"Mum got the photos out yesterday. She doesn't really understand all this. They've got so old. The past is safer than the future. There's a picture of me the summer after it happened. We went to a B&B in Devon. I look like a child, this gangly child, and I looked into his eyes, trying to see it, and I could, so why couldn't anyone else? But then, there was a picture of you, Andy, a page or two on. That picnic we went to at Alton Barnes, do you remember? And you're just a little girl, I mean, so small, and so fighty, and you've got a big plate of chicken legs and potato salad, and there's that patch on your scalp you always covered, but you can see it, and the hair's coming back, and you have this tender, hopeful look. I would do it again, a hundred times. A hundred times a hundred times."

"Did Marcus know?"

"No. But I told David, but then it was you, not me, he fell in love with. And he wanted to tell you. The way you want to tell people things when you love them, when you don't want anything between you. I have resented you at times. Things came easy to you, Andy.

People always liked you. Didn't matter how rude or appalling you were. I was never sure if Em and Marcus would have been my friends without you, so I was waiting, waiting for my own someone. For life to begin, for love, for the great reveal, the grand reversal. But it happened to you instead and it was my turn."

"When you saw him? Did you still love him?"

"No. You make people into what you want them to be when you're that age. He was just a charming boy who wanted to be liked. Besides, Andy, once you've had the real thing, nothing else is ever going to do."

"The real thing?"

"Love. Sex. David wasn't disgusted by the fact I fancied him. That was the benchmark back then. I got called a queer from the age of seven. I used to get changed for PE in the corner facing the wall, because if I so much as accidentally looked at someone I'd be in for it. So a bit of kindness from David, a bit of flirtation, I mistook it for the real thing. Only it wasn't. I found that with Karsten. Later, Patrick and I had it for a while too."

"And burning down the phone box?"

"I knew you were there. Waiting. I called it and you were there so quickly, your voice so hopeful, and I knew if I didn't do something, I was going to tell you. I wanted to tell you so badly. Not just about David, but about Joe too."

* * *

We stayed there till dawn. As it broke, the colors in the stained glass windows emerged like jewels from the darkness. There, in the east window, was the blue-robed bowing figure who I had once chosen as my secret, special friend.

Peter told me more about the leaks.

"Why? It's not like you suddenly woke up one day and realized what your job was."

"Do you remember my angel?"

"The one with the book?"

"Yes. For years, I used to talk to him. I don't know, till about ten, maybe? It was a secret game. I'd talk to my angel, telling him about the things I'd done, good things, bad things.

"Then last year, I was very low. I tried antidepressants but they didn't work. It was like being very far away, in a boat at sea, alone. And I had rowed to exhaustion. I had nothing left. I couldn't sleep half the time. In the evenings I would sit there, looking out, and sometimes I would talk to myself. Then I tossed the pills. You're supposed to taper off, but I just stopped. And I started talking to the angel and the angel started talking back, Andy. But not like I was imagining it, not making up his side of the conversation. I could hear his voice, as clearly as I can hear yours."

"Weren't you scared?"

"No, no. It was wonderful. He was so angry, and the anger was like this cold, beautiful fire."

"Angry with you?"

"No. Angry with God funnily enough. Angry with people, with the world. And I wasn't alone, and it was the best feeling. I didn't go to work. I cannot remember being so happy. Making plans with the angel about what I was going to do.

"It stopped after a few days. I stopped hearing him. I went back to work and started downloading and making copies of everything. I thought it might come back. I miss it. I miss the clarity. I still talk but there's no reply. I thought if I did it, if I exposed what I knew, whatever happened, it would be something. I've got more now, more files, more documents. They're going to lose millions. It could bring down banks. It can't be stopped now, whether they catch me or not. I've made sure of it. I'm tired, Andy. I want it to be over. All of it. I'm glad you came. I knew you would, as soon as the bells started ringing."

There was nothing between us now, and despite all the trouble he was in, my heart was light. We would escape to France on a fishing trawler. Raise highland cattle in the Hebrides. I would never go back to my job. When I said these things, Peter smiled and squeezed my hand.

We fell to talking about the game, about Alice's insistence that Em had hidden the diamonds somewhere near the front of the manor that morning, nowhere near the temple. But if that was the case, then what had we found? Peter couldn't add much to what I'd learned about the night Em died.

"I sat in the boot room with a bottle of whiskey petting the dogs. I pissed in Rob's shoes at one point. Then I went to bed. The room cold and spinning like a merry-go-round."

"Shall we go see her? Perhaps she'll tell us what happened."

We went out. The sun was pale, sending long-fingered rays through the yew trees. Em was some distance away and we ambled down the path together to where the more recently departed were laid to rest. Her grave was well tended. There were flowers less than a week old. A jackdaw cawed.

"He's waiting for his sandwiches," I said to Peter, and then, "I wish you could be with us, Em. I wish you were still here."

Not possible. Not possible . . .

How thin Peter looked. How careworn. He seemed lost in thought, his brow knitted as it did when he was puzzling over something.

My mother's grave wasn't far away. After the funeral, I'd not been back. Now I was surprised to find it neat, neither mossy nor overgrown. Crouching, I traced her name with my fingers upon the headstone. There was no dedication, only her name and the dates. I hadn't known what to say then. I still didn't know what to say now, but I was willing to talk to her.

"Hello," I said. "Hello."

When I turned away, Peter was no longer alone. Two men were standing with him at Em's graveside. One of them was in the act of stepping forward and taking something from his pocket.

And the girl said *NO*, and I was running, running toward them. A hissing sound escaped my mouth. The two men turned to me. I saw a look of confusion pass over the nearest one's face. As I covered the last remaining distance between us, he stopped in his tracks. All three frozen, as I bore down on them, hissing like a gorgon, talons outstretched.

* * *

"No, it's not . . . It's all right, Andy." The two men had retreated, putting a large marble headstone between us. I advanced. I would give them dearly departed. I would show them resting in peace. "Really, Andy," Peter said, taking my arm. His lips twitched in a smile. "So small," he said, "so fighty."

The taller of the men had been at his pocket again. Now he proffered an identity badge. "John Hollis," he said. "MI5. This is my colleague David Lamb."

"You're not taking him."

"We've just been explaining to Mr. White that he is under no obligation to speak to us whatsoever."

"What was the name of your private detective, Andy?"

"Mr. Hutchinson. Why?"

"I think you'll find he's in the hospital," Hollis said. He seemed to have recovered himself. The other man, Lamb, kept one hand inside his jacket. "Fell out of a car on the motorway. He'll be all right though. Eventually. Now, as I was saying, Mr. White, we can only recommend, for your own safety and the safety of your loved ones, that you willingly enter our custody. There are, of course, matters we hope you will choose to assist us with."

I took hold of Peter's arm tightly.

"It's for the best if you come with us straightaway, Mr. White. Yesterday we encountered what you might term hostile parties in the area."

"Tried to run us off the road."

"I'll need to get a few things. Have a word with my parents," Peter said.

Hollis and Lamb went with him. I waited, sitting on the wall. The birds were singing, but my spirits were at a low ebb. Peter would be safe. Peter would be gone.

When they came back, Patricia and the vicar were with them. The vicar had Patricia's hand. She was in her dressing gown and her face was pink and swollen with tears.

Peter put his bag in the boot of a silver Audi and then came over to where I was sitting. "I'll see you soon," he said. "Don't look like that." He bent and pressed his lips against my cheek. "You should see Marcus, ask him . . . ask him about Mrs. Duncan."

"Mrs. Duncan the dinner lady?"

"Mrs. Duncan the dinner lady who also worked in the charity shop."

Then he went and got in the car with the men from MI5, and his parents and I watched as they drove Peter away.

CHAPTER 21

REVISITED

WE GROW UP BUT THE GAMES GO ON. WORK, RELATIONSHIPS, belonging to a religion, being left or right, having a class or gender, or interests, a personality even, they all seemed like games begun long ago, far back among the mists of time, played ceaselessly, routinely, and with neither end nor prizes in sight. Each day, less convincing. In the days after Peter went away with the men from MI5, I could not have told you anything about myself and been certain it was true. I stayed at the vicarage; finally the spare bedroom with the daisy curtains and matching bedspread was mine.

"Do you like fish, dear?" But the question seemed too hard, so Patricia made me chicken, every night, for two weeks. After they went to bed, never later than ten p.m., I would sneak into Peter's room and lie on the bed and take up something of his in my hands; a falling-apart paperback edition of *Crime and Punishment*; a scrapbook into which we had once stuck clippings from the local paper. One reported a missing donkey, rustled from its field. Another was a piece about a spate of car thefts, where the cars had been mysteriously returned, washed and waxed, the insides given the full valet treatment.

Each day I went out walking. The river was racing, the streams and ditches bright and overflowing with water. Then there were three warm days in a row, and as though responding to a blare of trumpets, spring broke like a wave surging up a beach, foaming into blossom and bud, rippling into green. I climbed up Liddington Hill and stared at it. A part of me that was not my mind cried *Green! Green!* and pressed to the front of my eyes. I watched the cows being let out to pasture after their long winter in the sheds, watched them run, udders flying, tails whisking, across the fields, and I understood. And part of me said, *Go on, have a catatonic breakdown. You've earned one.* But another part said, *I want to feel.*

Peter called one night, after dinner, and the three of us huddled around the phone taking it in turns to talk to him, although he would not say where he was or what he was doing, only that he was going to travel, to do *something for them,* as he put it, and then he would not be in touch for a month or two.

"Then we'll do something together, Andy. A trip. We'll go somewhere beautiful and fox-trot round a fountain." But his tone was compensatory as it had been when we were younger and he'd had access to a treat—a visit to some puppies, an excursion to London to see a show—to which I wasn't invited. I sensed he'd found a new game, one I wasn't allowed to join in.

I did the washing up while Patricia hovered. Would I like a glass of sherry? The vicar wouldn't, but she would have one if I had one. The questions trickled, and then poured. She was so hungry to know her son.

"We were surprised that he chose law in the end. Because," she cast me a sidelong glance, "he was so artistic."

She wanted to know about Peter's special friends.

"Karsten?"

"Karsten von Kloss."

"Von," she mused. An evangelical light shone in her eyes. "You know, Andy, the Gospels say very little about, well . . . sex. Much, much more about money, about helping one's neighbor, succoring the poor and weak." And then, "Because the Bible was written by man, inspired by God but written by man, so it's flawed." Till it burst out of her, "Peter can love who he wants. No one is better than Peter, no one has the right to think they're better than Peter!"

* * *

I went to church with them, taking Patricia's arm as we navigated the cracking, uneven path. The congregation was small and elderly, the organist tone-deaf, the singing thin. Richard mounted the pulpit and read from the Gospel of Matthew about Jesus turning over the tables of the money changers in the temple. Later, he asked us to shake our neighbor's hand. When it was over, I went and talked to Em and to my mother. Marcus didn't call, and I gave up expecting him to, but in the town, I turned every corner with the thought that he'd be there.

I went to the house. The council had sold them off and the whole row had been done up; new windows and doors, an unblemished cream paint job from end to end. I lingered outside Mrs. East's with my hands upon the wall and then walked down to where I had once lived with my mother, with Joe. A shiny bottle-green Mini was parked outside. Beside the front door were two sets of muddy wellies, one adult-sized and green, the other small and pink. The curtains were pulled back in the front room and I took a few steps forward to peer in. As I did so, the door opened and a woman came out, and then a little girl.

She was more or less my age, with shoulder-length brown hair and a jumper all the colors of the rainbow. The girl was about four. Upon seeing me, she took a step back behind her mother's legs. I wavered.

"Can I help you?" The woman's smile was friendly, open.

"It's just . . . I used to live here."

"Oh! Are you Mrs. Jevons? I don't think we ever met, but the estate agent—"

"No, I left twenty years ago. I grew up here." The door was still open and I could see the carpets had been taken up and the floorboards polished. A print of a Matisse hung at the end of the hall.

Beneath it was a walnut chest of drawers with a turquoise ceramic pot on it. A pause. I tore my eyes away.

"Listen . . . Would you like to come in and have a quick look?"

I thanked her, but said I had to be on my way.

"We came down from London. Couldn't get a studio there with what we had. We wanted Ella to have her own room. It's been an adjustment, but we love it now. And the house, it's a happy place. We've always felt, well, that people were happy here."

Not trusting myself to speak, I nodded.

She unlocked the car and started getting the girl strapped into her booster seat. I waved goodbye to them both and went over to where the telephone box had once stood. It had been taken away, but the concrete plinth remained, weeds pushing their way up through the cracks. Where were the children now, the ones like I had been, now that the turquoise ceramic pot owners had moved in?

When they'd driven off, I went back, staring at the house like I could incinerate it, thinking what it must be like to have lived the kind of life that allowed you to invite strangers into your home, to believe the walls within which you lived radiated happiness.

* * *

The car slowed down up ahead and then reversed until it drew level with me. The passenger window slid down and I heard a voice say, "Is that you, Andy?"

It was Em's mum. I leaned down to mumble hello.

"So it is you!" But then, seeing my eyes red from crying, she said, "What's all this then? Oh Andy, come on, get in."

I tumbled into the car. It was a moment of need, a moment where what I needed overrode my self-control. I fell across the passenger seat into her arms, pressing my face into her jacket. June did not push me away. She was not angry with me. Instead, she stroked my hair while I wept and shook.

"I'm all right. I'm all right." I don't know how many times I said it.

"You been up to your mum's?"

"Yes." I sat back, with my hands over my face.

"Oh, Andy. Come on, love. Let's go home."

* * *

Not my home, of course, but Em's. We sat in the kitchen, under the low beams. Out came the tea and cake. It was June who looked after Mum's grave. She went up to see Em most weeks.

"Used to see your Marcus up there sometimes. I invited him back, but he never wanted to come. He's done well with his uncle's business." She paused. "Got married a while back. His wife, Lisa, is friends with my Faye. Kids the same age. The boy's a sweet little thing, but his girl is an unholy terror. Wild as the wind. Gorgeous, of course. Lisa says her dad worships her."

We talked for a bit about her grandchildren. There were two, with a third on the way.

"I'm sorry I never came."

"I thought you might visit. Even if it was just to see Peter's mum and dad. Sometimes Mrs. White would pass on a bit of news if she'd spoken to him. Then I got to thinking what's she got to come back for? There were times I'd have run off too if I could.

"Nothing ever makes up for it, Andy, for losing Em. Some days I'll remember a falling-out we had, because she borrowed my best earrings without asking or locked herself in the bathroom for three hours so I'd had to pee in the garden. And I'd cut off all my limbs to have her back. But you make a place for it. That's what I tell them—Jack, Faye, the rest of the family. Because I'd get angry sometimes, like they wanted to pretend she was off on holiday somewhere, or hadn't existed. Oh, that made me hopping mad. People cope differently. I told them, you have to let me do it my way. Faye understands now. She had a miscarriage between her first and the second, and idiots kept saying things like 'Well at least you've got your Shelley,' or 'You'll have another one.' Like you're not allowed your grief."

I swallowed hard. June cut me another slice of cake and slid it across. She asked me about London, about what had brought me back.

"That was Peter? Well, I never. I remember the two of you, right back to infant school. That was a love affair like no other! Em would be 'Andy this,' and 'Andy that,' and 'Oh but Andy only likes Peter.' She was so pleased when you finally became friends. Never shut up about you. Then you started coming round. Do you remember? And she'd whisk you off upstairs so she could have you to herself. It was like having a little wolf about the house. Then I started noticing, after you'd been, all the Tampax would be gone from the bathroom. And I wondered, 'What's going on that she's got to help herself to Tampax?' And I'd see your mother in town sometimes. I wanted to talk to her, but . . ." Her face darkened, "Unhappy woman. That's what I used to think. That's an unhappy woman."

June was heading out to pick the littlest one up from playgroup.

"Do you want to see her room? You can let yourself out, or I can give you a lift, after we're back from swimming. Some days I sit in it, but less now. The girls sleep in it when they stay over. I wasn't sure about it. But it's better. They love it. They call it Dead Aunty Em's room. Horrible, but then kids are horrible, aren't they?"

I followed her upstairs as if to my execution.

The sun was slanting in under the thatch through the latticed windows, strewing diamonds of light across the floor. The shoebox of My Little Ponies that Em'd kept hidden under her bed was out. Small jumps had been built out of twigs and the cardboard tubes from toilet rolls.

"Might see you in a bit then, Andy."

Sitting on the bed, I listened to her footsteps descending the stairs. After a few minutes, the door clicked shut. All of Em's things were there. The red teapot on the window ledge. A pencil tin with I ♥ MF still visible in Tipp-Ex on the lid. Martin Frost or . . . Marcus Fisher? I picked up her hairbrush for a bit and held it. On the dressing table was a black eyeliner. I got it going on the back of my hand and then, in the mirror, I did first one eye and then the other, aiming for flicks, but I'd never been able to get them right. I knocked over two of the ponies and knelt down to set them straight. With one hand, I took the one with the rainbow mane and tail over the jumps, then placed it back on the carpet, but so it was humping the pink one with hearts on its bum. In my head, I heard Em laugh.

The Christmas tapes were on the side by her CD-Double-Cassette player. There was one for each of us. I slipped mine into the machine and lay back on the bed with my head on Em's pillow, reading through the track listings. Some of the songs she'd taped off the radio and there would be the last second of John Peel introducing them before the music started. She knew what I liked. Seattle sounds, girl punk bands, Leonard Cohen, Elvis Costello. When side one finished, I turned it over and this time I closed my eyes, and for a while I could feel myself held in Em's mind, could feel her reaching out to me. *Songs for Andy*, the cassette said, and on the inlay card, she'd drawn a cartoon in pencil, the figure of a girl from behind, looking out into a landscape of Christmas trees and snow, a small moon, hanging like a lantern in a sky studded with stars.

* * *

When it came to an end, I took the tape out and put it back in the case and then into my pocket, along with the one for Peter. I looked around, ready to go. In the alcove by the wall was her art stuff, the plastic toolbox full of paints and brushes, sets of pastels and crumbling sticks of charcoal. On the shelf above, her sketchbooks were lined up. I pulled one down, recognizing the cover, and put Marcus's tape into the player. He liked his music loud and shouty. Didn't matter if it was rock or rap or rave, just so long as you could take a corner fast to it, shifting up and down the gears with the engine revving.

The sketchbook was the one she had started that summer at the manor. She always left the first few pages blank.

Too much pressure, and if I fuck up the first page, I won't want to use it anymore.

You could tear it out.

Not possible Andy, not possible.

I remembered her saying that after she had drawn something, she never forgot it. She could close her eyes and see the thing exactly as it was, not the drawing she had made of it, but the thing itself.

There was one of the fountain, and another of the manor from the front, not quite right so she'd ruined it by drawing two smiling stick figures on the roof. A few of the sketches were from art class, a still life, a copy of a painting of a platter of fruit and what looked like a baboon, a miniature picture of the temple and the lake—and there were sketches of us. I knew she had done them, indeed I had seen them before. Peter wearing a daisy chain. Me. Marcus. *Why are you doing this to me, Em?* Me again, on the lawn looking away, the shoulder wrong but the eyes right. A half-finished portrait of David, all wrong; you could see why she had given up.

But there were others, others I hadn't seen. A sketch of Marcus. And then another. And then a lot more. Different poses, quite a few portraits of his face. Proper finished pictures, time spent on them, time and love. I had the sketchbook on my lap. Lead had come off on my fingers and I wiped them absently on my trousers. Marcus sitting half in and half out of the shade with his eyes closed. Marcus lying in the grass.

I hadn't really been listening to the tape, but the music swelled now to fill my ears, not shouty but soft, soft, full of longing. I picked up the case and looked at it, properly looked at it, reading the listings.

Love song, after love song, after love song.

CHAPTER 22

THE SECOND SET

I DID NOT KNOW WHAT TO DO WITH THE TAPE EM HAD MADE for Marcus. In the end I took it, and let myself out, and when the Whites had gone to bed, I listened to it, over and over on the stereo in Peter's room, with the volume low in a way that I had not listened to music in years.

After much deliberation, I left it in Darren's room, inside the visitor's book, on a Friday evening, knowing Marcus came in on Saturday mornings.

On the walk back, Oliver called again. Sometimes he tried to woo me back. A couple of times he'd threatened me with violating the terms of my contract.

"What are you going to do? Volunteer in Liberia? Build yurts in Mongolia? Start a cheese farm? A yoga camp? Are you going to train in the art of vaginal steaming? It's all bullshit and you know it."

I let him run. When he'd finished, I cleared my throat. "I don't know, Oliver, really I don't know. All those pictures you sent. Remember? I want to find the things behind them."

"What things?"

"The things behind the pictures. I can't see them because the pictures are in the way."

"You're not making any sense." He sighed. "Listen, take a holiday if you have to. But you've worked so hard. Don't throw it all away. We can talk about your hours. Money. Work-life balance or whatever. Are you listening, Andrea?"

"Yes."

"Will you think about it?"

And I said I would. And I did, among other things.

David alive again in my head. Spectral company. Turning to gesture to the man selling coffee, legs stretched out from a red plastic stool. His face in shadow in the tiny Florentine chapel. David's lips touching mine in a display bed in the empty IKEA.

I had always wanted magic from David, and he had supplied it, as best he could, with what he had. A part of me had reasoned that if there were people like Joe, blight men, wrecking balls, that there must exist the opposite. The ragged ancestors who raised the standing stones at Avebury and Stonehenge must have believed in magic, or why did they cart rocks weighing tens of tons from Wales to Wiltshire before the invention of the wheel? The early Christians shivered in their stone churches waiting for Viking marauders, believing in their God's protection. I had needed magic too, but I had wanted David to perform a spell that only I was capable of. I didn't want to make the same mistake again.

At night, I lay in bed in the vicarage spare room, fretting. I had the idea I might go south, to Cornwall, to the sea cliffs. I researched courses in climbing, battling the specter of Oliver laughing over my shoulder. I had a vision of myself, suspended on ropes over the foaming sea, stretching for a handhold somewhere high above. There, alone, I would find my nerve. I fed the image, and struggled to believe in it, held captive by the other images that came: of indifferent, much-younger climbers cold-shouldering me, of a sarcastic group leader, macho and posturing, an impatient man with an unkind laugh. Even when I imagined the ropes holding me, my thoughts turned to falling, to falling and not being caught.

The episodes were held in check by the presence of the vicar and Patricia, but I could feel them stacking up, like a series I had committed to watching that would run for years and years. I gave the Whites the answers they wanted—a short period traveling, followed perhaps by a course of some kind. I helped the vicar set up a Facebook page for the church. In the evenings, I returned to aimlessly clicking and scrolling, feeling a sickening lurch as I resumed my role as an investor in the attention economy, the rewards small—those tiny dopamine hits—the losses imperceptible, but cumulatively significant.

I wanted David, knew it, but my fear of falling off a cliff was nothing compared to the fear of giving myself to another person. I couldn't think of romantic love as anything other than a wild speculation, an investment in an economic bubble that would inevitably burst.

I considered love's economy—its currency of gestures, its debts and crashes. I thought of girls in summer dresses wheeling barrows full of worthless notes. I thought of couples exchanging foreign notes with one another. I thought of love's bad checks and black market, its lost fortunes and bubbles. I thought of men staring up at screens in devotion, watching love's market value rise and fall. I thought of love's vault, its gold reserves, its overdrafts and exchange. Love's loans and repayment plans. Its bankruptcies and defaults.

A risky business, a bad investment. I had done the sums, over and over, and they did not add up.

But love is not money . . . I heard a quiet voice say. *To compare love with money is a great mistake.*

* * *

England was playing football. A big game, the biggest for years. The roads were empty, and as I took the lane into the Savernake, from somewhere far off I thought I heard cheering. Deer had eaten the green bark from some of the younger trees, leaving torn patches. Their hoofprints patterned the mud at the side of the road. A van approached and I stood aside to let it pass.

It slowed to a halt and the passenger window rolled down.

"Get in," Marcus said.

I only hesitated for a moment before opening the door and climbing inside. The van was new. It had that smell. On the dash there was a screen. Digital radio, USB ports, air con, the works. Marcus was listening to Radio Six these days. I closed the door and he pulled away, eyes on the road ahead into the forest.

"Did you get the tape?"

Marcus seemed to flinch at my voice, then he nodded. He was beefy now, thick about the neck and shoulders. You could see his uncle in him.

"I wish you'd leave us alone."

"I thought you might want to have it. She made it for you."

"I have a family. A wife, children. You can't come back stirring it all up."

"I was looking for Peter."

"Did you find him?"

"Yes."

"So you can go then."

"What makes you think you can tell me what to do?" A knee-jerk reaction.

Abruptly, Marcus pulled in, to the side of the road, to one of the widenings that allowed cars to pass one another. He turned off the radio.

I had thought of things to say to Marcus. There was a speech I'd given in my head. In it, I thanked him for the care he'd taken of me. I acknowledged that what had always been wrong between us had been my fault. That he had tried, and I had failed, but I hadn't known better, and we had been so young. When I'd pictured it, Marcus had nodded and let me say sorry for being such a nightmare—for the rage and depression, for cheating on him, for not loving him better and not letting him go so he could be with Em. The way I'd pictured it, I hadn't imagined Marcus saying anything back, speeches were not his style, just him letting me speak, the sense of a weight lifting.

I wondered if we might talk about Em. Not about what had been between them, but her, how she had been, that we had loved her, and missed her.

Met with reality, the fantasy evaporated. Marcus had a way of not letting you speak, if what you had to say wasn't what he wanted to hear.

Beneath his jaw, the skin of his throat was throbbing, like there was something in there, threatening to hatch. In the back, I caught sight of a tarp. A long wooden handle was protruding out from under it.

And I knew. All of a sudden I knew.

I put my hand to the door handle. When it wouldn't open, I slammed my shoulder against the door.

"Don't bother. It's got child locks on."

It did something to me. Being in a car with a man, not being able to get out. Like someone pinching my windpipe. I stopped moving and went very still inside. I looked down at my hands. On the floor, peeping out from under the seat, was a cuddly toy, a little pink pig I recognized from the Facebook photos, and I wanted nothing more than to go, *Wee, wee, wee, all the way home.*

"She'd had enough. Back off to London, wanted to be making quilts out of sanitary towels or whatever it was they were doing up there."

Suddenly I didn't want him to tell me. Not only because he'd come out with a tarp and a spade in the back of the van, but because there are some things you just don't want a share in.

"After the shoot, after I got hit by those pellets, I went over to see her. Promised I was going to leave you. Promised me and her could give it a proper go. Won her round. That's why I wanted to go to the manor when those pricks asked us. What Em and I had was normal. It was how people are supposed to feel. You and me, the way I felt about you, it was a fucking disease. But I never hit you, did I?"

"No, not once."

"But I hit her—just that one time."

"Peter said to ask you about Mrs. Duncan."

"Surprised he remembers that," Marcus said slowly.

"Remembers what?"

"We bumped into her once. Me and Pete. I'd bought another necklace from that charity shop she worked in, just like the first. She was asking me if my girlfriend had liked it, and I tried to pretend I didn't know what she was on about.

"I wanted to get rid of David that summer. Knew if he thought we'd found the real ones, he'd be off quick smart with them, and you'd see him for what he was. I hid the second necklace. The statue of Athena. But he was gone before we could play and I forgot all about them. Only he did find them, three fucking years later. Em knew they weren't the ones she hid. At first, she said she thought David had moved them. But then later, she went back and fetched our diamonds from the fountain where she'd put them. The icicles, remember? That's where they were. So now there's two sets. Everyone had gone to bed and she came to me. Excited. Eyes shining. Thinking we might have found the real ones. I had to tell her, only I hadn't told her before. At first she was just disappointed but then she was angry. She got it in her head I was hiding things from her, not being straight. She said she'd had enough. Took it as a sign. I said I'd leave you, but I'd said it before. Half the night. Going round and round. We'd all been drinking, hadn't we?"

"For a while, I thought it was Peter. I thought Peter . . . maybe he thought it was me. She was wearing my coat. It was dark."

Marcus's hands were tight on the wheel. "She stormed off. I let her go. Then I changed my mind. I went downstairs. I heard you. I heard you and David. I was just this mug, not just to you, but to all of you. After that I don't know. It was black as pitch, like a nightmare. I was looking for her . . . blundering around all those rooms." Marcus turned to me. His eyes were still that hardwood brown. "I heard the front door click. I couldn't find a pair of boots that fit. By the time I got them on, she was halfway down the drive."

He shook his head like a man trying to free himself from a dream. "I caught her up. I got hold of her arm. She said to let go. She said it was too late. She said it was over. And I hit her. Just once. She went down and smacked her head. She was lying very still. It was so quiet. They said it wasn't immediate, but Christ she seemed dead to me. Floppy. All the heat leaving her. It was like, I just couldn't take it in. I . . . I literally tiptoed away. I went back to bed and got under the covers and went straight to sleep. Like a child who thinks when they wake up, it won't have happened. Didn't sleep another night after for years. And now again. I can't sleep. Can't work."

"Why didn't you tell? It was an accident."

Marcus frowned. "No. I hit her. It wasn't an accident. I lost control. Just for a second, and then I ran away and left her there. I couldn't tell anyone that. I couldn't have my mum know I did that. I just couldn't do it to her. Not after everything she'd been through with my old man. And Darren, you know what he was like. I'd have been dead to him. I want it over. I want it over. It's like you always had this hold over me. Even now. It was your fault. This . . . this is your fault."

"That's what Joe used to say."

Marcus wasn't looking at me anymore, but staring out through the windscreen at a thick patch of brambles beneath a beech tree. Maybe he was thinking it would be a good spot to hide my body. A vein was popping in his temple.

Afterward I would wonder if what Marcus told me was just a dream he'd had that night at the manor, or in the years since. Guilt for having loved her, for not having saved her. But in the van, I believed him and I knew he meant me harm.

"Can't let you threaten my family. Not Lisa, not Nick, not Maggie." I had the sense I was listening to a track he had going on repeat in his head. Instinct told me not to move, not to speak. Then the fight kicked in.

"The only thing that is going to threaten your daughter is men like you—" I had a lot more to say, nearly three decades' worth of fury.

Marcus lunged for me, but the seat belt held him back. He moved to undo it, fumbling with the buckle, as I shrank back, pressing myself against the window.

The phone rang. It was connected by USB to the van and the name Lisa flashed up on the screen on the dash. Before Marcus could stop me, my hand flicked out and accepted the call.

"Marc, Marc, where are you? Maggie's lost her pig. She's creating seven kinds of hell. Are you watching the game? I know it's a pain in the arse, but she seems to think it's in the van." Lisa's voice softened, became more intimate. "If you've got it, would you be the world's best dad . . . Marc?"

At the sound of her voice, Marcus had frozen. As she chatted on, he sat there blinking like a man ripped from a dream. I don't know why I didn't say something. Now all I can think is that we had always kept one another's secrets, Peter, Em, Marcus, and I.

Slowly I reached down, picked up the toy, and placed it gently in Marcus's lap.

"Marc, can you hear me? Fucking football. Your daughter's going mental. She's desperate for the pig. She's like Genghis Khan today." In the background, a scream, starting low, ascending through the octaves.

At the sound of his daughter, Marcus snapped to. "I'm on my way." He turned the keys in the ignition. The van jumped forward. Marcus made a U-turn, swerving half off the road, leaving ruts in the leaf mold.

"You won't be long, will you?"

"Fifteen minutes tops."

"All right then, love. Thanks." Lisa hung up. I sat there not moving or saying a word, willing him to keep driving with every ounce of my being.

When we got to the bottom of Postern Hill, clear of the forest, I told him to let me out. Because of the child locks, he had to come round. Many years ago, I had always kissed him before saying goodbye. But I would never kiss Marcus again. I made an effort not to touch him as I got out. He was trembling. I wavered for a moment and I thought he might have something more to say to me. In the event, he said nothing at all, got back in the van, and drove off. When he was out of sight, my knees went and I crumpled to the pavement in a daze, hyperalert giving way to stupor.

Very soon the doubts would start. It had been something else in the back under the tarp, not a spade at all. Or Marcus had been off to do a bit of gardening at his mum's. He hadn't planned to do me ill. His hands hadn't been reaching for my throat.

That's still what I'd like to think. But it's not what I believe.

CHAPTER 23

INVITATION TO A GAME

THE EMAIL SAT INNOCENTLY IN MY IN-BOX, THE ADDRESS A string of numbers. I was about to send it to spam, but there was something, something familiar.

I looked at the numbers. 4203417. It was a call, a call to a number that no longer existed, the number of the telephone box. The email contained nothing but a link. I clicked and a new tab opened to an article, now some years old.

The story was about a man who, while walking his dog in the South of France in the 1950s, had discovered a system of caves, secret within mountains of limestone. The dog—a black-and-white photograph showed a border collie, eyes laughing as if at a marvelous joke it had perpetrated—had disappeared. The man had called and called, eventually following the dog inside a narrow crack in a cliff wall. The crack had led to a passageway, the passageway to a chain of caves, each darker than the one before, each heading deeper into the mountain, as in a fairy tale.

In his pocket, a torch. Imagine the moment of illumination, the darkness coming to life! The animals streaming across the stone walls pursued by hunters, woken from their sleep after thirty thousand years. Even in photographs, the cave paintings were urgent, muscular, twitching with life. Another image showed ocher handprints, child sized, found in the deepest recesses of the furthest caverns. Looking at them, I had the sense that they were pressing forward, as though emerging from within the walls and, sitting at the desk where Peter had once so diligently done his homework, I itched to lay my palm against them.

Another email, another link to another article, again about the caves, about the dark cells within the honeycomb of limestone, sacred places reserved for ritual purposes. Once I could have gone and seen them, but now they were closed; the breath of the present would obliterate the past. But there were more, the article said, inevitably more caves, more paintings, yet to be discovered.

The next contained another set of links—to a documentary by a famous German director, to articles that speculated about the role of the paintings in Paleolithic society, what they might have meant, beautiful speculations about rituals and hunting grounds and Ice Age star maps, description of great cathedrals under the earth, with wild beasts in the place of saints: bison, stags, ibex, deer, bears, and big cats. There was a basilica, an apse, a hall of bulls, a painting of an aurochs five meters high. Next, I received a link to a Flickr album, photographs of rivers and forests, ruined castles, gigantic limestone escarpments.

David. But why didn't he speak to me? Because he was incapable of sticking to his word, because all of his promises were made to be broken? Enchantment, seduction, disillusionment. They were the stations and the train only went in one direction, and disillusionment was the end of the line, a final station at the foot of a mountain of impassable rock. But I kept looking.

Then, for a few days, there was nothing. And the fear I had, the fear of a return to the old paralysis, was replaced by terror that the emails would stop. I knew the panic well: the phone was ringing in my bag, the life-changing call from someone who would ring once and withhold their number.

Another email: A link to a map. A train station. A date. I wouldn't go. I would. I wouldn't. I deleted all the messages and went to the manor.

It was a warm day. The sky was thick with dense white clouds that trapped the heat. After I had signed him out, Darren and I walked around the grounds in silence. We paused before the fountain. Someone had scrubbed off the moss, but the cherubs were still there, still beckoning.

"Peter told me what happened with Joe. Where is he? Where did you put him?" But Darren only mumbled something about an invoice.

It was entirely possible that Mortimer's diamonds were still here. Faintly, as though from very far away, I thought I heard their call. Perhaps the price of some things staying buried was that there were others you would search for and never find.

When it came time for me to leave, I kissed Darren's cheek, and he smiled, a sweet vacuous smile, the kind a toddler gives to its mother.

That night I dreamed again. Em and I were on the Ridgeway, hurrying along the track in broad daylight. She was two steps ahead and no matter how I tried, I couldn't draw level with her.

"We're not going to the manor, are we?"

She shook her head, half turning toward me so that I caught a glimpse of her face in profile.

"Where then?"

"You'll see." In her voice, I heard the smile I could not see.

But Em went ahead, her feet barely touching the earth, till she was ten steps in front, then a hundred, then a thousand. And no matter how I struggled I couldn't keep up.

* * *

The day before I left, I found the vicar in his study among his books. Patricia was out. The years hung on him. There was talk of a bungalow.

Always spare, his long limbs put in mind dry branches. I put a cup of tea down beside him and he looked up from the page.

"Are you leaving, Andy?"

"Tomorrow."

"Ah. A holiday then?"

"To France, to see a friend."

"We will miss you. Patricia and I are very fond of you." He closed the book. Plato. He had always had a weakness for the ancient Greeks. Patricia had referred to them as his old pagans, as though they were a rabble of unshaven, rowdy pub drinkers.

"I never felt quite up to Patricia's standards."

"Well, that goes for all of us." He picked up his book and then put it down again. What alcohol had been to my mother, books were to the vicar. Always the sense that even when he was with you, he was aching for them. He sighed and his eyes wandered away out over the lawn.

"It was a different time. Her family was very poor. Her brother died when he was five. Before the NHS and not enough money for the doctor. Always haunted by relatives who'd ended up in the poor house. Her mother wouldn't let her visit the library, said it was above them. Class, the rubbish about class. Her family had nothing, but they were respectable. Even so, my family opposed us getting married. It's so easy to love the past, as long as you don't actually look at it. And so easy to regret it, of course. I do, Andy. There are things I regret, failures . . . I failed you and Peter, and I have known it for a very long time."

My throat was very thick. I didn't want him to think he had failed. This anxious, shy man, laboring over his sermons, greeting the children and adults at Harvest Festival with a great booming welcome, hands shaking, but why always God the Father, God the Son? Why not God the Mother, God the Daughter, why not marry the gays? I tried to say as much.

"I gave him books. Oscar Wilde. Auden. I didn't want to invade his privacy. But I suppose that is an excuse too. I sometimes wish Jesus had endured the world just a bit longer. Thirty-three. It's not a lot, is it, Andy?"

I made noises to go.

"You will come back and see us, won't you? You won't leave it so long?"

I promised. Before I went, he took my hand.

"You know, I cannot count the evenings we have sat here and talked about you and Peter, remembering your little ways. I would watch you, out there in the garden. I always thought God was in the games you played; they gave me faith, like when you watch the wind fill a sail and the boat leaps forward. Grace. It showed such grace."

* * *

The last night together, we watched television. It felt an old-fashioned thing to be doing, sharing a single screen between three. I thought how one day people would look back on communal television watching with the same nostalgia they reserved for charades and playing cards.

The program was an ITV Sunday night special. There had been a murder. And it was the best kind of murder, a middle-class murder somewhere beautiful, neither gruesome nor graphic, with a pleasing array of suspects, and a detective who drank too much, but quietly, and had been wounded by life. In one of the breaks, Patricia made cocoa, missing the first minute of the next part, and never quite catching up again, so she asked questions at important moments and it was a great act of will not to shush her.

Nevertheless, we were gripped. Ten o'clock came and went without mention of bed. In the ad breaks, we discussed who we thought had done it, and which suspects were the red herrings, and the whole thing rose to a tense denouement, in which the detective had to race against time to prevent a further murder and was nearly offed himself.

"Look out!" we shouted at the crucial moment. The detective looked out, the murderer was apprehended, and in the final scene the detective shared some melancholy reflections on human nature with his partner, a bright-eyed sergeant.

We sat there spellbound till the final credits rolled, and then went to our beds consoled, and I lay there in the darkness, thinking how different the program was from life. How life was full of mysteries that would not be solved, not ever, while we lived. But that each of us would play the detective nonetheless, and the life and death we would investigate, whether we knew it or not, was our own. And the thing was not to become deadened to them, to the mysteries.

CHAPTER 24

THE CAVE OF DREAMS

I TOOK THE BUS TO SWINDON WITH A NEWLY BOUGHT RUCKSACK on my back and a tin on my knees, a whole sponge cake inside that I had to balance on my lap on the way to the train station. I would eat it piece by piece over the next twelve hours, sharing slices with the mum and daughter off for a day's shopping in London, the dancer who was on her way to Paris for an audition.

"Just a sliver, then, but only a sliver."

A couple on the train south through France.

"Un gâteau anglais? C'est bon!"

I muttered the names of the stations under my breath. So many years since French class! There was only one slice left, when I finally arrived at the little station deep in the Ardèche. A single car, battered and dusted in ocher, was waiting in the car park.

David put his hand on my waist, leaned in for a kiss.

"What's in the tin?"

"Cake."

"I see." He lifted it for weight. "Feels a bit light."

"Sacrifices had to be made."

My face was so pleased to see him, it hurt.

"And Peter?"

"On her Majesty's secret service."

* * *

The summer was as dry as the spring had been wet. A forest fire in the hills above the campsite at Malbosc. The night turning red, smoke blowing up toward the sickle moon.

"Why cave paintings?"

"There are some things you can't get out of your head, Andy." David was standing behind me, his arms loose around my waist. He dropped a kiss on my bare shoulder. "You may as well get on with seeing what they mean."

A bad driver, humming as the locals tailgated him in a fury.

At the guesthouse, the ancient landlady fell in love with him. *Cheri, Cheri, Cheri!* She had a black cat—*putain!*—forever weaving through our legs.

School French: La fraise. Le framboise. J'aime beaucoup des glaces. J'aime beaucoup la nuit.

There is a ruined castle of the Knights Templar, an abandoned village. A rope swing out over a gorge. The jade waters beckoning. The cold green gulp.

We are hunting aurochs, the aurochs underground.

What comes after disillusionment? Can it be lived with? Can it be accommodated? Can you say to someone, you broke my heart and will break it again, and know any peace? Can that someone be life itself?

David bending over the camping stove, chasing a tea bag round a saucepan with a spoon.

The red and white way markers. The forest trails. The cliffs where the climbers come every summer, leaning out over the river, imitating the angels.

"What will we do when the money runs out?"

"What have people ever done?"

The tent in the glade, a brindled dog darting in from out of nowhere and stealing the sausages.

On a forest path at dawn we meet an Afghan man with two Somali companions. He is walking to Paris, his friends to Calais. They fear the farmers and their dogs, the police, for those left behind, the coming winter. One has a laugh rich as August sunshine.

Oh, I have ta'en
Too little care of this!

* * *

Deep play. I love you. I love you. Of course, it is a game.

* * *

The bulls are waiting under the earth in total darkness. In my sleep, I hear them stamping, their hot breath.

We buy torches, rope, begin startling bats among the rocky overhangs. In the caves, there is often the smell of water, pooled and stagnant.

Sometimes, there are dark mouths high up on the cliffs. I climb up but most of the caves are shallow. In many there are places where the walls are blackened by smoke. I crumble the soft ash of a fire between my fingertips. *Who were you, traveler?* It blows away on the wind.

"Come down from there."

"You come up."

It pays to have something to hunt, something outside ourselves.

"What if it caves in, the cave? What if we're buried down there with the aurochs?"

It pays to have something to fear, something outside ourselves.

* * *

This one is deep. We dare each other, a little further, a little further again. We whisper for no reason. David swings the torch and the light jerks wildly, and for a moment we're on a boat and the deck is pitching under our feet.

A little further, just a little further. Laughter, fear and laughter.

"Turn off the torch."

David turns off the torch and the darkness is complete. I cannot tell my eyelid from my eye. At my side, David smells like river water and campfire smoke. It is cold here, the heat of his body is like a beacon.

Now the whole world is a dream: the houses and offices, the supermarkets and IKEAs, Selfridges, the Savoy, the churches and chapels, the manor. The commuters gazing at their phones are dreaming, the climbers ascending the cliff walls. The cities are dreaming, and the Downs, the gorges and forests, the sea gripped in a pulsating, churning dream. The world dreaming all of it back.

I feel the millions of tons of rock pressing down. The ancient darkness. And yes, the aurochs!

So still, so quiet, I think I can hear David's racing heart. His mouth swims against my ear.

"So, can you see it yet?"

"What?"

"A future."

Fragile, the vision. Wet and trembling in the mind's eye, yet to unfurl. I cannot look at it directly, but it is there and it is mine.

"Yes," I say. "Yes. I think I can."

ACKNOWLEDGMENTS

To be frank, the journey to this page has been long and plentiful in orcs (but oh, the views!) and I'd need another book to name everyone who helped along the way.

I would like to thank my family, especially my parents—for the books, the understanding, the endless support, and for giving me the kind of childhood that is a gift to a writer and allowing me to share it with so many friends. I'd also like to thank Toby and James for the art therapy. See beloved nephews, here you are in a book! Nor do I know where I'd be without Gijs Van Koningsveld, my heart's companion and the greatest source of magic I know.

My heartfelt appreciation goes to Suzannah Dunn, Debra Hills, Jen Hewson, Abbie Holmes, Susanna Forrest, Traci Kim, Brigid Delaney, Leighton Cheal, Jenna Krumminga, Lucy Jones, Odysseas Vasilakis, Kenneth Macleod, Kristin Harrison, Ulrike Kloss, and the Berlin writing community, particularly all the Reader Berliners. Thanks to Tom Pugh for the Hasenheide strolls, feedback, and encouragement when I needed it most, and to Jane Flett for apparating in my life, bearing so many gifts, like the very good witch she is.

I am hugely grateful to Judith Murray at Greene & Heaton for her insight, kindness, and unwavering enthusiasm; to my brilliant editors Rebecca Gray and Leonora Craig Cohen at Serpent's Tail and Caroline Zancan and Kerry Cullen at Henry Holt; and to Lucy

Carson and Molly Friedrich of The Friedrich Agency, whose belief in this novel was such an unexpected delight.

Finally, I would like to remember Andraya, one of my very first friends. Andraya's death during the writing of this novel changed its shape. In her name, I say to anyone affected by intimate partner violence: you are not alone; it is not your fault; please seek help. Your first loyalty is to yourself.

To Andraya I would say this: I have thought of you often in these last years. The memories of our adventures on the farm have returned to me with such clarity, I cannot believe they are really over. Instead, it seems more likely that we are still out there, risking our parents' wrath as the sun sets, perhaps in the barns, or sitting on a tractor, or down by the stream. The whole summer lies ahead. Tomorrow let's make a campfire. Knock on the back door and I'll be waiting . . .

ABOUT THE AUTHOR

Victoria Gosling is a British author, currently living in Berlin. She grew up on a farm in Wiltshire, studied at the Universities of Manchester and Amsterdam, and has lived in London, Australia, Brazil, and the Czech Republic. Victoria is the founder of The Reader Berlin and the Berlin Writing Prize.